NO CHILD'S GAME
REALITY TV 2083

ANDREA WHITE

An Imprint of HarperCollins*Publishers*

No Child's Game: Reality TV 2083
Copyright © 2005 by Andrea White

www.harpereos.com

Library of Congress Cataloging-in-Publication Data
White, Andrea, date.
    No child's game: Reality TV 2083 / by Andrea White.— 1st ed.
        p.   cm. — Eos.
    Summary: In the year 2083, five fourteen-year-olds who
were deprived by chance of the opportunity to continue their
educations reenact Scott's 1910–1913 expedition to the South
Pole as contestants on a reality television show, secretly aided
by a Department of Entertainment employee.
    ISBN 0-06-055454-1 — ISBN 0-06-055455-X (lib. bdg.)
    ISBN 0-06-085100-7 (special edition)
    [1. Survival—Fiction.   2. Television programs—Fiction.
3. Education—Fiction.   4. Contests—Fiction.   5. Antarctica—
Fiction.]   I. Title.
PZ7.W58177No   2005   2004006249
[Fic]—dc22   CIP
                                                        AC

Typography by R. Hult
1 2 3 4 5 6 7 8 9 10

First Edition

Permissions: see p. 326

Also published as SURVIVING ANTARCTICA.

To the memory of Birdie Bowers—
and to the kids of Marni Hettena's
fourth-grade class, who helped bring
his name alive again

*We are not going forward like a lot of
schoolboys on a holiday picnic but rather
as a party of men who know what they have
got to face. I for one am sure that the journey
will be no child's game but a hard one, as
hard as any have ever been[,] and the
Pole will not be gained without a terrible
struggle. . . . If man can make for success we
have the right stuff with us, but as I say[,]
when man has done all he can do he can only
trust with God for the rest.*

—H. R. Bowers,
from a letter to E. Bowers,
October 27, 1911

PROLOGUE

What chance did Stephen Michael have of winning his Toss? In the year 2080 there were so many fourteen-year-old kids and so few scholarships. And if he lost—he hated to think about his choices then. Sweat poured down Steve's face as he stared at the poster on the wall in front of him: WELCOME TO THE EQUAL OPPORTUNITY EDU-DICE TOSS, SPONSORED BY THE DEPARTMENT OF ENTERTAINMENT.

"Candidate 9426!" the Scholarship Advisor called out. She was a short, chubby woman, with a face pitted like the dice.

Steve opened his fist to stare at his number again. His sweat had drenched the slip of paper and smeared the ink. Number 9429. It wouldn't be long now. Soon he would know whether he could go to high school and college or if he would have to find a job, any job at all. But this was silly. Why did he doubt the dice? He would win his Toss. He was going to be able to continue in school.

Candidate 9426 fought her way through the crowd. He watched her blond hair bobbing through the sea of people. The room was suddenly quiet.

The Scholarship Advisor consulted her hand-held. "We need a double six," she said into her megaphone.

The blond girl groaned. "Not a double."

"You all get an equal statistical chance," the Advisor chided her.

The blond girl took a deep breath and rolled. The dice spun around on the concrete floor before stopping. Steve craned his neck to see the dice, but couldn't. He heard the girl's scream.

The blonde fell back.

"We have a winner," the Advisor said into her megaphone.

A few kids cheered, but mostly Steve heard groans. The blond girl's luck had reduced everybody else's odds.

The Advisor handed the blonde the coveted green ticket and pointed toward the registration desk. "Now for Candidate 9427," she said to the crowd.

Steve didn't watch the next Toss. He was too busy reassuring himself that he could win. He had been there since early morning, and twice two kids had won back-to-back. It didn't mean anything that 9426 had won. He could win three rolls later.

The next candidates would lose, and Steve would win. That's just how it had to be.

In fact, 9427 already had lost. The discouraged-looking boy shuffled past him, and Steve worked to shut out the boy's disappointment. He couldn't let himself be distracted. He repeated the promise that he had made to himself: If I win my Toss and I'm able to get an education, I won't be like most of the educated kids. I won't just try to make money with my life. I'll try to make things better for everybody. Please, dice, let me win.

Candidate 9428 held his head high, but he, too, had lost.

Steve was next. He sucked in his breath. He heard the Advisor chant his number, and as if in a dream, he stepped forward. The black-and-white dice waited for him, only him. They gleamed with hope and the promise of his future.

"You need a five and a three," the Advisor said.

Five was a good number. He had a special feeling for fives. But the three . . . He didn't feel anything for that number. There was still time. *Three. Three. Three.* He didn't know if mind control worked, although some kids swore that it did. What else could he do?

Steve's hands were shaking as he picked up the dice. They were cold and hard, and he pressed them deeply into his palm, memorizing the moment. Perhaps it was the last moment in his life when everything was still possible. He dropped the dice on the floor. He heard them clatter before he shut his eyes.

A kid next to him shuddered. Steve opened one eye.

Two white fives stared up at him.

Steve didn't move. He couldn't move. Both eyes were glued to the traitorous dice. How could they do that to him?

"Everyone can play the game. There are winners and losers. Everyone has an equal chance," the Advisor chanted into the megaphone. She touched his shoulder and said to him, "Now go. It's someone else's turn."

His feet wouldn't budge.

Then the Advisor shoved Steve. He had no choice but to head back through the crowd, most of it eager or crying parents.

At least his mom and dad wouldn't be disappointed. They had died in the last Superpox epidemic, along with his little brother, Sam.

The thought of his family's death made him mad. "The Toss is not fair!" he shouted.

In the hordes of people pushing past him, only one person bothered to reply. She was carrying a clipboard.

"I played the Toss and won. Stop whining, loser!" she snapped.

Before Steve could protest, she disappeared into the crowd, and Steve did the only thing he could think of.

He headed for the door, his wet number still clutched in his hand.

1

THREE YEARS LATER

Andrew Morton was lounging in the soft spot in the tattered couch where he always watched television. He tried to feel cozy and warm, as he usually did in his hollow, but he couldn't. His dad was screaming at him.

His father, a big man, wore an undershirt and pants. "If you fail teleschool again, your mom and I will have to watch sixty hours of parenting classes. Sixty hours of idiots telling me how to get my son to do better on his television tests. Do you know how boring those parenting classes are?" His voice dropped. "You read me?"

Andrew nodded.

"The law says you have to pass eighth grade. You're the unluckiest kid I've ever known. You're sure to lose your Toss. You only need to make a sixty-five or above. After you pass, you're finished studying for your whole life. Are you ready?"

"Yes, sir." Andrew had watched reruns of *Historical Survivor*, *Dialing for Dollars*, and *Tele-Novelas* for the past week.

"I'm going to turn on the test." His father clicked the remote. RETAKES FOR EIGHTH GRADE FINAL EXAMS, July 15, 2083 appeared on the screen.

A voice broke in. "But first a special message from the Secretary."

The redheaded Secretary of Entertainment was young to be so important. She leaned toward Andrew and seemed to be speaking only to him. "I'm sponsoring something very special for eighth graders this year. Apply to be a contestant on my new upcoming *Historical Survivor* series for kids. If you finish the game, you'll be paid ten thousand dollars, and if you're voted Most Valuable Player, you'll win an extra ninety thousand dollars, for a grand total of one hundred thousand dollars. The series is set in Antarctica, one of the coolest places in the world. Press ENTER now if you're interested."

"Press ENTER!" Andrew's dad barked.

Andrew pressed ENTER on the keyboard.

"After the test, an application will appear on the screen," the Secretary concluded. "Complete it and submit it, along with your test. Good luck."

"Do it!" Andrew's dad ordered. "Maybe your mother and I'll get lucky and you'll go to Antarctica. You know you had an ancestor who was an explorer there?"

Andrew had heard his aunt speak of a distant uncle, a man named Bowers.

EIGHTH GRADE HISTORY FINAL RETAKE appeared on the screen.

"When did Bowers explore Antarctica?" Andrew asked.

His father pointed sternly at the question on the screen. "You can't put your test off any longer."

Andrew read: QUESTION 1: WHICH PHARAOH BUILT THE MOST PYRAMIDS IN ANCIENT EGYPT?

He should know this answer. He had watched every episode of *Egyptian Pyramid Historical Survivor.*

"Remember!" his dad thundered before leaving. "A sixty-five or above!"

It was a cool day, but Andrew wiped the sweat off his face before he began to work.

From her stall at the flea market in Times Square, Polly Pritchard watched the bustle of the vendors behind aging stands, the brightly colored signs of all shapes and sizes, and the crowds of worried-looking people carrying shopping bags. She reminded herself that she didn't know what else to do. Although she had been a nationally recognized student on EduTV, she had lost her Toss. Her mother was disabled. A few years ago, her father had died of tuberculosis. Without the help of a Toss scholarship, she had no money to continue in school. When the flea market offered her father's old stall, she had to take it. So here she was today, working as a memorist for the first time. Mr. Pebst, her father's former partner, had willingly given her the money for the stall in exchange for an agreement that she would give him twenty percent of her take.

"Are you as good as your father?" Mr. Pebst had asked her. Before she could speak, he shook his head. "Nobody was as good as him. In the twenty years that I knew him, he never once got anything wrong. He was the best."

Her customers might ask her anything—the date of George Washington's death, the distance to the moon, the calories in a peanut. She had learned many of her facts from reading the World Book encyclopedia. But most of her business would be from shoppers. Polly's head was full of jumbled phrases from the morning's paper and from the bulletin boards she had read on her way to work: "Instant Travel, the world's first human fax." "Fastgrow: Watch your hair grow one foot each night or your money back." "Dream Hat: Finally you can photograph your dreams." "Help the victims of the Urban Trash Wars by donating to . . ." And she found herself wondering, not for the first time, if the kids on her street were right, if the Memory was a curse. Casey Duncan claimed that Polly's brain would explode before she was twenty.

A customer, her first, hobbled toward her.

The old woman scrutinized Polly's face for a second before bursting out, "I need to know if there are any used televisions for sale. They'll take my grandkids from me if I don't have a television."

Polly nodded. Everybody knew that the law required all kids under the age of fourteen to watch thirty hours of teleschool a week.

"I'll pay you a dime. That's all you're worth." The old woman's teeth were the brown, unhealthy color of the endless smog that blanketed the city.

"Okay." Polly tried to ignore the woman's rudeness. Once her mother had been unable to afford a television repairman, and her fear had made her grouchy too.

The old woman flung the dime into Polly's empty jar.

"There's a basement sale on the corner of Broadway and Fifty-first that lists a used television along with an EduTV attachment," Polly said.

"You're sure?" The old woman shook a bony finger at Polly.

"I saw it on a bulletin board."

"I want my dime back if you're wrong," the old woman warned her.

Polly shrugged and wondered how her father had worked at this job for thirty years.

A boy her age walked up. He had long, shaggy hair and a broken front tooth.

Polly tried to look serious, as a memorist should.

"I lost my Toss," he said in a quavering voice.

Polly knew how he felt. She had lost hers, too.

"I was wondering, are there any other scholarships for kids advertised?"

"Why, yes," Polly said. There had been one in the newspaper. It felt strange to realize that she hadn't even thought about it for herself.

"What do you charge?"

"Oh, give me what you have," she said. Charging a boy as poor as herself would make her feel bad.

He threw a nickel into her jar.

"So?"

"The Secretary of Entertainment is producing a *Historical Survivor* show with kid contestants."

"What age?"

"Fourteen." Polly's exact age. The age when teleschool ended and only the rich, along with the lucky few who won their Toss, got to continue their education.

"Tell me more," the shaggy boy said eagerly.

"It's going to be a simulation of the Robert F. Scott expedition. Five kids need to make it to the South Pole with the supplies Scott had. There's prize money."

"Where do you apply?"

"The application is on EduTV."

"Gee, thanks!"

As he jogged away, she couldn't resist shouting, "Those *Historical Survivor* shows are dangerous!"

"What do I have to lose?" he called over his shoulder.

Polly listened to the *clip, clip, clip* of Mr. Jones's toenail clippers in the next stall and the shouts of a roving food vendor: "Hot dogs, hot dogs!" She watched swarms of ragged people passing by. What do *I* have to lose? Polly wondered.

Robert Johnson pressed his nose against the fence of Motorworld. For forty-five dollars a boy could spend the day at Motorworld driving any of its "thousands of vehicles specially outfitted for young teens."

Peeking through the fence, which was all Robert had ever done, was free.

A kid his age was working the controls of a miniature red-and-black helicopter, which rose up and then settled back down on the landing pad.

A few Jaguars, Ferraris, and Corvettes sped around the track fast enough for the kid drivers to feel they were driving the real thing.

One trailer truck plodded along on the track. Behind the windshield, a boy's face shone with excitement.

If Robert ever got the chance, he'd drive one of those race cars. But wishes were for babies. Wishes were for people of the twentieth century, not the twenty-first.

"Robert!" Joey Washington hollered at him from across the bayou.

Robert turned away from the shiny vision of Motorworld.

"Come on and tell me where to look, Robert!" Joey shouted.

Last year a giant mud slide had submerged a parking lot a little to the east of Motorworld. Robert had dug up a pickup truck there. He could probably use some help dismantling it. "Meet me at the bridge!" he yelled back to Joey. The bridge was a water tower that had fallen across the bayou.

Robert dodged the mud-encrusted trash piled on the banks of the bayou until he came to the silver water tower. He climbed onto the trestle at its base and surveyed the smelly brown water passing underneath.

Joey was already there.

"Someday I'm going to break into that Motorworld and drive every car I want," Joey said. He straddled the *H* of HOUSTON, the name inscribed on the fallen tower.

"You're dreaming," Robert said.

"You dream too," Joey said.

"I just scavenge."

The boys heard a buzz. An ad airplane was circling overhead. A banner burst loose from its rear. It read: "KIDS: TRY OUT FOR ANTARCTIC HISTORICAL SURVIVOR. $100,000. APPLY BY AUGUST 14."

"You should do that, Robert," Joey said.

"Has it ever snowed in Houston?"

"Naw, you're a bayou man, but . . ."

"You got it. I'm a bayou man."

"I'm stuck here," Joey said sadly, looking at his dirty shoes. "But if anybody could get out, it would be you."

Robert didn't answer him. August 14 was this Saturday. He wondered if he could afford to take the afternoon off.

"If you do, remember us here in ol' flooded Houstontown."

"I'll remember your lazy self for all my life," Robert said. "Do you have any tools with you?"

Joey shook his head.

"Go home and get some tools, and I'll meet you back on the bridge in a couple of hours."

Joey walked off slowly, whistling. He was never in a hurry to do anything.

The ad plane circled again.

One hundred thousand dollars!

With one hundred thousand dollars, Robert could buy several motorboats and start a hauling business.

But he couldn't remember: Was Antarctica north or south?

Billy Kanalski stared at the Compu-gametable. His father had designed the round table with a computer top. Every game in the world was in its memory. When a player selected his game, the colored board and game pieces appeared on the screen.

The table was a great idea, a cool invention. It was just that the toy companies were stupid losers who didn't know a great game when its bright lights flashed in their fat faces.

At first the Compu-gametable had promised success. In those early days, Billy and his parents had vacationed in the largest indoor mall in the world and had once ridden in a white limo that was so long it had trouble turning corners. But those early days were over, and now Billy was hungry almost all the time.

Billy pushed a button and the table lit up with reds, blues, and purples. "What game do you want to play?" the table asked him.

I don't want to play any game, Billy thought. I want to have lunch. I want to go to high school and college. Since he had lost his Toss and his father hadn't been able to sell his invention, Billy couldn't hope for further schooling.

Billy punched the button for Navigant. The fake starry background and bright purple compass appeared on the screen. It had been one of his favorite games since he was a child. Players traveled across the globe, navigating by the location of the sun and stars, and using simulated compasses and a gauge capable of reading longitude and latitude. He had played the game so much that he no longer needed to consult the instruments.

A news bulletin flashed across the top of the screen: "Trying to top her popular *Alamo Historical Survivor*, the Secretary of Entertainment has announced a new *Historical Survivor* series. This one will involve fourteen-year-old kids. The MVP—the contestant voted Most Valuable Player—will get one hundred thousand dollars. All contestants . . ."

One hundred thousand dollars?

Billy's mom and dad appeared at the door. Billy noticed first that his mom didn't have a grocery bag in her arms, then that his dad still looked discouraged. "Hey," Billy said. The map of the world lit up next to the purple compass. Idly, Billy's finger traced a path south.

It was Grace Untoka's turn to be "it." She counted to one hundred in the central plaza of Pueblo Village, looked around for her cousin, and almost bumped into a family of tourists.

The family all had cameras dangling from their necks. The daughter wore a flowered shirt that matched her beret. "My parents want a photo of a Hopi. Can we snap your picture?"

"I'm an Iñupiat Eskimo, not a Hopi."

The girl smirked.

Grace didn't say anything. Hopis and Iñupiat Eskimos both had straight black hair. But the Hopis' skin was reddish while the Eskimos' was yellowish, and Grace's cheeks were full, not hollow like the Hopi kids'.

"You sure look like a Hopi."

Grace turned her back on the tourists. As she listened to the girl march away, she tried to calm her anger. Of course the girl mistook Grace for a Hopi. Grace was standing in the plaza of a pueblo in the middle of an Indian reservation in Arizona. Some days even Grace thought that she was a Hopi. But her grandfather had always reminded her, "You are an Iñupiat Eskimo with a proud six-thousand-year history."

"Grace, I don't want to play hide-and-seek anymore." Her cousin Aleqa crept out from her hiding place. "Look what I found."

Grace stared at the animal Aleqa held in her outstretched hand. Grace had raised baby kangaroo rats before. "It's got a broken leg," she said, noticing the naked bone.

"Eskimo, Eskimo, Eskimo . . ." Tommy Screechowl, one of her many tormentors, was shouting at her from behind an adobe building.

"Take it to my clinic," Grace whispered to Aleqa, "and I'll meet you there in just a minute." She was sure that if presented with a choice, Tommy would chase her, not her smaller cousin.

"Okay." Aleqa started down the path to the discarded refrigerator carton that housed Grace's clinic. Right now her patients were a blind dog and a bald goat.

"You can't catch me!" Grace called to Tommy.

His footsteps pounded the trail behind her.

Grace ducked into her family's shack and almost knocked her mother down.

"Whoa! What's wrong?" Grace's mother put a pile of T-shirts and one old pair of sealskin socks on the table. "Those boys were after you again." She shook her head.

It was a statement, not a question, and Grace didn't have to answer. Years ago Grace's family had been subsistence hunters in Alaska, roaming an area that was among the least populated on earth. Because there were so few people there, Congress had voted to turn her tribe's land into a nuclear waste dump, and the government had offered the tribe a deal. It would pay to move them to a Hopi Indian reservation in Arizona. They would be given a few acres of land and a tractor.

Grace had been born on the reservation. All she knew about the ways of the Iñupiat were what her grandfather, her parents, and the elders of the tribe had told her. But every day she was tormented and bullied by the Hopis for being an Eskimo and mistaken by the tourists for a Hopi. It didn't seem fair.

Her mother hugged her. "I'm sorry. They're just ignorant kids."

A rock sailed through their one small open window and clattered onto her grandfather's table. His tools and skinning knife crashed onto the floor.

Her mother screamed.

Grace knelt by the scattered objects. She missed her grandfather so much. He had died only a few weeks ago. Tommy Screechowl was lucky that her grandfather's knife wasn't broken.

Grace ran out the front door to look for Tommy.

Tommy smiled at her from behind the neighbor's beat-up truck. When he was sure that Grace had seen him, he disappeared.

Grace returned to her mother, who was holding the rock.

"Those boys are getting worse and worse," her mother complained.

Grace leaned over her mother's shoulder. Her mother

unrolled the piece of paper that had been wrapped around the rock.

"*Historical Survivor*. Set in Antarctica. For the first time, taking applications from kids," Grace read slowly. She looked into her mother's broad face. "I guess Tommy wants me to move to Antarctica."

"That's silly. There've never been any people in Antarctica." Her mother turned away to finish the laundry.

Grace slipped the flier into her pocket. Antarctica. Even the name sounded white and clean.

2

"You lucky, lucky kids." The Secretary of Entertainment was beaming at Andrew, Polly, Robert, Billy, and Grace. "You have been chosen from a pool of 4,825 applicants."

Polly sat with the other winning contestants around a long table at the Department of Entertainment in Washington, D.C. The walls of the room were lined with photos from *Civil War Historical Survivor*, *Bubonic Plague Historical Survivor*, *Titanic Historical Survivor*, and *Egyptian Pyramid Historical Survivor*, to name a few. Staring at the old-timey rifles, crushed and missing limbs, and pocked and bloated faces, Polly didn't feel lucky at all.

Billy wondered what lies the other kids had told to be chosen. It was true that he was almost an Eagle Scout, but he wasn't the snow-and-ice expert that he had pretended to be on his application. He had gone skiing only twice.

Andrew had a stomachache.

Robert had a million questions to ask the Secretary.

Grace wondered if snow still tasted good, as it had when her grandfather lived in the Arctic. Her parents had moved to the reservation just before Grace was born. Her father had died shortly after her birth, and her mother couldn't remember what snow tasted like.

"You all know one another, don't you?" the Secretary said.

Robert nodded. If you called shaking hands and saying "hi" knowing one another, he thought.

"And you've all seen our popular *Historical Survivor* series?" the Secretary asked.

Polly nodded. She hated the shows.

What a stupid question, Billy thought. Since the public schools had closed, every kid fourteen and under who wasn't enrolled in private school was required by law to watch teleschool.

"Then you know that *Historical Survivor* can be dangerous," the Secretary said.

Andrew thought of the Texans lying in bloody heaps all around the Alamo. But those were adults, not kids. Surely for kids the show would be different.

Robert guessed that of the five, he was the only one who understood danger.

Grace willed the idea of danger to become a snowball, and she tossed it away.

"But since you've chosen to apply, you must all be fearless." The Secretary smiled. One of the Secretary's many aides handed her a slip of paper. "Excuse me," she said to the kids. She began speaking to the aide.

Billy strained to listen. He overheard the words "special meeting" before her voice dropped to a whisper.

The Secretary had called Polly fearless. Actually, she was terrified. Polly and Mama had never dreamed she would be selected for the contest. When she was chosen, they both had wanted her to back out, but the recruiter who had phoned with the news had said, "It's illegal to withdraw from a government-sponsored contest."

"I didn't know," her mother had pleaded.

"Ignorance of the law is no excuse." The man hung up.

The Secretary turned her attention back to the kids. "Of course, in the original *Survivor* shows the television host traveled with the contestants. But in *Historical Survivor* you travel alone." She smiled again. "In fact, except for the camera crew, throughout your adventure you will be completely alone."

The Secretary acts as if she's describing a beach vacation, Polly thought.

Several men and women in white coats entered the room and stood against the wall.

Why are those people staring at me? Andrew wondered.

"You'll spend a few days here in D.C.," the Secretary continued. "The doctors need to perform some harmless tests to make sure you're fit to go. Then the *Terra Nova*, your compucraft— which has the same name but otherwise is completely unlike the leaky whaling ship that Scott used—will sail, with all five of you on it, for Antarctica."

Robert held up his hand.

The five doctors stepped toward the kids.

"We'll have plenty of time for questions later. But first I need you to go with these nice physicians to start your tests. They won't hurt you." The Secretary smiled. "I promise."

Stephen Michael, the newest member of the day shift, sat in the auditorium with the other employees. He still couldn't get over his good fortune. He was working on television production at the Department of Entertainment, or DOE, learning a lot and receiving a good salary.

Of course, the job had some drawbacks, and one of them was the Department head.

Dolly Jabasco, or Hot Sauce (his coworkers' nickname for the redheaded Secretary of Entertainment), had called a special meeting of the day shift. In her excitement she was practically hopping up and down on the stage.

"As I was saying . . ." Hot Sauce giggled. "It's so thrilling that I'm having trouble talking." She took a deep breath. "Our new series will feature kids."

Kids! How terrible, Steve thought. But Chad Atkins, his dad's friend, who had gotten him this job, had warned him not to let his thoughts appear on the screen of his face. He worked to keep his expression even.

Besides, Steve comforted himself, this series had to be different from the *D-Day Historical Survivor* that Steve had been forced to watch for teleschool. Two men had died in that simulation. In the *Alamo Historical Survivor* series that Steve had just finished editing, a whole slew of men had been killed. Men desperate for money and opportunity might be allowed to make dangerous choices, but the Secretary would have to protect kids.

"Some of you have heard about the original expedition to the South Pole led by Captain Robert F. Scott." Hot Sauce scanned the audience as she spoke.

Steve hadn't, and because the Secretary was the only college graduate in the room, he doubted whether anybody else had, either. After Steve had lost his chance for an education three years ago, he had pressed his dad's old photographic equipment into service, moved to D.C., and scraped by as a freelance photographer.

A few months ago, while photographing a wedding, he had run into Chad Atkins, his father's boyhood friend, who had offered to get him a job at the DOE. His chance meeting with Chad was the only lucky break that he had gotten in a long time.

"So no one in this whole auditorium has heard of this famous explorer?" the Secretary asked.

Steve hated the way Hot Sauce lorded her education over them.

"Well," the Secretary began, "in 1912, the Robert F. Scott expedition attempted to be the first to reach the South Pole. But they were beaten by a Norwegian, and the five men all died." She paused to let this fact sink in. "Now we are going to have five kids reenact Scott's expedition on *Antarctic Historical Survivor*!"

Mechanically, Steve clapped along with the rest of the crowd. As he looked around at the eager faces of his coworkers, he noticed that some of them were cheering. A few truly seemed to love the *Historical Survivor* series. He had overheard them talking about watching it on their off-hours. Steve had lived without friends or family for a long time, but on his weekends he still had better things to do than watch people suffer on television.

"The kids will have much of the same food and equipment that Scott had. But since they're kids, the Department is going to give them a number of breaks."

Steve breathed a sigh of relief. Without a doubt, the Secretary would make sure that the kids had a hair-raising adventure, but as he had suspected, it sounded as if *Antarctic Historical Survivor* would be a safer, kinder *Survivor* series. A "good" *Survivor* series. A *Survivor* for kids.

"Our job is to convince everyone in America to watch our

shows. We have carefully screened each contestant. To increase viewer interest, each of the five kids will have a special gift. You can bet the audience will be guessing.

"Of course, our series will include lessons and exams about the Scott expedition." Hot Sauce stared at the audience. "Any questions?"

The woman in front of Steve raised her hand. "Will the camera crew travel to location, or will we use the corneal implants?"

"We will rely completely on corneal implants," the Secretary said confidently.

On Steve's first day of work, Blair Provenzano, the day-shift manager, had solemnly explained the classified science of corneal implants. Because members of the camera crew had gotten shot (in *Civil War* and *D-Day Survivor*), had been gored (in *Hemingway Bull Run Historical Survivor*), and had died of hypothermia (in *Donner Party Historical Survivor*), government scientists had figured out a way to implant tiny digital camcorders in the corneas of the contestants. As long as a contestant had his eyes open, the camcorder recorded and transmitted to headquarters a movie, complete with sound, of the contestant's experiences. The digicameras had been used on the just-completed *Alamo Historical Survivor* without the audience catching on. The penalty for disclosing the Department's biggest secret was having to go on *Court TV*. Of course, Steve would keep the corneal implants secret. No one in America wanted to go on *Court TV*.

Hot Sauce smirked. Steve could tell that she was getting ready to tell one of her little jokes.

"We don't want to kill any more of you," she said, laughing.

A man in the audience raised his hand. "But since there's only ice and snow in Antarctica, won't the kids wonder where the camera crew is?"

What? Steve was shocked. Blair Provenzano had explained that the Secretary had plans to reveal the secret of the corneal implants in a dramatic way in a future game. For now, Hot Sauce preferred the viewers to believe that live cameramen faced some of the same risks as the contestants. That the Secretary was notoriously secretive was well known. But Steve had assumed that the Secretary had informed the contestants about the implants. That seemed only right and fair.

"That's one reason that we decided to use kids," the Secretary said. "The kids believed me when I told them that a hidden camera crew would be there. Adults might get suspicious."

"Kids aren't stupid," Steve muttered. Then he quickly looked at Toby Kyle, who was sitting next to him, to see if Toby had noticed his outburst. Toby was chewing gum and staring at the Secretary as if she were the most interesting person alive. But Steve chided himself anyway. He had to be very, very careful to keep his temper under control. Everything he said was recorded. He didn't want to lose the best job he'd ever had or get his father's friend into any trouble.

"Ever since the government got into the entertainment biz . . ." Hot Sauce said.

Here comes the speech, Steve thought. In the three months that he had worked for the Department, he had already heard it many times.

". . . we've cut the crime, murder, and assault rates and eliminated war. We've saved our taxpayers billions of dollars by getting rid of the public schools. We teach history through *Survivor*, English through *Tele-Novelas*, and math through *Dialing for Dollars*.

"Together we have built the finest edu-entertainment program in the world. And now, with our kid contestants, we are going to make edu-entertainment history."

Listening to the Secretary conclude her speech, Steve had a horrifying thought. If the Secretary—a prominent member of the government—was so low that she lied to the contestants, could she be trusted to keep the kids safe?

The sad thing was that no one would care. These contestants were probably street kids who lived in one of those tent cities that seemed to be springing up everywhere these days. They were kids who didn't have much to lose. They were kids whom hardly anybody cared about.

Without the ability to make his own living with his dad's photographic equipment, Steve would have been one of those kids.

He quickly changed the channel of his mind so that he wouldn't have to consider the life of poverty he had narrowly escaped. He had almost been forced to play a real-life *Survivor*—a game with no rules, no fans, no prize money, and worst of all, no hope.

I have a job. A hut in Shanty Town. One hundred and fifty dollars in the bank, he reassured himself. Everything will be fine.

3

At exactly four fifty-nine P.M., Steve removed from his front tooth the microphone cover that recorded all his conversations and dropped it in the outbox. He put his cup of urine, with his name and the date written on it in bold black letters, on the conveyor belt to the lab. He slipped off his outer boots, designed to make loud footfalls so cameramen like himself couldn't sneak around without being heard. He put his camera in locker 908, pressed his thumb on the fingerprint detector, and turned to walk out the door.

A heavy hand clapped his shoulder. "Stephen." It was Blair Provenzano. Blair was an older man with a twitchy mustache and lifeless eyes.

Steve's heart was pounding. He prayed that he wasn't going to be fired for muttering about the Secretary. His dad had always told him that his temper would get him in trouble one day. He promised himself that he'd keep his mouth closed from now on. "Yes, sir," he said slowly.

Blair bent toward him and whispered, "You've been transferred to the night shift."

"The night shift!" Although Chad Atkins was head of the

night shift, Steve was aware that it had a reputation for being a strange team. Toby Kyle claimed that only losers worked at night. Steve examined Blair's eyes for a clue.

"Congratulations!" Blair said unconvincingly.

Steve tried to smile. "When do I start?"

"Take your usual weekend break and report at six P.M. Monday."

"Do I need the same gear?" Steve motioned to the piles of surveillance devices that the day-shift cameramen were expected to wear.

"Chad Atkins, your new manager, will tell you all about it. Good luck," Blair said before he turned away.

His mind racing, Steve stepped on the exit pad. The night shift and Chad Atkins were both mysterious.

Steve's dad and Chad Atkins had grown up together in the little town of Norwich, New York. When Chad Atkins had moved to the big city, he had told Steve's father, "If you ever need anything, let me know; I'll be there for you." Chad and Steve's father had kept in touch by e-mail, but they hadn't seen each other for many years. At the wedding a few months ago, when Steve had introduced himself, Chad had immediately guessed that Steve was the son of his friend. After learning about the death of Steve's family, Chad had offered to help Steve get a job.

Steve had asked Chad then, "Will I be able to work with you?"

"Only if you're a night-shift man," Chad had answered vaguely.

What exactly did that mean? Steve had wondered. But he hadn't pressed Chad, and when the offer of the day-shift job came, he had gladly accepted it.

The exit pad registered Steve's weight and shoe size, and the door opened.

Steve sniffed. Ever since the Nuclear Accident, the residents of Washington, D.C., swore that their air had flavors. Today's, Steve decided, was burning trash.

A little after six o'clock Monday evening, Steve followed Chad's flashlight and voice down the halls of the Department of Entertainment. The gray-walled corridors, which during the day were only dreary, became spooky at night.

"Night shift has front-line responsibility for viewing the contestants' lives," Chad explained. "Since the kids' team watch is set on studio time, usually we'll all be on the same schedule. We'll watch their evenings in real time, but we also have the responsibility of viewing the daily footage and cutting it by two thirds. Of course, if the action gets tense, the day shift broadcasts live. But under normal circumstances, the day shift creates the three-hour episodes from our product. Because our hours are so long—during production we work from six P.M. to six A.M. with no weekend breaks—when we finish the series, we'll have a month off. Now, any questions?"

Walking down the gloomy hallway, Steve stumbled over his feet. He asked the first question that popped into his mind. "Are you trying to save electricity?"

"Yes," Chad said. "We try to keep our budget low to avoid notice."

"Why?" Steve asked. He realized with a shock that during his day job he had never once asked that question.

Chad stopped in front of the editing room. "If the Secretary focused on us, she might make us wear the gear and follow the rules." He smiled at Steve. "Now we make our own."

Chad opened the door, and Steve saw the blank television

screens lining the walls. He had spent many hours in this room editing the footage for *Alamo Historical Survivor*. "What are *your* rules?"

Chad grinned at him. "To have a little fun."

"Fun?" Steve asked, surprised. Now he was certain that there was something very different about the night shift. He had liked his day-shift job, but he wouldn't have called it fun.

Steve followed Chad through the door into what seemed to be an empty room. Then, in the corner, Steve noticed an old woman sweeping. The day shift didn't employ aged people. This bent woman's hands were so arthritic that they looked like claws.

"Why me?" Steve muttered. Why now? he was thinking. Why had he gotten transferred?

Chad looked into Steve's eyes. "'Kids aren't stupid.'"

"You were listening?" Steve asked.

Chad shook his head. "It was in the report."

"What report?"

"The daily report that goes to all the supervisors. When I helped you get the day-shift job, I didn't know if you were a day-shift or a night-shift man. The daily report gave me my answer. You wouldn't last long in the day shift saying stuff like that."

Steve hung his head. "I'm sorry."

Chad shrugged. "A day-shift job is far safer, but if it'll make you feel better, I know your dad would have been a night-shift man, too."

Safer? "What's so different about the night shift?" Steve asked, feeling light-headed from the strangeness of their conversation.

"Well, first of all, there are not very many of us. Only nine."

"Where are the others?"

"Loafing."

"Loafing?"

"Some nights we sabotage. Some nights we work for Her Royal Highness the Secretary of Entertainment. And every night we loaf."

"What do you do when you loaf?" Steve couldn't imagine a job that included loafing.

"Play cards. Sleep. Read."

Steve willed his voice to sound normal. "What do you do when you sabotage?"

"It depends. We can't do much. We have to be very careful. But for every series"—Chad paused—"one of us volunteers."

Steve's heart thudded. Volunteers to do what?

Chad picked up a remote and punched a button. All the televisions came alive with scenes from a clinic ward. Chad touched the controls and a camera zoomed in on a sleeping child's face. A girl. She had a slight smile on her lips. Her open arms made her look completely defenseless. Steve wanted to hug her.

"Polly Pritchard," Chad said.

Chad touched the zoom lenses for the camera aimed on the second bed. A tough-looking African-American boy lay asleep. "Robert Johnson."

Steve had seen kids like this on the streets. Even while he was asleep, the boy's hard life showed in his scarred face and his leanness. Steve had the feeling that if he made a sound, the boy would leap up in an instant, ready for anything.

"The kids are heavily sedated," Chad said.

"Because of the corneal implants?"

"Of course." Chad smiled. "Just a bit of department trivia. The implants are always placed in the contestant's left eye."

Chad seemed to be in such a talkative mood that Steve decided to risk the question that had been bothering him. "Why aren't contestants told about the implants?"

Chad turned toward the next kid's screen. This boy was about the same age as the other two, fourteen, so he was much too old for stuffed animals, but he held his chubby arms as if a teddy bear were in his grasp. He had long brown hair and long brown eyelashes. Steve couldn't say why, but the boy looked kind.

"Andrew Morton." Chad identified the boy before answering Steve. "How long do you think Hot Sauce could keep the implants secret if she told the contestants?"

Steve thought about the celebrity-hungry contestants on *Alamo Historical Survivor*, and the answer to Chad's question was obvious. "She gets away with so much."

Chad shrugged. "If the night shift had its way, she wouldn't."

Maybe he *was* a night-shift man, Steve admitted to himself reluctantly. The poor kids already had enough problems. No one should be allowed to lie to them.

The next screen showed a girl whose long black hair fell over the hospital sheets. She had a broad face and yellowish skin.

"Grace Untoka."

Steve guessed that she was a Native American.

Chad turned toward the remaining camera. "Last is Billy Kanalski." Billy had brown hair like Andrew's, but he was smaller, leaner. He tossed his arm over his head and his whole body shuddered; then he fell quiet.

"They should wake up early tomorrow," Chad said.

Steve still couldn't believe that when the kids woke up, although they wouldn't know it, they'd have miniaturized camcorders in their eyes. "When do they leave for Antarctica?"

"Tomorrow night," Chad said.

"What are we supposed to be doing?"

"Well, we call this the 'test period.' Since we don't start the actual show until the kids reach the ship tomorrow night, we're supposed to be"—Chad continued in an exaggerated voice—"'monitoring the kids to make sure that the implants are working properly.' Of course, since the kids are lying in clinic beds with their eyes closed, this is an absolutely stupid assignment. When they wake up, we can quickly tell if the implants are working. After that, we monitor them loosely until they arrive at the ship." He shrugged.

"So what are you going to do?"

Chad nodded as if he understood that Steve was asking a bigger question than what he was going to do tomorrow or the next day. "We don't know yet," he said seriously. "I want to introduce you to our crew." He gestured toward the corner. "This is Pearl. She's our mascot."

Pearl didn't look up from the floor. Steve couldn't see her face; he saw only her hair, which looked like a dirty mop.

"Hello, Pearl," Steve said.

Chad stamped on a floor tile in the center of the room. The large square popped up.

Steve stared down into the hole. He couldn't see anything, but he heard laughter.

"The rest of the night shift," Chad said. "Go ahead."

Steve walked down the narrow metal steps. As his eyes adjusted to the light, he was able to make out a tiny room. The walls and ceilings were covered in old rusted pipes. Piles of pipes lay on the ground.

Five or six men sat in a circle lit only by a flashlight. They were playing cards.

A radio blared out a Fair Society commercial. "Each person gets a Toss. Some win. Some lose. But everybody gets a chance."

The government-owned stations played Fair Society commercials fifty times a day. Steve had heard its messages thousands of times.

"Cut that trash off," one of the men shouted.

Chad turned the radio off before identifying Steve. "Our new crew member."

"Do you play gin?" one man asked. His face was striped with shadows.

Steve shook his head.

"How about bridge?" another called out from a dark corner.

"No," Steve said.

"Then why did you take him on?" The third man had a big grin on his face.

"He's the son of a dear friend," Chad said.

The man nearest to Steve nudged him. "Don't worry, Steve. We'll teach you how to play cards in no time."

As the men played their hands, the cards flashed in the semi-darkness.

"Thanks," Steve mumbled.

4

Steve lay on the ragged mat in his hut. The light streamed through the chinks in the walls. It felt strange to be home during the daytime, but now that he was on the night shift, he wasn't due at work until six P.M.

A few weeks ago if Steve had been home during the day in the middle of the week, he would have gone bowling on the abandoned freeway or waited for his turn on a free computer at the local computary so that he could read comics. But today, for the sake of these kid contestants, Steve had stayed home to watch *Historical Survivor*. He turned up the volume. ANTARCTIC HISTORICAL SURVIVOR flashed onto the screen.

"Right now we want to introduce the contestants for our upcoming series." With her perfect red suit and matching lipstick, Hot Sauce seemed to glow with satisfaction.

"First, Polly Pritchard," the Secretary said.

The kids all had on blue jeans, white T-shirts that read ANTARCTIC HISTORICAL SURVIVOR, and flashy new tennis shoes from the Nike endangered-fish series.

Polly smiled and waved. The Secretary introduced the remaining kids one by one.

Billy stared straight at the camera, as if to say, "I deserve to be here."

Andrew squirmed in the small chair.

Robert gave a thumbs-up sign.

Grace scowled.

"Now, Polly," the Secretary continued, "each of you has been selected because you have a special gift. Can you guess what yours is?" Hot Sauce crossed her long legs.

Steve knew that she had a microphone set to pick up the crackle of her nylons. Only the richest women could afford nylons.

"I don't have to guess," Polly said simply, staring straight at the camera. "I have a photographic memory."

"What exactly does that mean?" the Secretary asked.

"It's hard to describe." Polly fidgeted. "It's like I have books in my head."

"You look too small to have a library in your head." The Secretary tittered at her own weak joke. Prompted by laugh cards, the audience laughed too. "But I'll take your word for it."

"And you, Andrew?" She turned to the pudgy boy on the end. "What is your special gift?"

The boy turned three shades of red. "I'm alive," he said.

Steve felt he had something in common with this awkward kid.

Except for Polly, the other children grinned.

"All of us are alive," Hot Sauce said irritably. "I mean a special gift that you alone in this room may have." She spread her arms. "That you alone in the country . . ." Before becoming the youngest Secretary that the DOE had ever had, the Secretary had been a popular talk show host on another show that Steve hadn't much liked.

Andrew's face grew even redder. "You may have the wrong guy," he said finally.

"No, I am telling you that you scored remarkably on one portion of our test. The scientists couldn't even believe it. Do you have any idea what I am talking about?"

Andrew shook his head. He looked so incredulous that Steve wanted to laugh.

"You will." Hot Sauce smiled at the audience. She turned to a small, quiet, dark-headed boy on the end. "What part of the testing did you like best, Billy?"

"The computer games," Billy said. His fingers twitched as if he were sitting in front of the controls for one.

Hot Sauce looked into the camera. "Our contestants faced real-life survival situations on a computer. Their answers were analyzed by hundreds of scientists. In addition, they climbed rock walls, used navigational instruments, and spent some time in a freezer and a day at a farm. We have a very special group here before you. Grace, why do you think you were chosen?"

Grace stiffened and tossed her straight black hair. "I'm not sure that I want to talk about it."

The Secretary frowned. "What do you mean? I've asked you a question. You're supposed to answer. I'm an important figure in your government."

"On the reservation, they call my people dirty. I'm an Iñupiat Eskimo. We are a people of ice and snow. I guess that's why I was chosen," the black-haired girl said.

Steve felt sorry for Grace. He knew how cruel kids could be. After his parents died, his old friends shunned him. It was as if they couldn't bear to be around so much sadness.

"Perhaps." The Secretary smiled in a way that made Steve doubt whether any of the kids had guessed his or her true gift. She turned to the strongest-looking kid, the only African

American. "Now, Robert, why don't you tell the audience about your very thorough checkup?"

"We've been examined by lots of doctors," Robert said.

You've been operated on, too, Steve thought grimly.

"And they've all given you a clean bill of health?" the Secretary asked Robert.

"Yeah. I'm fit for anything." Robert grinned. He was the only kid who seemed happy to be entered in the contest.

"Where are you from?" the Secretary asked.

"Houston, Texas," Robert said. Steve thought he detected in Robert's voice a slight twang.

"So you don't know much about snow and ice." The Secretary winked.

"No, ma'am." Robert grinned. "But once, when Houston flooded, my family lived on water moccasins for months. I caught driftwood as it floated by and pieced together a raft. We all sailed away on it. I'm ready."

Steve would bet on this kid's survival instincts.

"I'm sure you are," the Secretary said. "I think the only player with serious snow-and-ice experience is Billy." She turned to the slight, quiet boy at the end of the row.

Billy smiled uncomfortably. "That's right. I don't have to guess why I was chosen."

Polly raised her hand.

The Secretary frowned but nodded.

"I have a question," Polly said. "How can kids make it to the Pole if grown men couldn't?"

Smart girl, Steve thought. Like me, she ought to be able to afford an education.

"Glad you asked that question," the Secretary said in a sugary voice. "We'll go over this more thoroughly later, but we are going to give you a number of breaks.

"In Scott's day, the continent of Antactica was partly surrounded by ice. Much of the ice has melted, but since scientists haven't been there since the Big Bust, no one knows exactly how far inland the pole is."

Like every other kid in America, Steve had learned from teleschool that after the government went broke, it canceled all scientific research.

"To simplify," the Secretary continued, "we set our pole one hundred fifty miles from your landing point. Scott's team had to hike more than seven hundred fifty miles."

"One hundred fifty miles isn't a break!" Steve said to the television. The Secretary recited the mileage as if kids hiked 150 miles through ice and snow all the time.

"Second, Scott had to worry about returning from the Pole. If you make it"—the Secretary paused and smiled at the kids—"we'll pick you up in a helicopter."

Steve felt sick to his stomach, but Robert grinned as if the Secretary were doing them a big favor.

"Scott readied himself for the journey by storing food at various places for his return from the Pole," the Secretary continued. "You will need to carry food and fuel from the ship, but to make it even easier, we have deposited additional food and fuel for your journey. The depots will be twenty-five miles apart, except for the first depot, which will be fifty miles from the ship."

Despite the Secretary's so-called breaks, Steve wondered if the five kids would even make it to the first depot. He had been wrong. This series wasn't going to be a kinder, gentler *Survivor*.

It was going to be an icy hell.

"Third, Scott and his men relied on dogs, ponies, and a primitive motor vehicle, but for the final stage the men pulled their supplies to the Pole on sledges. You can go much faster than Scott, as you will have enough transport so that no one has to walk." She paused and smiled. "At least at first."

At least at first? Steve examined the kids' faces to see if any of them had registered the Secretary's carefully chosen words. They all looked dazed, not as if they were being briefed on a potentially fatal mission. Listen! he wanted to yell at them.

"Otherwise, to the extent possible, the journey will be authentic and true to Scott's original expedition. You will have the supplies that Scott had. You will eat the food that Scott did." The Secretary beamed again. "If no one has any more questions . . ."

Billy and Robert raised their hands.

The Secretary smiled at the camera, ignoring the boys. "As you all know from watching *Historical Survivor*, you'll find clues on the way, but the calamities will find you. Now, while the contestants and I chat about the ship, the audience will watch a video about Captain Robert F. Scott."

The screen suddenly went dark. First, a British flag waved against an icy background. Then a black-and-white photograph of a bedraggled group appeared as a voice intoned, "Robert F. Scott and the four men who died with him on the expedition to reach the South Pole in 1912 went on the worst journey in the world. . . ."

Steve flicked the television off. He was too upset to watch more. He had a terrible feeling about the series he would be forced to edit over the next month. His eyes traveled around his bare hut.

But if he quit his job, how would he eat?

To survive, Steve knew that he had to take care of himself.

If I had such fat lips, I wouldn't make them even bigger with lipstick, Polly thought, staring at the Secretary's red mouth.

Since the Secretary acted as if she didn't see him, Billy slowly lowered his hand. He had wanted to ask about their food. The Secretary had said that they would eat only what Robert F. Scott ate. Ever since he was a little boy, Billy had liked only three chip flavors: beef, chicken, and broccoli. Chips hadn't been invented in 1912; food then was soft instead of crunchy, and Billy thought it sounded generally disgusting.

"If you want, you can get up and stretch," the Secretary said. "We have a long ride to the ship."

"The ship?" Polly said.

I'll soon see ice and snow, Grace thought.

"You're leaving tonight," the Secretary said.

"Tonight!" Polly burst out. "But I need to say good-bye to my mother!" The Department of Entertainment had discouraged Polly's mother from coming. But she had managed to get train tickets somehow. Then her train had been delayed, and she wouldn't arrive until tomorrow morning.

"It's a compucraft." The Secretary acted as if she hadn't heard Polly. "The newest and the best. Your trip to the Antarctic will take five days."

Andrew hoped that the boat had a TV.

The sooner, the better, Robert thought.

I'll have to find something to eat soon, Billy thought.

"But my mother's come a long way. I want to say good-bye!" Polly cried out.

"The limousine will take us in an hour." The Secretary smiled as if she hadn't heard. "Everything that you need will be on the ship. You're not allowed to take anything but your backpack with a change of clothes."

A limo. Billy immediately felt better. Once he and his parents had ridden in a limo. While his dad had practiced his speech to the toy company executives and his mom had looked out the windows at the big houses, Billy had been astounded to find drawer after drawer stuffed with goodies. If Billy could figure out how to get to the limousine first, no one would be the wiser, and then he'd have plenty of extra food.

The Secretary held up one finger, and the various aides who had been hanging around sprang to attention. "Take them back to their hotel rooms," she ordered.

The hotel, Entertainment Headquarters, was adjacent to the Department of Entertainment. Andrew had loved the soft bed.

An aide dressed in gray jeans and a T-shirt fluttered around Polly. The woman had no expression on her face. She looks like an EduTV zombie, Polly thought.

One of the Secretary's assistants moved next to Robert's chair. "When does the show actually start?" Robert asked.

"We begin filming the episodes on the ship," the Secretary said. "I'll have a cozy chat with you on the way." She beamed at them. "It's one of our *Survivor* traditions."

Robert met the Secretary's gaze and promised himself that he would survive long enough to have a tradition.

An aide faced Grace. "Let's go," she said.

Grace stared at the aide's hair, which fell to her feet like a tent. She must use that unnatural stuff called Fastgrow, Grace decided.

A staffer tapped Billy sharply on his shoulder, but Billy was lost in thought, working out the details of his plan to find food.

5

"You have an hour to get cleaned up," Andrew's aide told him. "I'll be back for you at six o'clock sharp."

"Great," Andrew said.

"I'll knock when we're ready to go," the man said.

Andrew didn't answer. He had picked up the remote for the television and was headed for the bed.

After his aide shut the door, Robert counted to sixty and then slipped out into the hallway.

The elevator arrived right away. He stared at the advertisements playing on the elevator walls.

On one wall an old man with wrinkled lips and closed eyes smiled at him. "Dream Hat, a camera for your dreams," the man sang.

On the other wall a woman's hair was growing an inch per second. "With one dose you, too, can have floor-length hair," the woman in the advertisement promised.

The elevator stopped, and Robert walked into the lobby.

The elders of Grace's tribe had warned her about rooms like this, with luxuries like the mood-control ring next to the door.

41

"So you haven't tried the mood ring?" Grace's talkative aide was chattering away. "See, there are twenty different moods. If you push this button, the mood is Valentine's Day Romantic."

The aide pushed the button and sappy music played. Bright red hearts appeared on the window panels, but the lights in the room itself dimmed as if it were dusk indoors.

"Turn it off, okay?" Grace said.

"It'll go off in a minute," the aide said in a hurt voice. "Do you need anything?"

"No." Grace sat down on the edge of the bed.

As the woman left, Grace watched her step to the side to avoid closing the door on her unnaturally long hair. Sick.

Grace sat in the reddish light, listening to violins.

She couldn't believe how wrong modern people were. They didn't know that a person's mood came from the inside. She glared at the evil-looking ring.

Billy peered out the hotel window at the limo on the street below. It had to be waiting for them.

He peeked into the hall. The aides had all disappeared. He grabbed his backpack and snuck out into the hallway. If anybody saw him, so what? The flat-faced aide hadn't told him to stay in the room, had he?

Billy walked down the stairway to avoid detection, opened a door that led to the lobby, and headed for the grand front entrance. When he reached the lobby, he noticed Robert, who was standing with his back to him in a corner. Who's the guy Robert is talking to? Billy wondered.

"Everybody calls her Hot Sauce," Billy overheard the stranger say to Robert as he walked by.

Billy pushed his way through the revolving door, activating the exit pads. They played a few bars from the theme song of *Why Didn't You Tell Me You Liked Bananas?* This was a famous Department of Entertainment holomovie that was supposed to teach little kids to count. Along with hundreds of other kids at the theater, Billy had counted and danced with holobananas.

Outside, the chilly late-October air hit Billy as he exited. The long black car was waiting quietly at the bottom of the stairs. Billy circled it. The license plates read SURVIVOR! The driver was slumped over the wheel.

Billy tapped on the window.

The driver looked up. Billy realized that he had gotten lucky. The man looked beaten down, as if he didn't care about anything.

Billy smiled politely. "I'm one of the contestants. Mind if I put my backpack in the back?"

The driver shrugged.

Billy climbed into the backseat of the black limo.

The driver put his head back down on the wheel.

Billy unslung his backpack and opened a drawer. It was stocked with Billy's dream foods: nuts, beef chips, Chocobombs, crackers, and health-food bars. Billy loaded the contents into his backpack. He emptied the other drawers until his backpack was stuffed. Now, where to hide the swollen backpack?

The limo clock read 5:50. Billy saw that the Secretary, trailed by assistants, was walking up the steps of the hotel. He worried about what she would do if she saw him wandering around outside. But if he got some time alone with her, Billy felt he might be able to impress her. If he was her favorite, maybe he'd have a better shot at being MVP. Billy knocked on the glass partition and spoke into the microphone. "Can I keep my backpack in the front? I'm afraid someone will sit on it."

Billy didn't wait for the driver's answer before he opened the side door and hopped out. He stashed his backpack on the floor of the front seat and ran to catch up with the Secretary.

"Why, Billy, what are you doing?" The Secretary's fur coat was red, like her hair. She wore red leather boots and carried a red purse. Billy had never seen anyone whose parts all matched.

"You look great," Billy said. Since she didn't stop frowning, he added, "My head hurt. I was just walking around."

"I'll need to speak to your aide," she said crossly.

Billy followed her red fur coat through the revolving doors into the lobby. "Besides, I'm excited," he said to distract her.

Her green eyes brightened. "So am I."

They stood together in front of the elevator. "Are you going up?" Billy asked, pushing the button.

"Just to the second floor," the Secretary said. "I want to give my assistants some last-minute instructions."

Billy's heart was pounding. If his scheme was going to work, he knew that he needed to beat the Secretary to the limo.

"You seem like an intelligent boy," the Secretary said as they waited. "What are you going to do with the money?"

"Go to high school and college."

"And then?"

"Make a lot of money." Billy smiled his most engaging grin.

"You and I will get along just fine," the Secretary said.

The elevator bell pinged, and Billy felt as if he had scored. He followed the Secretary inside. "I've been a fan of *Survivor* for a long time."

"You're sweet." The Secretary smiled at him.

Whew! She didn't seem at all suspicious.

"See you in a minute," the Secretary said as she got off.

"Sure." Billy got ready to race to his room.

6

Polly followed her EduTV aide down the long flight of stairs to the street. Another aide was hanging out by the limo, and Polly wondered which of the kids was already there.

The staffer opened the limo door for her.

Polly didn't bother saying good-bye. As she slid in, she saw Billy. He was sipping a drink from a crystal glass.

"Polly." He smiled.

"How long have you been here?" she asked.

"Just a few minutes," Billy said. He felt it in his gut: His plan was going to work. His aide had accepted his story that he had gone for a walk and put his backpack in the limo. All he had to do now was transport the stuffed backpack onto the ship without arousing anyone's suspicions.

Polly watched Robert and Grace walk down the long steps toward the limo. Their assistants flanked them.

The Secretary followed behind them. She was talking on a cell phone.

Andrew and his aide lagged behind. Polly had counted how many steps it would take for the Secretary to arrive at the car and order the driver to begin their journey. Polly was one hundred and five steps away from the point of no return.

An assistant opened the car door, and the Secretary climbed in. "Everyone got their backpacks?" she asked.

The kids nodded. Andrew clambered in at the last moment.

"Do you need anything else, ma'am?" the woman who had accompanied Polly asked the Secretary.

The Secretary shook her head.

Robert's assistant rapped on the driver's door. "The boss is ready."

The Secretary's staff waved as the long car took off down the narrow street.

"I have a gift for your team," the Secretary said, pulling a watch out of her purse. "Now, who looks really responsible?" She searched all their faces.

Choose me, Billy prayed.

A Tantasm, Model 120. Polly recognized the watch from the ads.

I'm going to live by the sun, the moon, and the stars, Grace promised herself.

Nice watch, Robert thought, wondering how much it would sell for.

Andrew never got chosen in things like this, so he looked out the window.

"You." Her finger pointed right at Billy.

Billy beamed. He was her favorite. He had known it.

The Secretary handed Billy the watch. "Does anybody else have a watch?" She carefully studied their faces.

No one said anything.

Billy had pawned his a long time ago. He strapped the team watch onto his wrist. It looked really high-tech. He started playing with the buttons.

"Great," the Secretary said.

Billy looked up. "Hey. I can't change the time."

"That's correct. No matter what time zone you're in, you'll stay on what I call 'studio time' for the convenience of our production department."

Polly looked at the watch on Billy's wrist. Fantasy time. If only this survivor show turned out to be a fantasy and not a horror show.

"You'll make our lives easier if you live by its time," the Secretary finished.

Or die by its time, Polly thought.

Who cares about making the Secretary's life easier? Robert asked himself.

With the buttons disabled, the watch no longer interested Billy. He leaned back and enjoyed the soft leather seats, the headrest, and the heater. He tried to guess the number of packs of Chocobombs in his backpack. He had never had so much candy before in his life.

It was dark outside, but Polly saw lots of people on the street. A man carrying a few sheets of plywood paused and stared at their limo as it drove past him. Polly wanted to say, "Don't envy us."

A while later Andrew heard something and looked around. Billy was snoring with his mouth wide open.

It was strange that the kids had spoken so little to one another. Polly had already decided that Grace, the only other girl on the trip, didn't like to talk. Andrew looked as if he were going to cry if she smiled at him, and she seemed beneath Robert's and Billy's notice. The five of them could be together for months. She stared out the window at the buildings rushing by. The worst was that she hadn't even gotten to say good-bye to Mama.

Before Polly left, Mama cried over her and bought her favorite foods—blueberry and pickle chips—and damned the government. And then, in a final frenzy, she swore never, ever to watch television again—after the *Antarctic Historical Survivor* series was over, of course.

"We could win," Polly had tried to reassure her.

"Ah, you could," her mother said. "Wouldn't that be lovely? You know, the guy from *Civil War Historical Survivor* has his own game show." That man was at least six feet five, with a craggy face and muscles like mountains. "You don't have muscles, Polly, but you have the Memory." Her mother smiled sweetly at her.

"But what use will the Memory be at the South Pole?" Polly had asked. Terror rose in her soul at just the thought of long stretches of whiteness. The Antarctic had to be like blank paper.

Tears had rolled out of the corners of Mama's eyes and down her face. "Who knows?" she said.

Polly closed her eyes. She liked sitting in this limo. She wished that she could stay here for three months. *Limo Survivor* would be just fine.

The Secretary cleared her throat and pulled down her short skirt, but Grace noticed that it was still way above her knees.

"I like to get together with my contestants before the action starts." The Secretary patted her coiffed hair. "I want you to know that I'm on your side."

Robert had tried to talk a man in the lobby of the hotel into letting him use his cell phone. The man had refused, but they had gotten into a conversation about the Department of Entertainment. Robert had learned that the Secretary had a nickname. It fit her, and Robert wanted to call this woman "Hot

Sauce" now. Instead, he forced himself to use his most polite tone. "Ms. Secretary, I still have some questions."

"You mean that you were briefed for days and you didn't get your questions answered?" Although she was smiling, the Secretary's green eyes flashed with anger.

Polly could tell that Robert was struggling to invent a tart response. She broke in. "We were in the hospital, then I felt groggy, then we were on television, and now we're leaving."

The Secretary ignored Polly. "What can you possibly want to know, Robert?"

"Where will the cameras be?" Robert felt relieved that Polly had interrupted, but at the same time resentful. He didn't need a bookworm's help.

"Ah," the Secretary said. "*Survivor*'s secret."

"How will we know where we need to go? Will there be any maps?" Robert asked.

"You'll find out soon enough." The Secretary crossed her legs.

Polly choked out her most worrisome question. "If there's trouble, will the camera crew help us?"

Robert glared at her. He didn't want or need anybody's help.

"No," the Secretary said to Polly. "We never intervene."

"But we're kids," Polly said. "We don't deserve to die."

Robert corrected Polly: "We don't want special favors."

"Our viewers would not allow us to stop the simulation. It would ruin the game," the Secretary said. "Robert, Polly . . ." She smiled. "We have found that the less you know, the more exciting the adventure is. So no more questions about the game."

That's okay, Robert told himself. Hot Sauce was unfair, just like the world he lived in. He was used to it.

Polly wanted to pull out a hunk of the Secretary's red hair.

"But if you want to ask me anything about my personal life, I'd be happy to answer," the Secretary said. "I'd love to get to know you kids."

The Secretary only wanted to talk about herself, Grace realized.

"Do we get points for asking questions?" Robert asked.

The Secretary threw back her head and laughed as if he had told a great joke.

"Then I'm not asking any . . . Hot Sauce," Robert added under his breath.

Getting to know somebody before you hurt them was cruel, Polly thought. She wondered why the woman was so mean. "Were you always rich?"

"No. I wouldn't have had the money to go to college," the Secretary said indignantly, "but I won my Toss fair and square. After college, I lucked out and got a job as a TV talk show host. You may be too young, but did you ever see *The Grossest Jobs in the World*?"

Polly shook her head.

"Well, that was my show. I was young and idealistic back then. Now I try to face the facts. Games like the Toss and *Survivor* are the fairest way that I know to decide who gets a chance." She looked at Grace and batted her eyelashes. "Don't you think so, Grace?"

Grace turned away and stared out the window

"Grace?" the Secretary said sharply. "We like our contestants to have some personality."

"Sure," Grace murmured. She wondered what Washington, D.C., would look like dressed all in snow.

Andrew tried to wiggle his ears.

"Well, usually my contestants are more talkative. We are able to form a little bond that helps them get through the disappointments of the show. But if you all want to just sit there and stare out the window, fine."

Hot Sauce grinned at Robert as if to say, "See, I'm that cool."

Robert liked ignoring her.

Billy snored on.

"We're here." The Secretary shook Billy's shoulder.

"What?" Billy mumbled. He smelled her sweet perfume as he opened his eyes.

"We're at the dock."

Billy gazed at the Secretary's red lips and red-tinted sunglasses before turning to stare out the smoked-glass window.

It was dark outside. He noticed a sign that said NORFOLK NAVAL DOCK. He could see that the other kids were already climbing up the gangplank to the ship. It had been incredibly stupid of him to fall asleep.

"Your ship, the *Terra Nova.*" The Secretary smiled.

Then again, maybe not. Suddenly Billy was wide-awake. He faked a yawn.

"Take your time." The Secretary climbed out of the limo and began walking toward the ship.

Billy glanced at the watch. The glowing dial said ten o'clock. The limo ride had taken four hours. Without hesitating, he slid out of the limo, opened the front door, and snatched his backpack. He kept his eyes glued to the Secretary, but she didn't look back.

His one arm could barely lift the pack, it was so heavy with delicious food.

Billy didn't think the Secretary would notice the shape of his backpack in the dim light. But he couldn't take a chance. He rushed past her and up the gangplank. He didn't stop until he was facing her from behind the rail.

The other four had already disappeared.

Billy was the only one of the five to wave good-bye. The Secretary had said that the show started on the ship. Cameras were probably trained on him.

The Secretary smiled and then turned back to her dark limousine.

For the audience, Billy waved once more as the sea wind rushed through his hair.

7

Billy started to climb down belowdecks. He saw Grace and Polly on the stairwell. To hide his fat backpack, he stayed well behind them.

At the bottom of the stairs he found himself alone in a long, gray hallway. He heard noises to his left and walked through an open door into another corridor. He spotted a plain metal door with the name BILLY painted on it, as if he were a movie star. He opened the door and found a small cabin with a bunk against a wall and one round porthole. He looked inside the closet. Except for a few coat hangers, it was empty. Then he got down on his knees and peered underneath his bunk. This hiding place would have to do. He shoved his backpack against the wall.

Billy went out to explore the ship. His new tennis shoes slapped against the metal floor. The lonely sound reverberated in the hallway.

He heard a loud bang. Could they already be at sea?

Billy passed Grace's cabin. It was open. Grace's back was to him, and she appeared to be unpacking her skimpy backpack. He wondered if she was one of those girls who chattered away after you got to know them. So far he hadn't heard her say more than a few words. He walked past her door.

Andrew's door was closed. Billy looked into Robert's cabin. His backpack lay on the bunk, but the cabin was empty. Billy didn't usually want company, but right now he felt like talking. Anything to make him forget that he was alone on a ship sailing to Antarctica. He decided to go look for Robert.

Robert had already found the engine room. A computerized map hung from the ceiling. It marked the position of the *Terra Nova*. They had just put out to sea in the Atlantic Ocean, many miles from the South Pole, but riding a cushion of air above the surface of the sea, these compucraft traveled thousands of miles a day.

A door off the engine room was open. Robert went to it and turned on the light. Maps of Antarctica hung on all the walls. The continent looked like a squashed white ball. On one of the maps, "Safety Hut" was inscribed next to a dot near the shore. Four *X*s at various distances marked the depots. In the center, someone had scrawled "Pole" in large black letters next to a large dot. Underneath the map, Robert found a typed note:

> On the ship and in Safety Hut, you will find enough fuel and food to last you fifty miles. The dogs and ponies are on the ship. The motor sledges are in Safety Hut. The first depot is fifty miles away. Each depot will have sufficient supplies to carry you to the next depot.

How hard could riding 150 miles be? If this were a river expedition, Robert would have no doubts. Even though there was quirky and violent weather all over the globe, it had never snowed in Houston. Robert didn't know anything about traveling in ice and snow. But he'd learned everything he knew about rivers by watching, listening, and using his head. He'd figure out Antarctica. He had to.

Now Robert needed to survey the ship and decide on their next steps. For he was the captain of this ship, he was sure about that.

A metal door on the far wall of the map room caught his attention. The door opened onto a storage room. Shelf upon shelf was filled with boxes. Ropes hung from the walls, and skis from the ceiling. Two giant sleds lay on the floor, next to two smaller ones. He read the label on the end of one of the boxes. PEMMICAN. What was that again? With the pocketknife he carried in his wallet, he slashed open the box. It was brown and crumbly stuff. Maybe dog food. He sniffed it. Strange.

Robert touched a bag on the next shelf. A sleeping bag, covered in fur. He stroked the long brown and white hairs. Deerskin? Why couldn't they have Gore-Tex? But of course. Scott must have used deerskin.

In one of the boxes he found a folded-up tent and some modern-looking shoes. He felt a stab of relief that the Secretary wasn't accurate in every detail. He examined pairs of old-fashioned skis and a thermometer. He needed to make an inventory. Then he'd hand out supplies to each of the other kids. If the sea voyage was only five days long, he'd better get busy.

He heard a sound in the adjoining room and stuck his head out of the storage room.

Billy Kanalski, the intense guy, stood in front of the maps. He was staring at them as if he were Robert peering through the fence at Motorworld. "Come help with the supplies," Robert said. "We've got a lot to do."

Billy nodded, but his gaze lingered before he turned away to join Robert in the supply room.

From the moment Grace had stepped onto the deck, she'd had the feeling that something alive was on board. Walking down the stairs belowdecks, she took a deep breath and smelled paint and salt and water and . . . animals? After stowing her stuff, she followed the scent. Halfway down a narrow circular stairway she heard scuffling noises. Then a dog howled. She knew that she had been right, and was glad.

The room at the base of the stairs was crowded with barrels and harnesses. The sounds came from behind a closed door. She leaned her ear against it and guessed that there were ten or fifteen dogs, maybe more. She opened the door a crack. Gnashing their teeth, the dogs lunged at the door. She slammed it in their faces. They'd looked like huskies, white with brown and black markings. How long had they been down there? Did they have food and water? She cracked open the door again and spotted a barrel of water on the far side of the room, but no food.

As she slammed the door shut, she thought, Where would the government have put the dog food?

In the outer room, which seemed to contain most of the supplies, Grace pried a top off the closest barrel and stuck her head in. She couldn't identify the type of meat. The sides of the barrel were moldy, which worried her, but moldy food was better than none. How would she feed this pack? If she threw the meat to them inside the animals' room, the dogs would fight one another. A dog might get hurt.

She'd have to lead each dog into the supply room, harness it, and feed it separately. Which meant that she needed to go into that room of snarling dogs.

"An Iñupiat can think like any animal," her grandfather had told her. She thought like a husky as she cracked open the door again. The dogs lunged at her, but this time she braced her foot inside the doorway to keep the door from closing and sidled into the room.

I bring food, Grace thought. The dogs jumped up on her, but none bit her.

Then she noticed the ponies. Two white ones were in a pen at the back. She spotted a bale of hay but couldn't concentrate on the state of the ponies because the dogs were leaping and jumping all around her. Now that she was close to them, she realized that what she had mistaken for fury seemed to be only a frenzied excitement. What were ponies doing on an Antarctic voyage?

She grabbed one husky, a large brown one, by the scruff of the neck. The dog twisted and bucked, but she managed to drag it into the supply room. With her free hand she lifted a harness off the wall and slipped it over its head. Although most of her tribe used snowmobiles, her grandfather preferred a sled. He had told her many stories of sled dogs. She wondered if these dogs had worked together before.

The dog quieted down now that he was in harness. She took a cupful of the food from the barrel and poured it on the floor. The dog devoured it in a few moments and then looked up at her, hopeful that there would be more.

She stared into the dog's eyes. Okay. One more scoop. She poured it on the floor and considered where she would put this dog while she fed the next. And what were they going to do with ponies? The Indians on the reservation owned horses. Occasionally one escaped, and once Grace had kept a brown mare for a few days before she found the owner. She had a hard time believing that ponies would do well on ice.

She finally decided to tie the dog with a rope and fasten it to the stairwell. That done, she opened the door to retrieve her next dog.

The thought of what the other kids might be doing crossed her mind, but the dogs howled. She was needed here.

Polly noticed a stack of books on her bedside table. She had read thousands of books on her electronic book card, which she refilled at the computary. But only once had she read a book with an actual cover and pages that turned. It was *The Fellowship of the Ring* by J.R.R. Tolkien. She could still remember the pleasant hours she had spent with that book one summer on the steps outside her hut, fanning herself because of the heat.

She picked up *Scott's Last Expedition: The Journals*. It was surely no accident that the book was in her cabin. She knew a few facts about Scott, of course. The *World Book* had had a short entry on him. She turned to the back cover and read, *In November 1910 . . .*

It was almost November 2083, so here they were, starting out 173 years later.

. . . the vessel Terra Nova *. . .*

Their ship was named the *Terra Nova*.

. . . carried an international team of explorers led by Robert Falcon Scott, an Englishman determined to be the first man to reach the South Pole.

Why would Scott care about being the first to reach the Pole?

She didn't know about Robert, Grace, and the others, but here she was on the first kid-led expedition to the Pole, and she had no interest in record-setting.

Scott kept a detailed journal of his adventures until March 29, 1912, when he and the few remaining members of his team met their ends in a brutal blizzard.

"Brutal blizzard." She hated the sound of that. Her backpack still unemptied, she settled on her bunk, resting her head against the small pillow. She opened the book to the first page. She was used to reading adventures; she had read them ever since she was little: *The Wizard of Oz, Treasure Island, Into Thin Air.* She wasn't used to being in one. By reading, maybe she could forget that she was on this great big ship heading to Antarctica.

She sighed. Why, oh why, had she been chosen?

If a girl had a special gift for running, she should be in a track meet.

If a girl had a special gift for cooking, she should work in a restaurant.

But why send Polly Pritchard, whose special gift was the Memory, to Antarctica? She would be more of a freak in Antarctica than she had been on West Ninety-eighth Street in New York City, where her neighbors all hated reading.

She felt vaguely nauseated and rubbed her stomach. Just in case, she grabbed her book and went into the bathroom.

Sunlight flooded through his porthole, but Andrew Morton lay inert on his bunk. He had been miserable ever since he had boarded this ship. As far as he could tell, there was no TV anywhere. So last night, after searching for one, he had just gone to sleep.

"I don't care! Go!" his dad had screamed over the noise of the TV when Andrew confessed that he didn't know why they had picked him.

"They must have made a mistake," Andrew moaned.

His mother tightened the sash on the thick bathrobe that she wore all day long. "They probably did, but go anyway."

His parents wanted a chance at the contest money. One hundred thousand dollars was a lot. For thirty years, his dad had worked as a shoe salesman, but his mom complained that he didn't make enough money to keep his own kids in shoes. Andrew didn't mind going barefoot, so his parents bought shoes for his little brother, Bart.

Andrew got up and looked out the porthole at the gusty sea. Boring.

This was the first time in his life that he would ever be without a television. Before this, he had hardly ever missed an episode of his favorite show in the world, *Lives of the Rich*.

His dad had explained that as life grew harder in America, as the rich grew richer and the poor poorer, the poor people rebelled. To protest their hard lives, they waged the Urban Trash Wars. The politicians decided that better programming was the way to make Americans happier. So the Department of Entertainment was created. The Secretary encouraged everyone to enjoy television. Through television, each viewer could be anyone and do anything.

Andrew totally agreed. Day after day and night after night, Andrew watched reality television, showing on close to one thousand channels. On *Lives of the Rich*, his favorite character was Craig. Craig had a room of his own much fancier than even this cabin of Andrew's on the compucraft, and Craig had plenty to eat and drink and a closet full of clothes.

Sometimes, at home, Andrew would eat his bag of roast-beef chips while he watched Craig eat real roast beef and mashed potatoes, and he would be fooled and think that it was he, Andrew Morton, who ate roast beef off gleaming plates, and not Craig Collins.

Craig had a go-cart and nice parents. Craig's parents would never let him enter a kids' survival contest.

Andrew idly wondered where the other kids were, but he didn't really care. As long as he stayed hidden in his cabin, they wouldn't find out that they had been saddled with a mistake.

Craig had had some adventures. Once he had gotten locked inside a department store all night and played with the robots. Craig always had a good time. If Craig were on *Antarctic Historical Survivor* and in this cabin, what would he do now?

Ah, Craig would never be here, Andrew reminded himself. Never. Never. Never.

Andrew's mom, his dad, and Bart were probably sitting on the couch watching television, trading bets on whether he was going to make it to the Pole or not. They might even be watching him right now. They had cameras everywhere on these survivor shows. "Hi," he mouthed, just in case his family was watching him.

He looked around the room but couldn't spot the lens.

He wasn't sure whether it felt better or worse to be all alone.

Polly's stomach turned, and she tried not to retch. She hoped that Mama couldn't see her now. She didn't want her mother to know that she was seasick. She examined the mirror again for a hidden camera but saw only her own serious face.

This was the first time she had ever had a bathroom to herself.

She wished this morning that she could enjoy it in some other way besides hugging the toilet.

A loud bell clanged, and Robert's voice sounded over the intercom: "Meet in the mess hall in five minutes."

What a bossy boy! He was acting like he was captain or something. Casey Duncan and the other boys who lived on her street had been bossy. Over the years she'd learned to deal with them by staying away.

"Polly Pritchard comes to town; her fat brain weighs her down" was just one of the rhymes they taunted her with.

She sighed and stood up. It was going to be hard to avoid Robert.

8

Robert stood at the head of the small table while the other kids sat around it in the room labeled MESS HALL.

There's got to be a camera on us right now even if we can't see it, Billy thought. Involuntarily, his eyes swept over every inch of space in the small white room. He would give anything to know where the camera was hidden.

"Okay. We all know how these things work from other shows," Robert said.

Billy nodded.

Grace was sewing a torn harness.

Polly was reading.

Andrew just looked miserable.

"This is day one. We have a total of five days on this ship to 'bond together as a team and get ready for the challenge.'" Robert's voice sounded more sarcastic than he had intended.

Polly put her book down. Her stomach still felt unsteady, but she steeled herself. "Excuse me. Who appointed you leader?"

"I appointed myself."

"What are your qualifications?"

Robert smiled as if she had asked the easiest question in the world. "I'm going to survive. Any more questions? Anyone else want to be leader?"

"Grace? Andrew? Billy?" Polly studied each kid's face. "Don't you want to talk about this?"

Billy's plan was that Robert would do all the work and then, at the end, he, Billy, would do some amazing thing and be voted MVP. So he was happy for Robert to wear himself out as leader.

Grace didn't care.

"I think Robert's great," Andrew said.

"You can be leader, Robert," Polly said, since Robert was set on the title and no one else wanted it. "But on the big decisions, I think we should vote. One person, one vote. Does anyone disagree?"

No one said anything.

"Be leader, then," Polly said. "It's fine with me." She picked up her book. Scott's ponies had gotten stranded on an ice floe that floated out to sea. Henry "Birdie" Bowers, Titus Oates, and Apsley Cherry-Garrard were trying to rescue them. Polly was happier than usual to have a good book to help her escape from her life.

"Billy and I worked on the supplies," Robert said. "How about the rest of you? What did you do last night?" Except for Billy, he guessed that they were a worthless bunch.

No one spoke. "How about you, Polly? Did you read all night?" Robert tried unsuccessfully to keep the sneer out of his voice.

"I did," she said calmly. She held up the book, *Scott's Last Expedition: The Journals*.

"So?" Robert said.

"There are books about polar exploration in my cabin," Polly said. "I know it's part of the game. You should read one."

Robert had never learned anything worth knowing from a book, but before he could respond, Grace interrupted. "Did you hear the animals?"

"Yeah," Robert said. "I was going to bring that up next. We need to figure out how to take care of them."

"I already have," Grace said.

"You fed them all?" Robert asked, surprised at her efficiency. "What's on board?"

"Twelve dogs and two ponies."

"Ponies?" Billy said.

"I don't understand." Robert scratched his head.

Polly cleared her throat. Here was her first chance to show how useful the books were going to be. "Captain Scott used ponies, dogs, and a primitive form of motor sledge for his polar expedition. Of course, his faith in ponies and motor sledges was misplaced. Roald Amundsen beat him to the Pole in 1911 using only dogs."

"Ponies hauling on ice and snow?" Robert asked. The idea sounded strange. "How did they do?"

"They slipped a lot, and the weather was hard on them. They did better when they wore snowshoes," Polly added.

"Snowshoes for horses?" Billy asked incredulously.

"Any weird-looking snowshoes down there, Grace?" Robert asked.

"Yeah," Grace said, thinking of the round things hanging next to the ponies' bridles that had puzzled her. "Now that you mention it. I didn't know what they were."

"That's the Secretary of Entertainment for you, accurate down to the last little detail." Billy was anxious to do everything he could to remain the Secretary's favorite contestant.

"Let's get one thing straight," Robert broke in. "I hate the suck-ups on the reality shows. The wonderful Secretary of Entertainment this. The wonderful Secretary of Entertainment that." He tried to imagine a camera in the corner and looked straight at it. "I don't mean any disrespect, ma'am. I'm glad for this chance to earn money." Robert turned and glared at Billy. "But we won't have any sucking up while I'm team leader, you got that?"

"I didn't mean . . ." Billy's voice trailed off.

"So let's get back to our plan. Billy and I are going to handle supplies." Robert looked at Grace. "You, animals?"

Grace nodded.

"Polly," he said deliberately. "I guess you should be Director of Research." He smiled at his joke. She was prim and executive-looking, like her title.

"I think everybody should read these books," Polly said.

Robert shook his head. "No time. Find out all you can about Scott's mistakes. Maybe we don't even want to bring the ponies."

"Scott and his men brought them along and then killed them as food for themselves and the dogs," Polly said.

"Killed them," Grace echoed, with too much emotion in her voice as far as Robert was concerned.

"Another thing," Robert said. "Grace, those animals are our tools. We're not going to cry over ponies or dogs or anything." He stared hard at her. "You got it? Or I'm going to take you off animals and stick you with the supplies. Understand?"

"I'm going to need some help," Grace said.

"What about you, Andrew? What did you do last night?"

Might as well tell the lazy truth. "Slept."

"I'm getting a sense of what the other team members'

strengths are. What do you bring to the team?" Robert said. He tried to keep his voice level and not mocking.

Andrew shook his head miserably. Sometimes his family teased him and called him "couch worm." That's what he felt like, a soft, flabby worm.

"Where are you from again?" Robert asked.

"Nashville, Tennessee." Andrew hung his head.

"You get snow there, don't you?" Robert said.

Andrew nodded.

"Are you a good skier? A good ice fisherman?" Polly suggested.

"No." Andrew shook his head. "There's not enough snow to ski."

"Maybe a hunter? A friend of mine told me that there'll be seals in Antarctica," Robert said.

Andrew sighed. He was good at watching television. That was about it. When he was a little boy, his mother told him that everyone had special gifts, but he had long since given up on finding his.

"Okay," Robert said. No sense humiliating the guy. "You help Grace."

Andrew nodded.

"Now, we have just five days on this ship. We've got a lot to do to get ready . . ." He snapped his fingers. "I know. Polly, could you be our navigator?"

"Sure," Polly said.

Grace stood and walked over to a slot in the wall labeled KITCHEN.

"What are you doing?" Robert said.

Robert acted as if each of them needed permission to move, Polly thought.

"I'm hungry," Grace said.

Me, too, Billy thought. Please, let breakfast be a good bag of chips.

Grace punched a large button that said BREAKFAST. Five trays popped out of the paneling.

"Compliments of Shipchef," said a creaky voice.

"Good button-pushing, Grace," Robert said. The smell of eggs and bacon filled the cabin. Like most kids in America, Robert rarely ate hot food, so he savored the aroma.

"Is it egg-and-bacon chips?" Andrew asked Grace.

"No," Grace said. "It's the real thing." She walked back to the table with a breakfast tray.

"You say that like you eat real bacon all the time," Billy said.

"We do. From hogs." Grace took a bite of her food.

"Where do you live again?" Billy asked as he stood to get his breakfast. As far as he was concerned, a bag of bacon chips was better, but since this bacon was crunchy, bacon and eggs would do just fine.

"On a Hopi Indian reservation," Grace said. "My mom tries to keep the old ways as much as possible." Grace and her family didn't live like her Iñupiat ancestors had. But that didn't stop her family from being proud of the fact that they grew or raised most of their own food.

Robert returned to the table with his tray. He loaded up his fork with a huge piece of bacon and eggs. He loved bacon and eggs and rarely got to eat them.

"Better than water moccasin?" Billy said to Robert with a touch of sarcasm as he sat down next to him.

Robert decided to ignore Billy's jab. "Moccasins aren't that bad."

Polly and Andrew rose to get their trays.

"I bet your gift has something to do with animals," Polly said to Grace as she passed her.

"I hadn't thought about that," Grace said. "I'm the reservation's animal doctor."

"What did you do the day of the farm test?" Billy asked Grace.

"Played with the pigs. Why? What did you do?" Grace said.

"My tester told me that the farm test was optional, so I sat in the car," Billy said.

"I drove the tractor," Robert said. He looked at Billy and made a guess. "Did you ace the snow-and-ice computer games?"

"Yeah," Billy said. But he knew snow-and-ice games were very different from real snow and real ice. "What did you do at the farm, Andrew?" he asked, to change the subject.

"I watched TV," Andrew said.

Robert laughed along with the others. "You watched television?"

"Yeah, there was a TV in the farmhouse. They said that I could go anywhere and do anything." Andrew blushed.

Grace pointed to a small black box in the corner of the room.

"What are you looking at?" Robert said.

"Is that a camera?" Grace asked.

"I already checked. It's a smoke detector," Robert said.

"The thought of the cameras gives me the creeps," Polly said.

"We've got to put the cameras out of our minds," Robert said firmly, as much to himself as to the rest of them.

Billy touched the top button on his shirt. "Maybe the cameras are in our clothes."

Robert pointed to his shirt. The buttons were missing.

"What happened to it?" Billy said.

"Smashed them in my room last night," Robert said.

"And?" Polly looked up, interested.

"They're buttons," Robert said. "Which reminds me: After breakfast, I want us all to try on the gear."

"If there are cameras, there have to be cameramen," Polly said.

"Yeah, remember when those cameramen got blown up in *Civil War Historical Survivor*?" Billy said.

"Well, there's no camera crew on this ship." Robert had searched the whole ship and was sure of that.

"I think that they've wired the ship in some way, but when we get to Antarctica, there have to be cameramen," Billy said. "Otherwise, how would they know which way we're going?"

That was what Polly had been thinking. Adults. Adults had to be near them. They couldn't be all alone.

9

Later that same day, the kids were in the supply room, modeling gear in front of a mirror.

"You look huge," Andrew said to Polly.

"You look funny, too." Polly giggled. She wore a parka, waterproof pants, three layers of long underwear, a pair of goggles, a pair of undergloves, a pair of fur mittens, a neck warmer, two hats, three pairs of socks, and some fur boots tagged FINNESKOE. A vocabulary word for the schoolkids, Polly decided.

"These clothes look old," Billy said.

"It's not Gore-Tex or any of the fabrics that we're used to," Robert said.

"Animal furs are warmer," Grace told him. "And better."

"I'm burning up." Andrew tugged at his turtleneck. Sweat poured down his face.

"You'll be glad for these clothes in a couple of days," Billy said. In the polar gear he appeared twice his regular slim size.

"At least it's late spring there," Polly said.

"It is?" Robert spoke without thinking. He hated to admit that he didn't know something, even a fact about a land as remote and foreign as Antarctica.

"Yeah, we'll be landing in November when Scott started his trek," Polly said. "The days will be long. The sun may not set."

Robert felt stupid. He should have remembered the seasonal difference in the hemispheres. What else had he forgotten?

Polly laughed and pointed at all of them in the mirror. "We look like that photo of the Scott expedition on the video."

"Polly, those guys were losers," Robert said sharply.

No one said anything else, but for Polly the fun of dressing up was over. Robert's rebuke hurt her feelings and angered her at the same time. She had read enough to learn that the Scott expedition boasted accomplished scientists. Among them were surgeons, a physicist, a zoologist, geologists, and a biologist. They were not losers.

"My clothes are fine," Billy said quietly. He slipped out of the heavy garments and stowed them in a bag marked BILLY. While the others were still fooling with the gear, he turned to go. Robert had kept him so busy last night that he hadn't had time to study the maps.

Billy looked at a 1911 map of Antarctica and saw that Scott had landed on something named the Ross Ice Shelf. Comparing the 1911 map with a map dated 2057, the last year that the government had sent scientists to Antarctica, he noted that the ice shelf appeared to have melted. They would land on Beardmore Glacier.

He heard someone fidgeting and turned to see Polly standing next to him.

"So these are the maps, huh?" she said. "What are you looking at?"

"The Beardmore Glacier," Billy said.

"Oh," Polly said. "So that's the Beardmore."

"What do you know about it?" Billy asked.

"Scott began his ascent of the Beardmore on December 10, 1911," Polly said, remembering the facts from one of her books. "Three groups of four men carried 200 pounds of supplies per man up its slopes. It was really rough going."

"Do you always sound like an encyclopedia?" Billy said.

Polly sighed and fought the impulse to turn around and rush back to her cabin. Why were these boys so rude? Didn't Billy realize that to win the game, they all needed to get along?

Billy figured that if he ignored Polly, maybe she would leave. He studied the next map. It showed the placement of depots. They were in a straight line to the Pole, but since compasses didn't work well in Antarctica, he'd have to keep track of the longitude and the latitude to calculate the distance traveled.

Polly stirred beside him. Why hadn't she left?

"Billy, Robert's made me navigator."

What an idiot! She was going to tell him to get out of her map room.

"I guess he thought that because I could read books, I could read maps." Polly laughed. That's right. Keep your voice light. You need Billy.

It was obvious that Polly couldn't navigate her way out of her bathroom. Billy could have told that to Robert, but the fool hadn't asked his opinion.

"I can't," Polly concluded. "I mean, I've never even tried." A part of her wanted to kick Billy in the shin, but she managed to say, "So could you help?"

"I was planning to do it anyway." No one could keep Billy out of the map room.

Polly sighed with relief. Holding her tongue had paid off.

"And . . ." Billy turned back to stare at the maps.

"And?" Polly said.

"I don't need any help, so you can leave," Billy said.

Polly turned around and walked out the door. She couldn't stand to be in the room with that boy another instant. "We have five days to bond together," Robert had said at breakfast. Five days to hurt each other's feelings, Polly thought.

The kids had been so busy that they hadn't sat down for lunch, but for dinner Shipchef spit out sandwiches, chips, and concentrate from real oranges. Billy had never had real fake orange juice before, just orange drink. He took a sip of the juice. It was not as sweet as the drink, which he liked better.

"Polly, how many motor sledges did Scott have?" Robert asked. Robert and Billy had been making an inventory of all the gear before deciding what to load into the big sacks that were going to be strapped to the sleds.

"He started with three," Polly said. "But he lost one unloading it from the ship on the thin ice. I think I told you, the motor sledges weren't reliable."

"It will be great if the Secretary has given us three," Billy said. "Otherwise I don't know what we're going to do with all our stuff."

"If Scott had them on board," Robert said, "I wonder why the Secretary didn't put them on the ship." He took a bite of his peanut butter sandwich.

"She's not always accurate," Polly said. "I read that the Alamo guys carried guns that weren't invented until the Civil War."

"It's probably that simple," Robert said, "but I keep looking for meaning behind everything. For instance, did any of you guys think that DOE clinic was spooky?"

"What do you mean?" Andrew asked. He had liked sleeping in the clinic, with its fresh sheets on the beds and a television mounted on the wall.

"It's like they knocked me out." Robert tore into his bag of chips.

"Now that you mention that clinic—" Polly said, biting into her sandwich.

Billy interrupted her. "I thought I was the only one. The whole stay seemed like one long dream."

"I remember doctors standing over me, talking. One came toward me, holding a long needle pointed at my eye; then everything went black," Robert said.

A needle aimed at his eye, Grace thought. She had cut tendons and muscles with her scalpel, but she couldn't imagine puncturing an eye.

Billy involuntarily touched his eyelids. They felt normal.

"I just remember voices," Polly said. "I kept trying to wake up and listen, but I couldn't."

Andrew remembered a nice nurse standing over him and encouraging him to drink a purple liquid.

"I'd give anything to know what they did to us," Robert said. He didn't have a good feeling about that clinic visit.

"Remember, we're on camera," Billy said.

"Use your head. Do you think that darn Hot Sauce is going to broadcast anything she doesn't like?" Robert glared at Billy. He finished his last bite of sandwich.

"'Hot Sauce'?" Polly asked.

"The Secretary's nickname," Robert explained.

* * *

Steve chuckled. "I wonder how that kid learned her nickname."

"I don't know," Chad said.

Except for Pearl, who was sweeping the same spot on the floor over and over, Steve and Chad were alone. The rest of the crew was on a break.

"We need to double delete that whole conversation," Chad said. "Hot Sauce is so paranoid about the corneal implants that she doesn't allow references to the clinic even on the backup system."

Steve reached for the DELETE button, but Chad grabbed his hand. "On second thought, sometimes we save some of these cut scenes."

"Why?" Steve asked.

Chad shrugged. "They could be useful."

"If you say so," Steve said hesitantly.

"Let's double delete the scene from the official records but save it in a separate file."

Steve pushed the TRANSFER button.

Chad leaned over his shoulder.

The computer asked Steve to name the file. "What's the file's name?"

"'P.B.'?" Chad said.

"What does that stand for?" Steve asked.

"Possible blackmail." Chad laughed.

Steve froze. Blackmail?

Chad clapped Steve on the back. "But we're very careful."

The *swish, swish, swish* of the broom competed with the thumping of Steve's heart as he nodded.

Jacob Petrello walked in and joined them at the screens. Jacob was a sandy-haired man around thirty-five years of age.

When Steve had first met Jacob, he had liked him instinctively.

On the screens, the kids were all working silently at their different jobs.

"Hey!" Jacob pointed at Andrew's screen. "He's talking."

Chad turned the volume up.

Andrew was alone with the ponies. "You know, guys," he said to the animals, "I have a confession to make. I've never been this close to a pony before. But if you help me, I'll help you." He held up a round contraption. "This is a horse shoe." He paused. "I mean a pony shoe. I need to put this on you." He looked into the eyes of one of the ponies. "So?"

"How long do you think it's going to take for Andrew to get that thing on?" Chad asked.

"I guess about two hours," Jacob said.

"I'll put it at three," Chad said.

"He'll figure it out," Steve said confidently.

Two hours and fifty minutes later, Steve had to admit that Chad was right. Andrew still hadn't been able to get the pony to raise its hoof long enough for him to secure the shoe.

Andrew looked as discouraged as Steve felt.

"You'd help him if you could, wouldn't you?" Jacob said to Steve.

What an odd question! How could he, a production editor, help any of the kids? But Steve didn't hesitate before answering. "Sure."

The pony kept still for an instant. Andrew jammed the shoe on.

Yeah, Andrew! It's a shame, Steve thought, that he can't hear our cheers.

10

It was the end of a long day, and Polly felt exhausted. The ship rolled in the impossibly vast sea. To calm herself, she clutched the sides of the deck chair and stared at the moons. The natural moon was pearl-colored. The second moon, which had been installed by advertisers years ago, was light green and shone with the Gap company logo.

Andrew plopped down in the deck chair next to her. He noticed the book in her lap. "Maybe you could write a book about polar exploration."

"Someone already did." Polly held up her book so he could read the title: *The Worst Journey in the World.* "Apsley Cherry-Garrard, one of Scott's men, wrote this in 1922."

"Our trip's not that bad so far, is it?"

Polly snorted. Hadn't he noticed the huge waves? The bottomless sea? But then again, the ocean was the least of their problems. "Do you think we're going to make it?" she asked.

"Yes." Andrew's voice sounded more confident than he felt.

"The camera crew is our only hope," Polly said.

"Why?"

"I can't believe that adults would watch us die."

"Kids starve all the time."

"I know, but no one has to watch them."

Andrew looked around the deck for the cameras. "Do you feel better or worse knowing someone is watching us?"

"It makes me feel better to think that God is watching, or my father in heaven, but it makes me feel worse to think that millions of people are watching"—Polly struggled to find the words—"our tragedy."

"I used to be one of those people," Andrew said. "I used to sit on my couch night and day and watch."

"Me, too. We all did. It's not like we had a choice."

"No. I mean, I used to like watching more than being a part of anything."

"And that's not true anymore?" Polly asked.

"Well, there's no TV here. I don't have anything to watch."

"I guess you're right. When I've finished my books, then I won't have anything to read."

"I hope we make it," Andrew said.

"We will," Polly promised, although she didn't quite believe it.

Billy and Robert appeared. Billy was holding a notepad.

"Have you checked the lifeboats for paddles?" Robert asked Billy.

"No," Billy said. He helped Robert turn a lifeboat over. Two paddles were hooked to the side.

Robert picked up each one and examined it. "They're in good shape."

Billy put a check on the inventory list.

Polly watched Billy and Robert pass by.

They're very diligent, Polly thought. I just wish they were nicer. "Andrew," she said slowly when she was sure that the two other boys couldn't hear her, "I've enjoyed talking to you."

"Sure," Andrew said.

"Have you talked to any of the others?" Polly adjusted the blanket on her shoulders.

"Like this?"

She nodded.

"No."

"Billy's mean and Robert's bossy," she said.

"They're okay." Robert and Billy were like all the boys he had ever known.

"Grace is nice. She just seems so removed."

"I know what you mean," Andrew said.

"Thanks for listening," Polly said.

"Sure."

She stared again at the ocean.

"It's a nice night," he said quietly.

For some reason, the big waves didn't seem quite as frightening as before. "It is," she agreed.

11

"We're going to cross the equator in twenty minutes!" Billy called out over the loudspeaker.

"Billy's sure good with maps," Steve said to Chad. The two of them were staring at the five screens. It was the second full day of the kids' ocean voyage. The Compucraft had passed uneventfully through the Panama Canal. All five contestants were busy doing chores.

"He is," Chad answered.

"The ratings for today's episode." Jacob came in and handed Chad the familiar blue ratings sheet.

Steve read over Chad's shoulder. "Seventy-three percent."

"Hot Sauce must be furious," Chad said.

"But these ratings are good. Most people are watching," Steve said.

"You don't understand. Last year, eighty percent of America watched *D-Day Historical Survivor*. This year's *Alamo Historical Survivor* pulled only seventy-five percent. The ratings are steadily declining," Chad explained.

"The viewers aren't hooked on this series yet," Jacob commented.

"The Secretary needs to create one of her calamities," Chad said. Steve laughed.

"You laugh." Chad pointed at the ratings sheet. "But she will."

"Oh, come on," Steve said.

"Our government depends on good ratings," Chad said.

"Of course. Good ratings mean that the crime rate stays low," Steve said.

"That's what they say," Chad agreed with a sly smile.

Steve was certain that Chad knew more than he was telling. "What's the real reason?"

"Did you know that less than ten percent of the public votes in elections?" Chad said.

"No." Steve wasn't old enough to vote yet. But he knew his mom and dad had never bothered to register.

"Well, the more TV people watch, the less likely they are to vote," Chad said. "Do you understand yet?"

Steve shook his head.

"We're still called a democracy," Jacob broke in. "But only the politicians vote. They control who's in office."

"There's a lot of pressure on the Secretary to keep the ratings up," Chad said.

"The stakes are high. She's got to be always on the lookout for a new gimmick," Jacob added.

The series made more sense now. "So that's why she's using innocent kids," Steve murmured.

Andrew had gone almost two whole days without watching television. He was surprised that he hadn't been bored, but when he thought about his routine, he realized that he had been too busy.

All of them had settled into their jobs. Robert and Billy sorted and inventoried the gear. Polly read her books. Grace trained the dogs. Andrew worked with the ponies and did the odd jobs that Robert and Grace requested. At night, he talked with Polly.

"We're crossing the equator in one minute!" Billy called out.

Andrew put down a sack that he had been packing. "I'm going to go on deck." He knew there wasn't a line in the ocean marking the equator, but he wanted to see for himself.

Robert nodded. "Break time." He turned off the camp stove—or Primus, as the vocabulary note had labeled it. The instructions said that an outer ring was used to melt snow for tea or cocoa while the inner pot was used to melt the snow to be mixed with pemmican. After playing with the Primus for twenty minutes, he felt he had learned how to work it in eighty-degree temperatures. The trick would be lighting it in subzero weather. He'd practice again this afternoon before training the others on how to use it.

Andrew walked up the stairs to the deck. It was late afternoon, but the sun was still shining. The water was bluer than Andrew had ever imagined it could be.

Grace was leaning over the rail, enjoying the feel of the wind.

Wearing a tank top, Polly was sitting on a deck chair, her hair blowing in the breeze.

A hit song was playing over the speaker system. Billy must have turned the radio on. "*I've got the hologram blues. Just when I think I know you, you fade away like some poor hologram that don't know how to play.*"

Robert stood next to Andrew near the rail. "I'd really like a swim."

"A swim would be great," Andrew said. He took off his T-shirt. The late-afternoon sun felt good on his chest.

"Of course, this ship is going so fast, by the time I took a stroke it'd be out of sight."

"Yeah," Andrew said. He balled his T-shirt up in his hand and tossed it in the air.

"Andrew!" Polly yelled. "Throw me your T-shirt."

Andrew tied his T-shirt into a knot before tossing it to Polly. Polly caught it and tossed it back.

Billy walked out onto the deck. He intercepted the toss. "It's a beach party," he said. "Robert!"

While still turned away from Billy, Robert caught the T-shirt ball in one hand. He called out, "Grace!"

Grace caught it and tossed it to Polly. Polly tossed the T-shirt to Andrew, but it was high. Andrew jumped to catch it. The sun was shining so brightly that for a moment he was dazed. But his fingers closed around the soft ball, and he landed back squarely on the deck.

Polly clapped.

Grace laughed.

"Good catch!" Robert called.

"He's a football player!" Billy shouted.

"Hardly," Andrew said, but he was pleased.

"The beach party was fun. When we start editing, I think we should leave in the whole scene. Don't you agree?" Chad said.

"Sure," Steve said. He hated to think about the reason the Secretary loved playful scenes. He guessed that they made the audience sadder when something bad happened.

All five kids were leaning against the rail. The wind was blowing through their hair. They looked as if they were on vacation.

"Steve," Chad said, "why don't you let Jacob take over? I need you to begin reviewing the e-mails from our viewers."

Jacob seemed to notice Steve's reluctance to leave the monitors. "Steve thinks he's the kids' baby-sitter."

Jacob was right. Steve didn't like leaving the kids; he wanted to see the rest of their day. But he couldn't disobey his manager's request.

Slowly Steve turned away.

12

On the third day, the dogs licked Grace as if they could read her mind and knew that she was thinking about the journey they would soon face. She wished there was a way to see how the dogs handled themselves in ice and snow.

Even so, Grace had begun to sort out the dogs' personalities. Brontosaurus, the dog with his nose under her arm, was a trouble-maker and a malcontent, but he also seemed very smart. Triceratops, the dog licking the back of her neck, had a sweet disposition but short legs. For different reasons, she expected to have trouble with both on the trail.

T-Rex stood next to her, looking dignified. He was a strong dog whose hazel eyes seemed human. He didn't let much bother him. He wasn't quite as smart as Brontosaurus, but he was steadier. The other dogs deferred to him; he was the leader.

In the tiny space of the compucraft, Pterodactyl almost flew, he was so fast, but he didn't seem to like Grace. Right now he was the only dog who wasn't waiting his turn to be petted. She sensed that he wasn't going to be loyal.

Dryosaurus, the dog with his paw on Grace's stomach, was the second fastest, and he was sensitive. When Grace scolded any dog, she saw Dryosaurus tuck his tail between his legs and pin his ears back in total submission. Like T-Rex, he came when Grace called.

Brachiosaurus, Apatosaurus, Diplodocus, and Ichthyosaurus, the biggest dogs, would provide the muscle to pull the sled. Iguanodon, so named because he was the ugliest of the dogs, was also the slowest. Polacanthus was the least playful of the dogs and perhaps the oldest. Ankylosaurus's massive tail, almost as big as a club, had impressed her, but this dog was easily frightened and during conflicts spent much of the time crouching on the ground.

She called T-Rex to her and stared into his knowing eyes. He looked at her as if to say, "Whatever you want, I'll try to do it."

There wasn't enough room to hook the dogs up to the sled, but tonight she planned to try to put them in formation. She slipped the harness over T-Rex's neck. "I'm counting on you," she whispered as she pressed her face into his fur.

"Andrew!" Grace called. He was in the pen with the ponies.

Andrew had worked hard all day, but he was eager to help Grace.

Grace held three big huskies on a leash. She patted the head of one dog. "T-Rex is the leader."

"You named them after dinosaurs?" Andrew said.

"Yeah."

"Why?"

"They found the bones of a dinosaur on our reservation a few years ago. Scientists came. They talked to us about dinosaurs. I liked the names."

Those few sentences were the most that Andrew had ever heard Grace say. "Have you named the ponies yet?" he asked.

"No," Grace said.

"I was thinking about calling them Milky and Cookie," said Andrew.

"That's great."

"Have the dogs pulled a sled before?" Andrew asked.

"I'm not sure." Grace stood up. "Can you hold these dogs while I go get the traces?"

"What are the traces?" Andrew asked.

"They're the straps that tie the dogs to the sled." Grace handed Andrew the leashes.

A communications computer sounded, and Jacob left to retrieve the message.

Chad and Steve huddled next to the screens, watching the kids' third day on the ship. The kids hadn't gone to bed yet. So, as Steve preferred, they were watching in real time.

"The ratings have slipped again," Jacob remarked as he handed Chad the blue slip.

"Hmm," Chad said. "Today's episode went down to seventy percent."

"I'd be surprised if Hot Sauce didn't cause some mischief tonight on the ship," Jacob said.

"Me, too," Chad said.

I hope not, Steve prayed.

Grace faced the straps of leather hanging on a peg. She pulled the tangled mess off the wall. In trying to straighten the traces out, she stuck her head through a loop. She looked as if she were in harness herself.

"Good boy." Andrew patted T-Rex's head. "You're going

to carry us a long way."

With a vicious growl one of the other dogs attacked T-Rex.

Andrew started and dropped the leashes.

T-Rex jumped on the other dog's back, and the dogs quickly became a snarling circle of bristling fur. He stared at the dogfight.

Grace started to rush toward the dogs, but her feet got tangled in the traces. She tripped and fell flat on her face.

To avoid the fighting dogs, Andrew had backed up against the wall.

Steve couldn't bear to watch the scene any longer. These kids were so unprepared. He turned to Robert's screen.

"Billy," Robert said. "Get a box of dog food from Grace so I can weigh it."

Even though they would have to unload the four sleds to carry them from the ship, Robert had partially loaded them. He wanted to know how much gear they could carry.

"Okay," Billy said. This was his third day of being ordered around by Robert, and he was getting sick of him. But he obediently turned toward the hold where the animals were housed.

Steve turned his attention back to Grace's screen.

An image of a dog lunging at another dog filled it. The dog's teeth were bared, and spittle dripped from its mouth.

A door opened, and Billy stepped in. "Grace, Robert wants to know—" Suddenly the dog veered toward Billy.

Steve closed his eyes.

Billy screamed.

When Steve opened his eyes, he saw only fur and skin. He heard only screams and snarls.

"Looks like Hot Sauce just got lucky," Jacob said.

Grace, her neck still in the traces, yanked the dog off Billy. Her camera focused on his hand. Blood oozed from between his fingers.

"Darn dog!" Billy shouted.

Grace shook the dog by the scruff of the neck. "Bad Brontosaurus!"

"This episode will be a blockbuster," Jacob said.

Steve hoped that the Secretary had arranged for a first-aid kit. Billy was going to need one.

"The dog is vicious," Billy said. His hurt hand lay on the mess-hall table. The dog had rushed at Billy as if he had wanted to kill him. "We should shoot him," Billy added.

"Hush, Billy," Polly said.

Grace cleaned his wound. It wasn't deep, but there was a danger of infection.

Billy's hand stung. He'd probably get gangrene and die, all because of the dogs. It was actually Grace's fault. "Why didn't you warn me to stay out of the room?" he shouted.

Grace covered his cut with a cotton pad. What a ridiculous question! She hadn't known that Billy was coming into the room in the first place.

"You wanted me to get hurt. You just want to be MVP."

Polly tried to soothe him. "Grace wants no such thing."

Grace taped over the cotton pad, picked up her coat, and started out the door.

"Grace, where are you going?" Polly asked.

"Out on deck," Grace said. "It's a small cut. Your hand should be fine, Billy."

Billy scowled at her. "Besides, she gave the dumb dog the wrong name," he mumbled.

"What are you talking about?" Polly asked him after Grace had left the room.

"Apatosaurus and Brontosaurus are the same dinosaur. No one uses the name Brontosaurus anymore. She's so dumb that she doesn't know it."

"What does it matter, Billy?" Polly said.

"You of all people should say that? You, Miss Encyclopedia!"

"Grace knows a lot." Polly realized that she had never understood this before. People who didn't read books could know a lot.

Grace hadn't expected Billy to thank her, but she didn't expect him to blame her, either. She walked up the narrow steps and pushed open the door. The biting wind hit her face. As she did every day, she checked the thermometer. It was actually sixty degrees Fahrenheit, but with the wind, it felt much colder.

She leaned against a railing.

Billy Kanalski was an idiot. That dog wasn't vicious. It was attacking another dog, and Billy got in the way. And what did she care about being MVP? What did she care about television? The only good part about growing up on the reservation was that the Hopi tribal elders forbade the kids to watch EduTV. Grace and her cousins had gone to tribal school, taught by an aged Hopi in a two-room schoolhouse. She had learned to read and write the old-fashioned way. Her teacher had also taught her Hopi rituals, rain dances, and legends.

But how could she make anyone understand that while she had danced rain dances in Pueblo Village, she had felt as out of place as a seal? People weren't supposed to live their whole lives feeling they should be somewhere else, were they? Alaska had provided her tribe's clothing, food, and song. But when her family moved from that land of ice and snow to desert, they had lost a part of themselves, a part that they needed to get back.

Why else did her mother still mark the month that the great ice melted each year?

Her grandfather used to tell her, "Ah, Grace, soon the ice will freeze over again, and if our tribe were still there, we would all quit our jobs at the oil companies and be hunting above the Arctic Circle."

If Antarctica had gotten warmer, if there was game there, if she could survive . . . then why not? Why not move her tribe to Antarctica? Her family could give back to the U.S. government their few acres of reservation land and their broken tractor. They could return to a land of ice and snow.

For all these years her grandfather, mother, aunts, uncles, and cousins had saved their animal-skin clothes. Her mother treasured their family's sled. Her grandfather had kept his hunting knife sharp. It was clear to Grace that they were all waiting to return.

Congress had made her home a nuclear waste dump, but no government had touched Antarctica because conditions were too tough for any country—it was too cold, too forbidding. But not for Grace's tribe. Not for the people of the North. They could be Antarctic pioneers.

But she couldn't ever explain even one tenth of this to Billy Kanalski or any of the other kids, who had all grown up with a television for a teacher, whose dreams were of money and sad honors like being MVP.

Grace dreamed of a new life beyond time in a land of ice and snow, light and dark.

Billy's hand throbbed. He stomped out of the mess hall and almost bumped into Robert.

"Hey, are you okay?" Robert said.

"I have a bad cut. Thanks to Grace and those animals."

"Calm down, man."

"They're vicious."

"Why don't you take it easy tonight?" Robert clapped him on the shoulder. "I can finish up in the storeroom."

Billy felt his eyes fill with tears. They were landing in two days and Robert wanted Billy Kanalski to go sit in his cabin, while Robert Johnson worked diligently and scored more points to become MVP.

"What's wrong?" Robert said.

"What's this story you told about eating snakes?" Billy couldn't stop himself from lashing out.

"What are you talking about?" Robert asked.

"Those lies you told the Secretary," Billy said.

"Those weren't lies." Robert glared at him. "I did. It wasn't fun. But I did eat snakes."

"Sure," Billy said.

"You know about the Houston floods?" Robert said.

"Your downtown is like Venice, with those skyscrapers half filled with water."

"Right. Well, our home got flooded in the middle of the night. My family and I climbed up onto the roof. When the water got real high, we caught a log and floated on the bayou. Later we climbed onto the branch of an old oak tree. We ate what we could." Robert shrugged.

So Robert had been telling the truth. This just made Billy madder.

"Listen, I need you," Robert said gently. "I know nothing about ice and snow."

"I'm in charge of the maps now," Billy said gruffly. He wished the kids would forget about his supposed ice experience.

"Sure. That's fine. I'm glad you're going to do that, too." Robert looked Billy in the eyes.

Did Robert guess that he was a fraud? Billy worried.

Suddenly Billy didn't want to talk anymore. He pressed past Robert. When he got to his cabin, he slammed the door to make sure that no one would bother him. He stuck his head under his bunk and pulled out his backpack. On second thought, in case there were cameras, he crawled underneath the bunk and gripped his backpack tightly to his chest. He was the only kid on the ship to have a treasure trove, and he felt rich, not poor.

Someday Billy would be rich. He was sure of it. With a smart game strategy, he could win the one hundred thousand dollars.

Andrew wasn't a contender; he was too clumsy and dumb.

Polly wasn't one, either; too geeky.

The kids to beat were Grace and Robert. All Grace had going for her were those horrible dogs. He'd wait and watch for an opportunity to get rid of the animals. With Robert, his strategy was simpler. He'd let Robert boss him around until they were about midway to the Pole. When Robert was worn down and exhausted from the responsibility, Billy would quietly take over.

Every night around ten o'clock, most of the night-shift crew went to the screening room to view the episode of *Antarctic*

Historical Survivor that had aired on EduTV that day. Tonight, while the rest of the crew went to see the latest episode, Chad had allowed Steve to stay and keep watch over the screens.

After the dog bite, the kids had scattered.

Grace had gone off to the deck by herself.

Polly had read in the mess hall.

Andrew had busied himself with the ponies, their sleds and gear.

Robert had finished the inventory.

Billy had fidgeted alone in this cabin.

Even though it was a slow night, Steve hated to leave his post. But he needed to go to the bathroom. The bathroom was in the hallway, just outside the production room.

On his way back, Steve heard voices coming from the production room.

"I'm telling you, Chad, he's so attached to these kids that you better give him the Voice." Steve guessed it was Jacob talking.

"He's a good kid. I just need to think through my responsibility to his father."

"If he's careful, he won't get caught, and you'll be doing him and all of us a favor."

"You're probably right," Steve heard Chad answer.

Steve opened the door and almost bumped into Chad and Jacob. It was too dark to see the expressions on their faces, but Steve sensed that he had startled them. They had been talking about him, he was sure of it. What's the Voice? he wondered.

"Where have you been?" Chad asked.

"Just took a quick break," Steve explained. "Is the screening over?"

"The others are watching a few replays," Jacob said.

"They'll be along soon," Chad added. He turned to Jacob. "Why don't you take care of the summary?"

"You got it," Jacob said.

Chad opened the door. In the glow from the screens Steve saw the two men exchange glances before Jacob walked off.

Chad stood beside Steve in front of the screens. "There's a matter I'd like to talk to you about, Steve."

"Sure," Steve said slowly. He took a deep breath.

John Matthews and Raymond Chiles, two of the night-shift employees, walked into the room. John and Raymond, like all the night-shift employees, were older men with graying hair and slight paunches.

Steve looked at Chad expectantly.

John and Raymond walked over to the screens. "What's our assignment?" John asked.

"John, you edit the first quarter. You do the second, Raymond." Chad said. He turned to Steve and shrugged his wide shoulders. "Let's talk tomorrow," he said in a low voice.

Steve exhaled. How could he wait?

13

"You're a bumbler!" Robert shouted at Andrew on the evening of day four. "There's no margin for error in Antarctic travel. None! Do you understand?"

Andrew just stood there. He had been supposed to separate water bottles into five separate piles, but he had started listening to music and had gotten the water bottles and the fuel bottles mixed up. The two types of bottle looked a lot alike.

"Oh, go to bed," Robert said.

Robert was right. There was no margin for error in Antarctic travel. And Andrew had made a mistake. In fact, he made lots of mistakes. Yet he was soon going to be in Antarctica, where there was no margin for error.

In Antarctica the bumblers probably died first.

Andrew walked up to the deck. He stood there and watched the waves roll toward the horizon.

Billy had told them that they would arrive in Antarctica sometime tomorrow night. It was as though maps talked to Billy. Andrew saw just a jumble of colors and lines, where Billy understood patterns and distances. Billy was amazing.

Polly knew so much. Grace was good with the animals.

Robert could organize anything, and he was usually kinder than Andrew's neighbors, the Cross boys, who jeered when Andrew struck out at baseball.

Except for tonight's outburst, Robert had always been patient.

Andrew sighed.

Andrew's sigh sounded sad. Steve looked over his shoulder to check on Chad's whereabouts. Chad was in the far corner of the room, keyboarding.

"It's okay," Steve whispered to Andrew's screen. "The two bottles looked a lot alike."

Robert was still sorting gear.

"He's trying as hard as he can, man," Steve said softly to Robert's screen.

Steve heard footsteps and looked up to see Chad join him. Steve had lain awake today wondering about the conversation between Chad and Jacob that he had overhead. There was something about the dim lights and strange hours of the night shift that made him feel as if he could have imagined the whole thing.

Chad turned up the volume.

On the screen, Steve heard a slap as a wave crashed against the bow of the compucraft. The wind gusted, but not loudly enough to drown out the sound of a human sigh. He and Chad had become part of Andrew's private world.

"He's the one," Chad said.

"What are you talking about?" Steve said.

"The outcast," Chad said. "There's always one."

"I guess you're right," Steve said, thinking about the sad

Egyptian in the pyramid show and the trigger-happy Texan in the Alamo show.

"If we decide to do an intervention," Chad said carefully, "it's safest to talk to the outcast."

Steve was puzzled. "An intervention?"

"You thought the time was past, didn't you?" Chad said.

"What time?" Steve asked. "I don't understand."

"The time when one person can make a difference."

Steve didn't answer. He had spent his life hoping that it wasn't.

"Remember that I told you we played games here?" Chad smiled.

"Yeah."

"Well, sometimes we play a game called intervention."

"You actually talk to the contestants?" Steve said, hardly able to believe his ears.

"Yes, but we have to be very careful."

Steve squirmed uncomfortably. Why was Chad using the word *we*?

"First we choose the contestant carefully. He needs to be someone who would never tell anybody else about the voice that he hears. Or he needs to be someone who wouldn't be believed if he did."

Chad sounded as though he had thought this through, but Steve had a basic question. "How can the contestants hear the production room through the digicamera implants in their eyes?"

"The implants are complete cameras, with audio and video recording capabilities and are audio receivers as well. With these new satellite long-range mikes, we can talk to the contestants thousands of miles away as if they were in the room with us."

But the long-range mikes didn't make sense, Steve thought.

"Why would the Secretary build digicameras that some rogue DOE employee could use to talk to the contestants?"

"Soon the Secretary plans to use the long-range mikes to dramatically change *Survivor*. She'll put contestants in desperate situations—say, facing a wild animal in gladiatorial combat—and let them talk to their loved ones in the studio. She thinks the long-range mikes haven't been activated. But"—Chad chuckled—"Raymond Chiles is as good an engineer as he is a card player."

Steve tried to imagine how the long-range mikes worked. "It's got to feel weird to hear a voice coming from your eye."

"As I understand it, if the long-range mike is used, the auditory receiver in the implant sends electronic signals to the brain. Otherwise the auditory receiver just functions as a recorder that transmits sound to the production studio. You probably saw the Alamo MVP on television after the series ended. When the reporters asked him how he escaped the Mexican bullets, he said, 'I heard a voice.'" Chad shrugged. "But everyone dismissed it as a religious experience."

"So you guys talked to the survivor on the Alamo series?" Steve was shocked.

"That's my next point. We select only one person in our crew to be the Voice."

"Why?"

Chad met his gaze. "If we're caught, that person takes the fall for the whole group. Are you interested?"

"Me?" Steve looked away. This sounded dangerous. He must not have understood. Chad couldn't be asking him to be the Voice, could he? Steve was new to the night shift. He had no family. No one to take care of him if he lost his job. He decided to change the subject. "What did you talk to the Alamo survivor about?"

"We never told him who we were, but we relayed to him where the Mexican line was weak."

"So that's how he cut through. I had wondered. How did you choose the Alamo survivor?"

"He seemed like the strong, silent type who would be so embarrassed by hearing voices that he would never mention them. Basically we were right."

"If the Voice is caught?" Steve answered his own question. "*Court TV* for sure."

"Or worse," Chad said.

Steve shuddered. What could be worse than *Court TV*? *Court TV* was the highest-rated show after *Historical Survivor*. After a quick trial, the punishment phase was carried out on television. Viewers voted. Common punishments were near drownings, beatings, occasionally even crucifixions. When critics objected to the inhumanity of the punishment, they were reminded that criminals were all terrorists, and as such had no rights. No one in America wanted to be a defendant on *Court TV*.

"Did you understand my question?" Chad said.

"Not really," Steve replied. His voice trembled.

"I asked you to be the Voice."

"But that sounds dangerous," Steve protested.

"You just need to be careful. I was the Voice for *Alamo Historical Survivor*," Chad said proudly. He looked Steve in the eye. "Jacob pointed out that you seem attached to these kids. When bad things happen to the contestants, sometimes it's easier on the Voice. He feels like he's doing what he can to help.

If you want, you could have this series."

Steve was silent. He had stared at the screen so long that the waves were starting to make him feel seasick, but he didn't look away.

Chad looked at his watch. "Well, you don't have to decide tonight."

Steve felt relieved. The topic made him uncomfortable. He wanted to help these kids, but not enough to risk his own future.

"Go ahead and cut Andrew from the footage. The Secretary won't be interested in twenty minutes of a kid standing at the rail."

Steve's fingers started flying over the computer keys, but his thoughts were stuck on their strange conversation.

"Andrew, you don't even have a coat on." Grace walked up to him.

Grace had on a parka and matching hat. Her face shone with good health, and when she smiled at Andrew, her dark eyes sparkled. Yet from the way she held herself, Steve could tell she didn't know that she was pretty.

"Aren't you cold?"

"No."

"It's freezing out here." Grace shivered.

Steve looked at Grace's screen and saw Andrew hatless, coatless, leaning against the rail, his face to the wind.

"Is something wrong?"

Andrew shook his head.

"Why don't you go to bed?"

"I will," Andrew said.

Grace turned to go below, but Andrew lingered on deck for

a moment. The spray from a wave splashed his face, and he didn't bother to dry it.

"Time to view today's episode," Chad said. He turned to rouse the crew in the basement.

Before Chad had a chance to order Steve to the screening room, Steve spoke up. "May I stay and watch the cameras until the kids go to bed?" he asked hopefully.

"No, you stayed last night. I'll stay tonight," Chad said.

Disappointed, Steve turned away from the screens.

"Let's go!" Chad called down to the basement.

The rest of the crew began clambering up the stairs.

Steve followed Jacob, John Matthews, Raymond Chiles, and the others down the dark hallway to the screening room. When he entered, the Secretary had already appeared on the screen. She began every episode by putting her hand on a tall stack of Bibles.

"We abide by the rules in this program," she said. "There is no outside intervention. You will see real people here make decisions that will cause them to live or die. Lean back in your armchairs and enjoy yourselves. You are watching the best programming in the world."

Steve settled in to watch the kids' third day on the ship.

"Hello," someone said to him.

When Steve turned to see who had spoken, he saw Jacob. Oddly enough, the cleaning woman, Pearl, was sitting next to him. Her eyes drooped as if she were half asleep. Steve realized that he had never seen her before without a broom.

"Did Chad offer you the Voice?" Jacob said.

"Yeah," Steve said. "He talked to me about it."

"I intervened seven times in the Egyptian series."

Steve needed to ask the question that had been gnawing at him. "Do you think that you made a difference?"

"I saved a woman's life. No question about that. Just to have someone who cares, even a Voice, means so much to the contestants."

"I can understand that," Steve said. On many lonely occasions in his shack, he would have loved to have had a Voice to talk to.

"Of course, Pearl started it all," Jacob added.

Steve stared at the old woman. A bubble of spit rested on her lip. It was hard to imagine her doing anything but sweeping and sitting. Jacob must have guessed Steve's disbelief, because he asked, "You haven't heard Pearl's story?"

Steve shook his head.

"She was a camerawoman on one of the early *Historical Survivor* shows, the one about World War I. She was filming a battle and didn't notice a soldier crawling toward her. He had been badly injured and was dragging one leg. He begged her for water.

"Pearl stopped filming, bent over, and gave the dying man a sip from her canteen. The problem is a camera picked up her act of kindness, and the Secretary saw it."

Steve had heard this story before—everybody at the Department seemed to know it. But no one had told him the camerawoman's name.

"Pearl didn't make it home that night. She got beaten up, then locked up, and they tried to break her spirit by starving her for a while."

"How do we know that the Secretary was responsible?"

"I didn't work here then, but Chad said that the Secretary

bragged that bad things would happen to anyone who intervened."

Steve looked over at the old woman.

"Chad's taken care of Pearl ever since," Jacob explained.

"I see," Steve said. So that's what Chad had meant when he'd hinted at a fate worse than *Court TV.*

"She's only twenty-nine."

Steve stared at Pearl. Although he didn't have a view of her face, he noticed for the first time that her skin wasn't wrinkled. It was just her gray hair and hunched posture that made her seem old. To be a young person living inside an old person's body must be torture.

The Secretary was a truly horrible person. Steve looked up at the screen. She was talking again.

"On board the ship today, we had quite a bit of excitement," the Secretary was saying. "Billy was bitten by a ferocious dog, but wait and see"—she put her finger to her lips—"I don't want to give anything else away."

In the production room, only fifty feet down the hall, Steve could be watching the kids in real time. He fidgeted in his seat. He was too preoccupied to pay attention to the show.

Steve closed his eyes. When he really concentrated, he could hear Pearl breathing. Her raspy breaths sounded like her straw broom raking the floor. He didn't even know these kids. But if Steve got caught helping them, he could turn into an old person, like the woman sitting two seats away from him.

"Did you see the ratings for this episode?" Jacob asked him.

Steve looked up and caught the end of a commercial for instant palm trees. "No."

"Seventy-eight percent," Jacob said. "Understand why she likes a little blood?"

"Yeah," Steve said.

"Have you decided?" Jacob's voice was low.

"Why me?" Steve whispered. "Why not one of the other guys?"

Jacob sighed. "It's hard to keep watching these shows year after year. If you want to know the truth, it's only you, me, and Chad who still care."

"So that's why the others spend so much time in the basement?"

"Yes."

"Do I need to decide today?"

"Soon," Jacob said. "Remember, they're landing tomorrow." He turned away.

Steve closed his eyes again and found Pearl on the screen of his eyelids. He quickly opened them.

Another Fair Society commercial was playing on the big screen.

To take his mind off Pearl, Steve watched the dumb commercial. He'd watch anything to try to forget about Pearl.

14

From what Steve had seen since he'd arrived at work, day five had been an uneventful blur of activity.

Grace had finally gotten the dogs attached to the dogsled. But they had moved two steps and the traces had knotted.

It had taken Andrew *only* an hour to get all eight snowshoes on the ponies.

As if he were a pro at arctic travel, Robert had finished stowing the gear in bags.

Polly had spent the time in her cabin, fitfully reading and staring out her porthole.

Billy had carefully packed the maps.

In just an hour or so, the kids would be in bed, and Steve would have to begin editing. Steve dreaded this time of night, when the kids' day was ending. He liked working with the live footage best, as he felt closer to the kids.

The kids sat around the mess table, eating a late-night snack of chips and juice.

"We should be landing tonight," Robert said. "Anybody have any comments or questions?"

Nobody said anything.

"How's your hand, Billy?" Robert said.

"It hurts," Billy lied.

"The dogs' food is moldy," Grace said.

"We need to shoot the dogs," Billy said.

"Please, don't let's start that again," Polly said sharply. "We haven't even seen the motor sledges."

"Maybe we can shoot a seal for the dogs to eat," Robert said. A friend had told him that there were seals in Antarctica. He hated to admit it to himself, but that was about all he knew about the wildlife there. "Why don't you brief us on ice and snow?" he asked Billy.

"Uh," Billy hesitated, "I've never been to Antarctica, so I don't know about conditions there."

Weak answer. Disappointed, Robert looked at Billy.

Polly's eyes were big. She was leaning over the table toward Robert, trying to get his attention. Robert knew that if he asked Polly, she would have lots of information, but he didn't feel like listening to her.

"Well, if nobody has any questions, I think we should finish up our jobs," Robert said quickly. "I want to be ready to unload as soon as we land."

Chad and Jacob walked over to Steve and looked at the screen.

"The kids aren't in bed yet?" Chad asked.

"No, they're finishing up some chores," Steve explained.

Chad checked his watch. "Jacob, why don't you go check that the screening room is ready."

"Sure," Jacob said, and walked out of the production room, leaving Steve and Chad alone.

"If you want to intervene," Chad began slowly, "there's no set formula. You just look for opportunities to help."

"So if the kids don't need help, the Voice stays silent?" Steve asked.

"That's right," Chad said.

This was good news. It was possible, wasn't it, that Steve wouldn't have to make up his mind after all.

As if Chad had read his thoughts, he reached underneath Andrew's screen and pulled out a snaky mike. "The long-range mike is simple to operate."

Steve's fingers were drawn to the shiny metal. He fingered the ON/OFF switch.

"Let me know when you're ready," Chad said.

Steve pushed the mike back under the screen. "The kids don't need me yet."

"True." Chad paused. "But at some point, they *will* need you."

Steve couldn't ignore the certainty in Chad's voice.

Polly stared out the porthole at the seagulls flying above the calm dusk sea. She held Scott's diary, which was open to the last chapter, loosely in her lap. They had crossed the equator three days ago, and according to Billy they were on schedule to arrive in Antarctica sometime tonight.

The back cover of her book referred to the "fatal" Antarctic expedition of Robert F. Scott. Fatal. Final. Scott and four of his men had reached the Pole over 170 years ago and had never returned.

Sixteen men had started for the Pole. On Scott's direction, eleven had turned back. Five men had continued on to march the last 150 miles to the Pole. On the way back, one, the strongest, had fallen into a crevasse and hit his head. He died a few days later. Another, one of the younger men, had gotten frostbite. He had purposely limped out into a blizzard to die. If he hadn't, he would have slowed the group down and endangered them all.

That left three: Robert F. Scott, Robert Wilson, and Henry R. "Birdie" Bowers. They were only eleven miles away from a depot of food when a blizzard hit. They set up camp and waited. They had two days' supply of food and water. Captain Scott started writing good-bye notes. They never once felt sorry for themselves.

Polly skipped several pages and forced herself to read Scott's last diary entry, dated March 29, 1912:

> *We had fuel to make two cups of tea apiece and bare food for two days on the 20th. Every day we have been ready to start for our depot 11 miles away, but outside the door of the tent it remains a scene of whirling drift. I do not think we can hope for any better things now. We shall stick it out to the end, but we are getting weaker, of course, and the end cannot be far.*
>
> *It seems a pity, but I do not think I can write more.*
>
> *R. Scott.*
>
> *Last entry.*
>
> *For God's sake look after our people.*

Polly dropped the book onto her lap. What must it feel like to starve to death in a tiny tent, with a blizzard going on outside? She rubbed her sweatshirt just to prove to herself that she was sitting in a warm cabin on a ship. She was safe, but that didn't make her feel better.

She wanted to bring Scott and his men back. If only they

could step out of the pages, across time. She would give them a cup of hot tea and share her warm blanket with them. She would ask them questions and seek their help. If they were on this trip with her, she wouldn't be scared at all.

But Scott and his men were frozen in their icy graves, and soon she, a fourteen-year-old, would be attempting a march that this smart and committed group of adults had failed to survive.

Of course, Polly's group had some advantages, but she guessed that many of the dangers would be the same. As she read the descriptions of the steep crevasses covered by ice and snow that the members of the Scott party plunged into from time to time, she shuddered. The sharp icy waves called sastrugi would certainly slow them down. One or more of the kids were sure to go snow-blind. Then, of course, there was the treacherous weather. Even if Antarctica was twenty degrees or so warmer now than it had been in Scott's time, blizzards would still blow in without warning and fill the air so completely with snow and ice that a traveler couldn't see her hand in front of her face.

She put the book down. She needed some air.

Grace stood on the deck and watched for signs that they were closer to the continent of her dreams. Billy had told them that they would cross the Antarctic Circle soon. She didn't need a map to know that they were going farther and farther from people, and from cities with their lights and confusion.

She had turned her face to the sky when she felt the first snowflake. It was like a cold, wet kiss. She brushed it off with her mittened hand and stuck out her tongue. Snow pattered away on it. She drew her tongue in and swallowed the icy drops.

The reservation had suffered floods and droughts from the

messy weather that ruled the planet. One year winter had skipped them entirely, while the next year winter was longer and colder than anyone could remember. But the Hopi Indian reservation in Arizona had never gotten snow. Just as her grandfather had promised, the snow on her tongue, the first she had ever tasted, was sweet.

"*Ayayay!*" She stamped the boat deck with her feet, and her fingers stroked the air. "*Ayayaa!*" On the reservation she and her cousins had danced to celebrate the rain, and now she improvised. "*Ayayay,*" she sang. "Bless us with this force of life; make these beautiful white drops fall faster and faster until I am covered in snow."

Polly stepped carefully onto the slippery deck. She watched Grace hop around. Was this some kind of dance? What did those eerie howls mean? What was going on in Grace's head? "What are you doing?" Polly asked finally.

Grace looked at the girl. Her trance was broken.

On the reservation all the Hopi kids made fun of Grace and her cousins except when an outsider came in, maybe the son or daughter of a doctor or a government official who had come to inspect the reservation. Then the Hopis and the Eskimos banded together to stare at the outsiders and make fun of them. The Hopis called these kids "zombies" because with their love of television, computers, and movies, they seemed like the living dead.

"I'm sorry," Polly said. "I didn't mean to bother you. I just came up here to get some air and"—she hesitated—"to escape some ghosts."

"Ghosts?" Grace said. They had plenty of ghosts—or spirits, as the Indians called them—on the reservation.

113

"When I read a book," Polly said, "it's like I'm in a different world. I love the characters, and when something bad happens to them . . ." Her voice trailed off.

Grace had never experienced a book that way, but she had lived an imaginary life in the snow and ice, so she understood.

Polly examined the empty deck. "Do you sometimes get lonely?" she asked.

"No." Grace looked at Polly curiously. This girl's head held so many books, but it contained no friends. Grace had her grandfather inside her head, and she could talk to him whenever she wanted.

"You don't talk very much," Polly said.

"It's snowing." Grace pointed at the sky.

"I hadn't noticed," Polly said. She couldn't focus on anything but the tragedy of Scott and his men. *"But this I know: we on this journey were already beginning to think of death as a friend,"* she mumbled.

"What?" Grace said.

Polly couldn't hold back her tears. "That's what one of Scott's men wrote. Oh, Grace, I don't think any of us are going to make it."

"Is that what your books tell you?" Grace said.

Polly nodded.

"Then throw them away." Grace had been wrong. Polly did have friends in her head, but they were dying friends.

"I can't."

"Why not? Didn't your mother tell you? You can know too much."

Polly shook her head. She believed without any doubt that her knowledge of what had happened to Scott could make the difference in whether they survived or not, but watching her book friends die was hard. "I won't bother you anymore. I'm going to go back in."

Grace had opened her mouth to the snow. She acted as if she hadn't heard Polly.

Polly settled back in her bunk with her book on her lap. She dared herself to flip the book open. She looked down at the page. It was Scott's journal entry for March 3, not thirty days before his death: *Amongst ourselves we are unendingly cheerful, but what each man feels in his heart I can only guess.*

She forced her eyes to move down the page. March 4. *We are in a very tight place indeed, but none of us despondent* yet.

She scanned another entry near the end of the journal: *Had we lived, I should have had a tale to tell of the hardihood, endurance, and courage of my companions which would have stirred the heart of every Englishman.*

And again she read Scott's last entry: *For God's sake look after our people.*

Polly put her head in her hands. Her tears came freely now. She pulled the pillow to her face. It was more than 170 years after Scott's death, but Polly cried as if Scott and his men had died that day in her tiny cabin.

Steve glanced at his watch. It was about time for him to begin his editing assignment. Chad and Jacob were sending their reports.

Billy's, Robert's, and Andrew's screens had gone dark. Grace's screen was filled with a starry evening sky.

Polly's screen looked like a windshield in a car wash.

"See you tomorrow," Steve said to the five live screens before he turned away to begin his other work.

* * *

After passing through security, Steve pulled his pollution mask out of his pocket and covered his face with it. A low-lying haze had settled over Washington. The radio said that long periods outdoors, like the walk from the DOE to Steve's home, should be avoided. But he didn't want to waste his money on bus fare.

Steve turned the corner and started down the front walkway of the DOE. It was lined with statues of television stars. There was Jorna Morgaday, with her long hair and long legs and the trademark umbrella that she carried as protection from the newly discovered ultra-ultraviolet rays of the sun. Lyle Allen's tough face was turned toward the street. Lyle, who had portrayed a policeman in a holomovie about the Urban Trash Wars, was holding an Urban Trash rifle. In his first film, *Food Fight*, he had battled the trash and food fights that had raged in cities across the country in the 2060s.

But the statues weren't all of actors and actresses. The display also celebrated teachers on EduTV.

In one prominent sculpture Tanya, one of hundreds of national teachers, held a pencil in her hand. She had been Steve's first teacher. He still remembered Tanya's refined accent and alphabet-patterned dress. "Now, class," she would say, "today we are going to study the letter *D*." Sitting in front of the television, four-year-old Steve would take out his pencil and his notebook and try to write a *D*.

The flashing lights of the Department of Entertainment brought him back to the moment. Its motto, LET'S HAVE FUN, blinked on a giant sign above the building.

I'm *not* having fun, Steve thought. Those kids are not having fun. "The Secretary is the only one having fun," he muttered out loud. Then, remembering his poor dead parents and the debt his family owed to Chad, he swallowed his anger and tried to make his face a mask as he passed under the shade of an emerald-green instant palm tree.

15

Robert heard a loud bump. He guessed that it was around one A.M. After only five days, the *Terra Nova* must have docked. He wanted to go up to check, but his cabin felt cold. Over the next few weeks, they were going to have to haul equipment 150 miles in this same punishing cold. He needed his sleep. They all needed their sleep. He pulled the blanket over his head.

A couple of hours later, Robert awoke and immediately remembered the bump. It was time to get going. He was ready, had better be ready, to lead the expedition. He threw on his layers of clothes. After ringing the ship's bell to wake the others, he walked to the mess hall. When he punched the BREAKFAST button, the shelf slid forward.

Shipchef had made them bacon and eggs again. As Robert ate at the counter, standing up, he mentally checked and rechecked the supplies that they had packed for the journey.

Billy walked in, feeling sleepy and grumpy. "Hey," he mumbled. In case the viewers had seen his outburst, he had been working harder in hopes that the television audience would forgive him.

"Hey." Robert grinned.

Even though Robert hadn't formalized it, he thought of Billy as his first lieutenant. Billy was a little temperamental, but sound. The rest of the kids . . . well, the rest of the kids were just kids. Not that they were totally worthless . . .

"How's your hand today?" Robert asked.

Billy looked down at his hand and was glad that the bandage hid the slight wound. "It still hurts."

"Watch it carefully. We can't risk an infection."

"Good bacon," Billy said, ignoring him.

"Yeah, I'm going to miss these breakfasts."

"Have you looked outside?"

"No, but I'm going to." Robert shoveled down his last bite. "See ya up there." He stopped at the door. "If the others don't show up in a minute, will you ring the bell again?"

"Sure." Billy dreaded seeing this land of ice and snow. Again he regretted pretending that he was an expert. But what was his choice? If he hadn't lied, he wouldn't be here with the chance to earn one hundred thousand dollars.

Robert ran up and almost slipped on the icy deck. He slowed his pace and walked to the rail. He spotted a hut a short distance away. This must be Safety Hut, as shown on the map. A line from a hymn ran through Robert's head: *"God loves me so much that he made the sun shine at midnight."* It was four A.M., and the sun shone down on him as if it were a hazy afternoon back home.

Except for the dull sun, everything looked white and frozen. In the flat light, details were hard to make out.

This land is not one color, Robert thought, training his mind to be alert to his surroundings. This is your new environment. You have to notice everything about it. Straining to see more clearly, he broke the whiteness down into lavender white, greenish

119

white, blue-white, yellow-white, rose-white. . . . He pulled a cord, and the gangplank slowly lowered.

As Robert waited, he wondered if he should say something for the cameras. He didn't want to suck up, but at the same time he worried that if he ignored the cameras completely, all the viewers would hate him. He had no idea if he was getting much footage. If he knew the Secretary of Entertainment, she was probably covering Grace and the dogs.

The gangplank hit the snow.

"Land!" Robert called out, and then felt so ridiculous that he promised himself he would never do anything for the television audience again. He raced to the bottom of the gangplank and stepped onto the snow. It crackled under his weight. His breath came out in white puffs that looked like Christmas tree ornaments hanging in the air.

As he hiked toward Safety Hut, his boots felt heavy, as if he were walking in sticky sand. He opened the door of the hut and nearly fell back in surprise. Two silver-and-blue machines filled half the shed. The term *motor sledges* had made him expect some old beat-up go-carts with big tires. These sledges looked like snow motorcycles with tow hookups. He heard someone running behind him and turned.

Billy joined him at the doorway. "Wow!" he said. They wouldn't have to use those dogs after all.

"Where are the others?" Robert asked.

"They're coming."

Robert looked back and saw Grace, Andrew, and Polly trudging toward them.

Robert climbed on one of the bikes and turned the ignition. It purred like a sweetheart. Perfect that there were two of them.

Billy and he could each ride one. Robert didn't have to tell Billy his idea, because Billy jumped on the other snowcycle.

The engine on Billy's cycle roared, then died.

The other three kids crowded into the hut.

"I hope there's more dog food," Grace was saying to Polly as they entered.

When Polly saw the shiny machines, she groaned. They looked like toys.

"What's wrong?" Robert shouted above the roar of the motor.

"I told you. Scott had some motors, too," Polly said, "but he had all sorts of problems with them."

Billy opened the panel covering the engine. "What sorts of problems?"

Robert turned his motor off and walked over to help Billy.

Grace pulled the lid off one of the aluminum boxes.

"The cylinders overheated, while the carburetors froze. They wasted a lot of time trying to repair them," Polly said.

Robert grinned. "Mine works like a charm."

Grace peered into the box. "There's no dog food."

"Stop whining!" Billy said sharply. He had never been a good mechanic. If there was only one working snowcycle, he didn't have to guess who would ride it, and it wouldn't be him.

"Billy!" Polly scolded.

Grace defended herself. "The dog food on the ship is moldy. I need some fresh food."

"I'm just sick of hearing about the dogs." Billy stared resentfully at the dead engine.

"Billy's right, Polly," Robert said as he tinkered with the motor. "We've got to focus. If we need to, we'll kill the ponies to feed the dogs."

We can't kill the ponies yet, Andrew thought. Maybe some-day we'll have to kill the ponies, but not yet.

Grace stared stonily into space.

"We do have to focus," Polly said. "And you shouldn't spend much time on those silly snowcycles. Motor sledges were losers for Scott, and I'm sure these cycles will be losers for us." Their trip was a simulation of Scott's. Something in Polly's gut told her the Secretary would have made sure that these motors failed.

Robert examined the motor. Polly was assuming that if Robert Scott couldn't do something, he, Robert Johnson, couldn't do it either. Wrong. He was a great mechanic. Hadn't he gotten more than one mud-drenched car to work? "How about if we drive the good one as far as we can and abandon it if it stops?"

"That's fine," Polly said. "But don't spend a bunch of time try-ing to get the other one to start if it won't."

"It's a deal," Robert said. "And Grace, about the dogs, don't forget that we might be able to kill a seal. Seal would be good for us to eat, too."

"Yeah," Billy said. "Better than that disgusting pemmican." He still had a hard time believing that people in the nineteen hundreds had considered pemmican food.

Robert looked up from the motor. "So, Grace, you and Andrew unload the dogs and the ponies. Polly and Billy can help me bring the supplies down and load them onto the sleds." He looked at Andrew. "Man, where is your coat?"

Andrew stood in the subzero temperature wearing only a woolen shirt. "It's on the ship."

"Am I going to have to be everyone's father around here?" Robert shouted. "Wear your coat! It's a matter of survival now that we are in Antarctica!"

Andrew reddened, and Robert reminded himself not to be too rough on the kid.

Polly put her arm around him. "Andrew, Robert is just telling you this for your own good."

Andrew nodded, embarrassed.

"Wait," Polly said. "We've never figured out what your special gift is."

Andrew sighed.

"I'm not trying to be mean," Polly continued, "but how long did you stay in the freezer?" In their tryouts for the contest, each of them had had to spend time in a freezer. When they got cold, they rang a bell to get out.

"I don't remember," Andrew said.

"I was in there for only a few minutes," Polly said. "Aren't you cold, Andrew? I mean now."

Andrew shook his head.

"He's our snowman," Polly said to Robert and the others.

"You're not cold?" Robert said.

Andrew shook his head again.

"How long do you think you stayed in the freezer?" Robert asked.

"I don't know. Maybe an afternoon," Andrew said. He had watched a small black-and-white TV in there.

"An afternoon!" Robert shouted.

Andrew nodded.

"That freezer was twenty below zero," Billy said, looking at Andrew in awe.

Robert shook his head. "I don't care. Wear your coat anyway. Just looking at you makes me nervous."

"I've never worn a coat," Andrew confessed. Now that he

thought about it, he realized that he couldn't remember ever wanting one, either.

"I'm freezing just standing here." Polly hugged herself.

"Let's go unload the ship, then," Robert said. "We need to leave first thing tomorrow morning."

Billy turned the ignition, and this time his machine roared. "Get out of my way!" he yelled.

The kids backed away. Billy drove the machine out of the hut and did a wheelie on the ice. *"Yeehaw!"*

Robert started his snowcycle and followed. Soon the two boys were making figure eights and kicking up clouds of loose snow.

Polly looked on somberly.

"I'm going to get the dogs," Grace said.

"I'll bring the ponies," Andrew chimed in.

Nobody had asked Robert what his special gift was. Everybody had assumed that it was his leadership skills. But maybe, just maybe, his special gift was mechanics. He bet that he could keep these engines going where Scott and his men couldn't. He'd work on them tonight. He did another wheelie.

Polly turned away to examine the landscape. She had experienced the great outdoors only through nature shows, and her first thought was that it was so, so big. Far away, she saw the jagged edges of icy mountains. The rest of the terrain was a flat white plain. The shed stuck out like a single word on a blank page.

She pounded her boot against the ground. The ice was hard, and she felt panic rise in her throat. The white expanse was endless. She could see for miles and miles.

"Andrew!" Polly shouted.

Andrew turned and stared at her.

"I need to talk to you," she said.

"What gives?" Andrew asked.

"Look." Polly spread her arms toward the horizon. "Where could a camera crew hide?"

"Good point," Andrew said. As he stared at the white land, he understood what Polly was saying. They were completely alone.

"I don't get it." Polly felt truly confused.

"How are they filming us?" Andrew asked. Surely Polly, who seemed to know everything, would figure this out.

Polly just shook her head. She felt so disappointed, she had trouble talking.

"The Secretary lied?" Andrew had sensed that the Secretary had been lying to them, so he couldn't say that he was surprised.

"I guess so. Because there's no camera crew here." Polly spoke slowly. Each word hurt.

16

"Trial run!" Robert called. He buzzed off, the gear on his sled bouncing jerkily up and down and producing bursts of snow. He loved his cycle. This contest was fun. He roared past Billy, who was riding the other snowcycle.

Grace had no idea what time it was. When she had gone to sleep last night, the sun was lying low on the horizon like some kind of lazy yellow dog, and since then it seemed only to have had the energy to crawl sideways. But it had to be late afternoon, because her very bones were tired. She surveyed her hard day's work: twelve dogs were fanned out in front of the loaded sled.

At the front of the team, T-Rex wagged his large tail as if ready to be off. Behind him Grace had placed Dryosaurus and Brontosaurus as her swing dogs. These two were smart enough to help T-Rex steer. The next several pairs of dogs were her team dogs. They didn't need any particular skill other than strong muscles. She had struggled with where to put Triceratops, with her short legs, and finally decided that she would cause the fewest problems in the middle of the pack.

Her two steadiest dogs, Ankylosaurus and Polacanthus, Grace put last. They would be the first to feel the burden of the sled as the team started or traveled uphill. They would have to bear the constant pounding of the runners close behind them.

The snowcycles circled her again, and Grace decided that it was time for her own trial run. She stood on the plastic runners at the back of the sled and held on to the wooden handles. In her ancestors' day sleds were sometimes made of walrus bone, and the handles were frozen fish.

Grace held no reins. She planned to use voice commands, as her ancestors had always done, and of course the whip. The handle of this whip was plastic. Her ancestors' had been made out of the leg bone of a caribou. Just in case she needed a brake, she had brought along a paddle to drag in the snow. She had no idea what her people had used in the old days to slow the dogs down.

Although they had spent the morning nipping at the snow and each other, now that the dogs were harnessed, she could feel their excitement. She sensed that they had pulled sleds before, though perhaps not together. She was sorry that she hadn't bothered to learn the Iñupiaq commands from her grandfather, but she slapped the cold air with the whip and shouted, "Go!"

T-Rex surged forward impatiently. Most of the team lurched ahead, but Triceratops didn't move quickly enough. Ankylosaurus tumbled into her. The traces knotted up.

"Stop!" Grace shouted, but with the confused mass of dog flesh behind him, T-Rex couldn't go anywhere. He stopped and looked at her. He seemed to be asking, Can't you do any better than this? She got off the sled to undo the tangle before one of the dogs choked to death.

She started with Triceratops. This dog was loose and relaxed, probably lazy from the trip. It was obvious that she didn't want to pull anything.

Andrew, who was holding the reins of one of the ponies, stepped alongside her. He had been working all day to get them used to the snow.

The snowcycles circled in front of Grace's team.

T-Rex grew confused from the roar of the cycles and tried to start running, but jerked the traces instead. Another dog collapsed into the growing heap.

"Are you okay?" Andrew asked.

Grace nodded and motioned him away. She was too frustrated to make small talk. When she had gotten the dogs into their places again, she climbed back into the sled and snapped the whip. The dogs ran a few feet forward. She snapped the whip to make the pack turn to the left, and for no reason that she could see, T-Rex slid and then pitched into the snow. This time he looked back at her sheepishly.

Grace took a deep breath before getting out of the sled. She heard her grandfather rooting for her: "Dogsledding is the greatest way to travel on the whole earth. Don't give up."

Robert circled back on the snowcycle and stopped. "What's the matter?"

Billy pulled up next to Robert and gunned his engine. His face was shining. It was clear that these two were having a great day.

"It's going to take me a day or so to make a team out of them," Grace managed to say to Robert as she knelt by T-Rex. It looked like the dog had just hit a patch of ice. She wondered if he was unused to the slippery white stuff.

"We can't spend days training these dogs," Robert said.

"What were you doing on the boat with them, anyway?" Billy said. "You've already had five days."

Before Grace could defend herself, Polly walked over with

her mouth set in that determined way that Robert hated.

"Robert, dogs are the most reliable form of polar travel," Polly said.

"These are good dogs," Grace protested, even though a few moments before, her team had been a hopeless mess of snarling bodies. "I just need a little time."

"We have only a week's worth of food!" Robert snapped.

"Didn't they teach you math on that reservation?" Billy chided.

"They'll be ready tomorrow," Grace said. That morning she had seen droppings that could only be from a large animal, such as a seal. If there were animals in Antarctica, Grace could bring her family back here. She'd learn dogsledding; she had to.

"Robert," Polly said slowly, "we're all tired. Why we don't talk about this over dinner?"

"Billy, what time is it?" Robert asked.

Billy glanced at his watch. "Five o'clock." It was later than he thought. Having the sun always in the sky was confusing. But then he felt annoyed when he remembered that all the watch told him was the time in D.C. He had no idea what time it was here. He hated imprecision.

"Okay. Let's get the dogs and the ponies in."

"The dogs should sleep in the hut, not on the ship," Grace said. "It will get them used to the cold." It did not amaze her that she knew these things; she was only surprised that on her first day she had driven a dog team so badly.

"What about the ponies? They won't fit in the hut with the dogs," Andrew said.

"We can stake the ponies next to the hut," Polly suggested.

"Andrew!" Robert called. "Take care of the ponies." He turned to Billy. "You check on Shipchef."

Billy nodded.

Grace cracked the whip over the dogs' heads and the ground became alive. As if they were one twelve-headed animal, the dogs raced toward the hut, pulling the sled effortlessly. She glanced over her shoulder, but Robert hadn't noticed. Her grandfather had, though. Out of the corner of her eye, she caught him smiling at her.

Billy pushed the big black DINNER button on Shipchef.

A bell rang. Then a note slipped out of the slot where they usually collected food. "No dinner tonight."

Billy sighed. The next stage of the trip must have officially begun. He went to the hold to get a box of pemmican. The box was heavy, and it stank. He dropped it on the floor of the mess hall, then pulled five tin plates out of the dishwasher and put them on the table. He filled five tin tumblers with water and put them on the table too. Then he took out his knife and hacked off a big piece of pemmican. Chunks of it crumbled in his hand. He sniffed it. Disgusting.

The five of them sat around the table, staring at their dinner plates covered with cold brown pemmican.

Although Polly was hungry, the pemmican was unappetizing.

"What did you say that Scott and his men did with this stuff?" Billy asked.

"When they could, they cooked it with melted snow, threw in whatever else they had, and called it 'hoosh,'" Polly said.

"We could try it mixed with hot water," Robert said. Like oatmeal, he thought.

On many days Scott's crew had no hot water because they

didn't have enough fuel to heat snow. The hardships that Scott and his men had experienced seemed unreal to Polly, but she felt that she was getting ready to walk in their boots. Each day she would have to give up something more. Each hour would become harder and harder to endure. These thoughts made her wish that she could see her mom one more time. Then she remembered that in some mysterious way she couldn't figure out, her mom was probably watching her.

Polly sighed.

To set an example, Robert took a bite of pemmican and followed it quickly with a swig of water. "Come on, guys, eat."

Grace popped a big piece of pemmican into her mouth and slowly chewed.

"We are alone in Antarctica," Polly said. Her voice sounded full of despair even to herself, and she wished that she had kept quiet.

Robert shook his head disapprovingly.

To calm herself, Polly took a bite of the stuff on her plate. It was dry and gravelly. Hard to believe that until she got back home—if she ever got to go home again—she would eat this stuff constantly. Scott and his men had eaten it for breakfast, lunch, and dinner almost every day on their polar journey.

There had been days when Polly had eaten chips for all her meals. Maybe after she got used to it, pemmican three times a day wouldn't be bad. But of course chips came in different flavors.

"I guess you're right that there aren't any cameramen outside, but there have to be cameras. Where are they?" Billy said. This was an urgent question. He needed to figure out the safest place to eat his junk food once they left the ship.

"Maybe they're not taping this one," Andrew said. "Remember, a few years ago they tried to get people to listen to the radio. This could be a radio broadcast."

"That radio show was a flop," Polly said. Even though she had no idea where the cameras were, she was convinced that they were being filmed.

Andrew took a big bite of his pemmican. "Not bad," he remarked. His mouth was full, and crumbs tumbled out of it. "Tastes like beef-flavored chips."

"So smile," Billy said. "For the camera." He faked eating a bite of pemmican and vowed to toss the rest.

No one smiled. All Polly could hear was the sound of the kids chewing their pemmican. She thought of her mother and what she would be having for dinner if she was at home. Her mother worked at a private-school cafeteria and often snuck food home in her apron. Sometimes Polly was lucky enough to have fried chicken and real mashed potatoes.

Billy stood and, with his back turned to the others, dumped his untouched pemmican into the open box. The bandage was loose on his hand, and in a way he was sorry to notice that his wound wasn't infected. "So what are we going to do about the dogs?"

"What do you mean?" Polly said.

"Well, they're dangerous. They nearly sliced my hand off." Billy held up his bandaged hand. "And if they're going to slow us down, shouldn't we ditch them? Take the two snowcycles and the ponies?"

"What happens when the snowcycles stop?" Polly asked.

"They're in great shape," Robert said. "I made a few adjustments to the motors."

"It's warmer now than it was when Scott was here," Billy reminded Polly.

"Our adventure is supposed to be a simulation of Scott's,"

Polly said. She wished that just one of them had bothered to read the Scott books. "These motors will die, and then we'll have to walk just like Scott did and pull those heavy loads ourselves."

"Modern mechanics designed those motors," Robert said calmly. "They aren't 1911 engines. Trust me, those DOE guys built a simple version of a snowmobile."

"What if you're wrong?" Polly said.

"Polly," Robert said, "you don't have street smarts. The Secretary is counting on us to ignore the snowcycles because motor sledges didn't work for Scott and to use dogs because they're tried-and-true. But we're smarter than she is."

"You said it," Polly said. "Tried-and-true. The dogs are tried-and-true. You keep repeating that there is no margin for error here. What if we leave the dogs and take the snowcycles, and the snowcycles stop? The dogs are our backup."

"Look at it this way," Robert said. "I bet the snowcycles can average six miles an hour. We're only one hundred fifty miles from the Pole. If three of us rode on the cycles and two of us rode the ponies, we could make the Pole in four or five days, easy. Speed is safest. We can get to the Pole fast, before a blizzard hits."

"Yeah, those dogs can't keep up with the cycles or ponies," Billy said.

Grace stifled a laugh.

"If the cycles are supposed to work the whole time, don't you think it's odd that the first depot is fifty miles away and the rest are twenty-five miles apart?" Polly asked.

"What do you mean?" Robert said.

"It's as if the Secretary is expecting us to make better time at the beginning."

Polly had a point. "The Secretary may want the motors to

fail," Robert added. "But I'm telling you, I can fix them."

"Scott's diary is a great gift. Are we just going to repeat his mistakes, or are we going to learn from them?"

Grace nodded.

Polly concentrated on Andrew. She stared hard at him. "Remember, we agreed. One person, one vote."

Andrew shifted uncomfortably in his seat. Polly expected him to side with her. He was sure of it.

"Two of us think that we ought to use the dogs and two of us think that we ought to press on without them. What do you think, Andrew?" Billy said.

Andrew was glad that pemmican didn't taste bad. He was glad that no one had yelled at him today. He was glad that he had found a place to tie up the ponies next to the shelter of the ship. He shrugged.

"This is where you could come in, Steve." Chad paused. "If you wanted to." Chad turned to look at Steve.

Steve felt his stomach contract. He was afraid he didn't have the guts to be the Voice. To change the subject, he asked Chad, "Do you think the kids ought to stick with the dogs?"

"No question about it. Robert may be right. Mechanics are so lazy these days that they probably didn't follow the Scott specs, and the kids may have better engines than the primitive ones that Scott used. But I know the Secretary, and she intended those snowcycles to be a hunk of junk. So I wouldn't trust them."

"The Voice makes the decision, then?" Steve asked fearfully.

"The Voice can consult with anyone he wants, but he makes the decision."

Steve knew that if he got caught, he alone would lose his

career and be punished. That was fair. He didn't want to get anyone else in trouble. But he reminded himself that he had never met these kids. The risk that he was considering taking was enormous. If he got caught, he could become another Pearl.

Besides that, he worried about accepting responsibility for the lives of these kids. What if his advice was wrong? He wasn't that old himself. "If," Steve hesitated, "the dogs don't perform, they might delay the kids a few days, and they could starve."

Chad nodded. "That's the way it is. All sorts of things can happen when you stop being just a viewer."

"Let's take the vote in the morning," Polly was saying on the screen. "Everyone's tired."

Steve glanced at his watch. Since the kids had gotten up so early, they were going to bed at eight P.M. If they kept to this schedule, the night shift would miss much of their daytime activities—a development that Steve would hate.

Robert was grunting his assent.

The kids got up from the table and trudged off to their cabins. Steve watched Andrew from Grace's camera. His shoulders were hunched. He walked like a boy much older than fourteen. He walked the way Steve had in that first month after his family had died. He walked like a defeated man.

Chad met Steve's eyes, reached under the instrument panel for Andrew's screen, and pulled out the long, snaky mike.

Steve stared at the gleaming metal. His face was hot and his palms wet. He dreaded disappointing Chad, but what else could he do?

Steve heard Andrew sigh as he fell onto his bunk.

"The perfect time to talk to contestants is when they're in bed," Chad said.

Steve procrastinated a little while longer. "Why?"

"So you'll sound more like an angel," Chad said. "Or God."

Steve understood that it would be safer if Andrew heard a heavenly figure talk to him. That way, if Andrew ever did tell anyone about his conversation with the night shift, they would think that Andrew had had a religious experience. But the thought that he would need to seem holy was another reason Steve didn't want to talk to Andrew.

Andrew's eyes were closed. Already his breathing had become deeper.

"If you don't act soon, he's going to fall asleep," Chad said.

Steve began his difficult confession. "Chad, I don't . . ."

A loud boom interrupted him, and then Steve and Chad heard the hum of the ship's motor.

"What? I thought Shipcaptain was turned off," Steve said.

"Calamity number one happens tonight."

"Before they even get off the ship?" Steve asked, his gut wrenching.

"Yep."

"How many calamities are there?"

"Six."

"Why so many calamities?"

"A version of all of them happened to Scott."

This was unfair. The Secretary planned to make the kids' impossible task even harder. Steve stared at Andrew's dark screen as he fingered the long-range mike's ON/OFF switch. "Why can't we prevent this one?" he pleaded. "Instead of talking to Andrew about the dogs, why can't we tell him to go stop the motor? Or go do whatever he needs to?"

"He can't stop the motor because Shipcaptain won't let him,

and do you really want him out on the ice floes in the dark?" He patted Steve on the back. "Besides, if you stopped all six calamities from happening, the Secretary would get suspicious—"

Steve interrupted him. "Scott was a grown man who chose to be in Antarctica. These are five kids wih no experience or preparation."

"We all know that the Secretary thinks calamities make for better entertainment."

Chad had the nerve to smile at Steve. Steve thought of the Superpox epidemic that had devastated his hometown and killed his parents. "For the people who have to live through them, calamities aren't entertainment," he answered grimly.

"You and I know that . . ." Chad said.

Steve finished Chad's sentence for him: ". . . but the Secretary doesn't." Angry, he reached for the mike. It felt cold and hard, like his own growing determination. *One. Two. Three.* He pushed the switch to ON. He felt as if he were jumping through the glass screen into the television as he forced himself to say, "Hello, Andrew."

Andrew didn't respond. Maybe the long-range mike didn't work.

Chad nodded encouragingly at him.

"Andrew?" Steve repeated.

"Yes?" Steve heard a small, scared voice answer back. "Is that you, Dad?"

"No," Steve said. His heart broke as he felt Andrew's loneliness. "It's not your dad. It's"—he paused—"a friend." Steve couldn't pretend to be God. It just didn't feel right. He looked over at Chad to see his reaction

"It's your call," Chad whispered.

"A friend?" Andrew answered in a bewildered voice.

"Yes. I know you're exhausted."

"How do you know?"

"But before you fall asleep, I want to tell you that tomorrow you should vote with the girls."

"You're sure?"

"Yes."

"Why are you so sure?"

"I'm older than you. Now good night."

"Good night."

Steve stared at Andrew's dark screen.

Chad clapped Steve on the back. "Good work. You've taken a big step tonight. Now why don't you come play cards?"

Steve shook his head. He worried about whether he had done the right thing. His dad had always said, "There's a difference between taking a calculated risk and popping off. Steve, you pop off." Had his temper gotten the best of him again?

"Come relax in the basement," Chad said.

"I'm fine," Steve said. He wished that his father were alive so he could talk to him.

"You're missing a good time." Chad stepped on the loose tile.

Steve could hear shouts and laughter as Chad climbed down into the basement.

"Put the tile back, would you?" Chad said. "It's easier to close from the outside."

"Sure," Steve said. Someone entered from the side door, but Steve turned back to the screens when he saw that it was only Pearl with her broom. Four of the five screens were the deep black of closed eyes. Only Billy's screen was gray.

Steve could hear the sound of Billy's feet pounding the floor.

Billy must be walking around in his dark cabin. Suddenly an object—Billy's dark-blue backpack—appeared on his screen. Billy pulled his backpack toward him and opened the clasp. Inside was a mound of silver- and gold-wrapped packages. Steve spotted health-food bars, Chocobombs, crackers, and peanuts. How had Billy snuck snacks on board? But then Steve remembered the testing period, when the crews had checked the screens only periodically. While no one was watching, Billy must have broken the rules.

The digicamera in Billy's eye focused on a long line of wooden slats.

Steve guessed that to hide from the cameras, Billy had crawled underneath his bunk. A candy bar filled the entire screen. Billy's hands slowly tore off the wrapping. He held the deep-brown chocolate bar close to the digicamera and stared at it before biting into it. Billy gave a long sigh of pleasure that made Steve wish he had a chocolate bar.

When Billy was finished eating, he scooted out from under the bunk. A white porcelain toilet appeared. Billy threw the gold candy wrapping into the toilet bowl and flushed it.

Normally, cheating made Steve mad, but cheating the Secretary was different. "This guy has enough to worry about. He ought to be able to eat a little candy," Steve said to Pearl.

Pearl didn't look up.

Billy lay down on his bed, holding his injured hand.

"It's your secret, Billy," Steve whispered to the screen. "Yours and mine and Pearl's."

As Steve pushed the button that would double delete the scene from the computer's memory, he was surprised by his own action. After a lifetime of passively viewing, he had intervened twice in less than one hour.

Billy closed his eyes.

All the screens were now dark and quiet, leaving Steve to his troubled thoughts. It bothered him that intervening the second time had been so much easier. His father had always warned him never to do anything to jeopardize his future.

The dark screens were no help.

If only I could watch the kids' dreams, Steve thought.

17

Oddly enough, Andrew was almost sure that he had heard the craft's motor come on during the night. Even though when he awoke he couldn't hear the familiar hum, he still rushed down to breakfast hoping for one last Shipchef meal. Instead of a hot breakfast, he had found Billy, Robert, and Polly waiting to resume their argument.

Although she was sitting with the group, as always, Grace held herself a little apart. All four of them seemed to have already eaten.

Andrew fixed himself a bowl of pemmican. As he sat down, he heard Billy mutter, "You can't vote with them."

Billy pulled his coat tightly to his chest. The heat had gone off in the middle of the night—another sign that the contest had officially begun. He turned and stared at Andrew. "Are you?"

The memory of a certain voice in his head was growing fainter, but Andrew answered bravely, "Yes."

"Hey," Robert said. "We don't have time to argue, Billy. He's made up his mind."

"We've already wasted a lot of time," Polly said.

"Okay, okay," Billy said. "Let's go."

Andrew shoveled down a few bites of pemmican.

Robert stood up and headed out the door. On deck, the wind whirled around him. The sky was gray, and the sun, which hung low in the sky, was blurred. Was it just a cloudy day, or was a blizzard coming on?

Waves lapped against the side of the ship, and Robert glanced toward land. Or he looked toward where land was supposed to be. Overnight the ice had broken up and shifted. Yesterday the ship's gangplank had been on firm ground, but now it was floating on a large ice floe next to the ship. The ponies were on a separate, smaller piece, floating out to sea. Land was at least a hundred yards away. "Incredible!" he whispered.

Polly and Billy raced up to the rail.

"What happened?" Polly asked.

"We landed at a glacier," Robert said slowly. "Last night the ship must have rammed it and broken off chunks of ice."

"I should have known. Something like this happened to Scott," Polly wailed.

"Good thing we unloaded our gear yesterday," Billy said.

Andrew rushed to join them. He stood at the rail, staring in disbelief at the helpless ponies.

"I told you to tie the ponies next to the hut, not the ship!" Robert said to Andrew sharply.

Andrew hung his head. Robert probably had. Andrew couldn't remember.

"We can't argue now," Polly said. She heard footsteps, then Grace's gasp as she stood next to Polly.

"Ice and snow are treacherous. Never forget," Grace's grandfather had always said. "I won't," she had promised him. But she had. This morning's icy betrayal was a surprise.

"What are we going to do?" Billy moaned. "The ship's motor is cut off. We'll never start it."

"We have lifeboats," Robert said. "We'll have to go ashore in those."

"But what about the ponies?" Andrew and Grace said in unison.

"We could tie a rope to an ice pick, toss it at the ponies' ice floe, and pull the floe in," Robert said thoughtfully. "But should we risk it?"

"We can't just let them die," Andrew said. It was horrible to think that Milky and Cookie might die just because he had made a mistake.

"Our rifle's on shore," Billy said grimly. "We could kill them."

Grace shot him a quick look of resentment. "We may need the ponies to make it to the Pole."

"So what do you propose we do, Robert?" Polly asked, ignoring Billy.

Fifty miles to the first depot. An hour to pack up gear. Two—no, better give it three hours to set up camp and cook dinner. He didn't know the terrain yet. The ponies and dogs would be slower than the snowcycles, maybe significantly slower. Better count on the whole group making only three miles per hour. To be super-cautious, Robert had loaded all the food from the ship onto the sleds, even though that would slow them down. Twelve to fifteen miles today was doable, but the clock in Robert's head was ticking loudly. "Okay, guys, here's the plan," he said. "Let's give the ponies two hours. If we can't rescue them in two hours, we'll shoot them. Is that fair?"

Grace nodded.

Andrew did the same, though he didn't agree.

Polly was worried. They had just arrived in Antarctica and

they were already threatened with casualties!

Robert turned away. The easiest solution was to shoot the ponies at once. You're a fool not to, he chided himself.

"I'll help you get the lifeboats," Billy said.

Andrew had had one job: the ponies. He had staked them to the ground next to the ship. If they lost Milky and Cookie, it was probably his fault—and besides, what would his job be then? Robert and Billy would never let him ride one of the snowcycles. Grace was the boss of the dogs. They had to rescue the ponies. . . .

They had to?

He thought about the rescue for a minute, and the clarity of his thinking surprised him. No one cared as much about the ponies as he did, not even Grace.

He had to rescue the ponies. He couldn't let them be shot or drift off to sea.

Robert and Billy picked up a big gray inflatable lifeboat from the deck.

It looks to be of modern design, Polly thought. Thank goodness the Secretary of Entertainment wasn't always accurate.

Or was she? Scott's expedition had lost ponies in similar circumstances. *As far as the eye could see there was nothing solid; it was all broken up, and heaving up and down with the swell. Long black tongues of water were everywhere. The floe on which we were had split. . . . Guts [the pony] had gone, and a dark streak of water alone showed the place where the ice had opened under him.*

But how could the Secretary have known that the ice would break up? Then Polly remembered hearing the ship's motor start last night. Had the Secretary programmed the ship to ram the shore? After Scott's pony had fallen into the water, killer whales, their black fins flashing, had appeared.

"Robert!" she called urgently. He and Billy were examining a lifeboat for holes. "I don't know if this is important."

"Then save it," Robert said. "This one looks fine," he said to Billy.

He couldn't put her off that way. "Robert, for your information, Scott and his men had this identical problem. They lost two of their ponies in the ocean."

So this was planned, Robert thought. As if hiking to the Pole with four children wasn't hard enough, the Secretary had created a calamity.

But how did Hot Sauce know that Andrew would mess up and stake the ponies near the ship? Robert wondered. Of course she didn't. But it was reasonable to guess that the kids would be too tired to lug everything to the hut. Actually, they had gotten lucky. If they had left food on shore, not "just" ponies, they wouldn't have had any choice but to chase after the ice.

"What would the viewers want us to do?" Billy mumbled.

"Who cares?" Robert snapped. "They're sitting at home watching TV. It's a game to them. It's no game to us." Didn't Billy understand what danger they were all in? They couldn't live in this cold without food and fuel, and they had a limited supply.

Grace, Andrew, and Polly stood at the rail, watching the ponies drift away, while Robert returned his attention to the lifeboat.

"I could lower myself down onto that chunk of ice," Andrew said, pointing to the ice mass directly below the ship.

"The chunks of ice are called floes," Polly said.

"Then I could hop those floes to the ponies," Andrew added.

"But what would you do then? How would you get back?" Grace asked.

"The ponies could jump with me," Andrew said.

"That's dangerous," Polly said.

"I can do it," Andrew said. "Some of those floes are really close together."

"Look, Andrew," Polly said. "Ponies are of little use in Antarctica. They sink into soft snow, hate blizzards, and generally are more trouble than they're worth."

Andrew stared at her. Sometimes Polly was such a know-it-all.

Polly didn't want Andrew to go onto the ice. She closed her eyes, and killer whales started cruising her memory.

> *Killer whales . . . were cruising about in great numbers, snorting and blowing, while occasionally they would in some extraordinary way raise themselves and look about over the ice, resting the fore part of their enormous yellow and black bodies on the edge of the floes. They were undisguisedly interested in us and the ponies, and we felt that if we once got into the water our ends would be swift and bloody.*

"We're ready!" Robert called. "We're going to launch the first boat. Polly, Grace, and Billy, head to shore. Andrew and I will see if we can rescue the ponies."

"But I want to try to save the ponies," Grace said, staring at the field of broken ice.

"I need you to get the dogs ready," Robert said sternly.

Grace thought about arguing, then changed her mind. She needed the extra time to work with her team.

With Polly following, Billy and Robert carried the boat down the gangplank. Together they launched the boat into the choppy water.

Grace climbed into it.

"I need to tell you, Robert," Polly whispered into his ear. "In Scott's time, killer whales cruised these waters. The Scott team stabbed a pony that fell in to keep it from being eaten alive by the whales."

Robert acted as if he hadn't heard her.

Billy climbed in beside Grace and unhooked the oars. He handed Grace one and kept one for himself.

"Come on, Polly!" Billy called.

"Did you hear me?" Polly said to Robert.

"Thanks for the info, Polly," Robert said quietly. The girl had no common sense. "But even the Secretary of Entertainment can't use a killer whale as a prop."

Polly stepped into the lifeboat. The boat skidded but didn't rock. She sat down on the plastic boat bottom. Robert was right. Her knowledge of the Scott expedition was just making her nervous. This morning she should try to forget about Scott and his men.

"Paddle, Grace," Billy said.

As Robert and Andrew stepped into the second lifeboat, Robert watched Billy and Grace turn their boat toward shore.

Polly pulled her jacket closer to her, but it wasn't the cold that bothered her. It was the burden of the Scott expedition. She glanced over the side into the murky water. It seemed bottomless.

Robert was angry with the Secretary for planning this emergency and worried about the ponies. He was also troubled by his own inability to read the environment. He had never dreamed that the ice could break up like that. Even so, the more he rowed, the stronger he felt. "To the left!" he called to Andrew, glad to feel in control again.

But his next few maneuvers were no good. The lifeboat was

trapped in a maze of floes. "Guess that's it," Robert said. He'd gotten the boat as close as he could, but the ponies were still staked to a floe thirty yards from them. Despite the rough ocean surrounding the floe, the animals looked peaceful.

"Listen, Robert," Andrew said. As usual, he was hatless. "From here I could jump from floe to floe until I reach the ponies. Then I could get them to follow me back to shore."

"Those floes may not be stable," Robert replied. Didn't Andrew realize that if he fell into the water, he'd probably die? Robert had made a pact with himself not to consider the viewers, but now he could feel their eyes on him. The viewers wouldn't want Andrew to risk his life.

"I've got to," Andrew said stubbornly.

Don't worry about those dumb viewers, Robert chided himself. Think for yourself. You know it will be safer if you save those ponies. What if the mutts never cooperate? The motors can't pull much stuff. How are you going to haul all the gear to the Pole? "Go for it," Robert said to Andrew.

Andrew could hear the creaks and groans of ice splitting in the distance. He stood up and cautiously tried the first floe. It seemed stable. He walked across it to the next one. There was only about a yard separating the two floes. He jumped and skidded onto the second floe.

The next floe was farther away, but he jumped the watery divide easily. Of course, if the floe moved before he started back with the ponies, his return trip might be harder. But he couldn't let himself think about that. All he could think about right now was that Milky and Cookie were drifting out to sea.

He jumped again, and then a fourth and a fifth time, but the space between him and the next floe, the one with the ponies, was too far for him to jump. He pulled out his ice pick, tied it to a rope, and threw it toward the floe. It caught the ice, and he pulled on the rope with all his might. Slowly the floe inched toward him. When it was close enough, Andrew jumped. The tip of his boot touched the icy water.

He wouldn't let himself think about what would happen to him if he fell in. He picked up each pony's rope. Holding the ends in one hand, he jumped across to the nearest floe. Then he faced the ponies. "This is it, girls," he said. He pulled on Milky's rope. The pony dug her hooves into the ice and wouldn't budge.

"Please, Milky. Please, pony. Just jump."

No, she seemed to say.

Andrew looked into Cookie's eyes. Maybe, she seemed to answer.

He put Milky's rope on the ground and stood on it. Then he pulled on Cookie's rope with both his hands.

The short, squat pony sailed across the water and landed so close to him that he almost fell back.

"It's safer to try to bring one back! Just leave the other one!" Robert called.

Andrew acted as if he hadn't heard. With Cookie next to him, he knew, Milky would come. He took hold of Milky's rope and yanked it, and this time Milky jumped. It was a powerful leap. She looked like she was going to clear the water, but she changed her mind midway and faltered. Her forelegs struck the ice floe, but her back legs landed in the ocean. Her forelegs slipped backward.

The splash of water hit Cookie, and she reared back. The ice floe tilted, and Andrew almost slipped into the water. He dropped Milky's rope, caught hold of Cookie's tail, and pulled himself to her.

"Let the pony go!" Robert shouted. "Come on back."

Milky was thrashing around in the cold water. Andrew had never felt so sorry for any animal in his life. He reached down, grabbed her wet rope, and pulled. She lifted her head out of the water. Her eyes rolled back until Robert was staring at big white globes.

He let the rope drop to his side.

She sank back down. He wasn't strong enough to pull her out alone.

"Robert, come help me!" Andrew called.

"No, we can't risk it!" Robert yelled. "Come on back!"

Andrew tied the end of Milky's rope to Cookie's halter and tried to get Cookie to step forward. She took a few steps, but the ice floe was small. This time Milky's head didn't even come up out of the water, only a cloud of blood.

Andrew stared into the water. He saw a dark shape dart from under the floe. More blood gurgled up, so dark that it was almost brown.

"What is it, Andrew?" Robert called.

"Just a fish!" Andrew yelled. Poor Milky.

"It could be dangerous!" Robert warned. "Watch out!" He imagined that Polly was there, scolding him as he argued with her: What am I supposed to say to Andrew? "Watch out for killer whales?" The poor guy is on a tiny floe and still has to lead the other pony back. I don't want him to panic.

Andrew looked closely into the water. Milky's guts were floating up to the surface like a string of blood sausages. He turned his eyes away.

"What are you staring at?" Robert called to him.

"Looks like sharks!" Andrew called back. The churning water

reminded him of a scene from a horror movie.

He sounds amazingly calm, Robert thought.

Robert, Andrew, and Cookie didn't make it to shore until four hours later.

Polly hugged Andrew.

Grace patted him on the back.

Billy shook his hand and said, "Good job."

"You're a hero," Polly said.

"But I lost Milky," Andrew replied.

"You're a hero anyway," Polly said.

In all his life, Andrew had never once thought that anyone would call him a hero. He was sorry that he had lost Milky, but he couldn't help beaming. Then he remembered the floating guts. "Sharks got her."

Polly looked sharply at Robert.

"Hey, I know. But don't make too much of the coincidence," Robert said to her.

"It proves that the dangers Scott and his men faced are the same dangers we face today," Polly said.

"Polly, Scott and his men didn't make it. We're going to," Robert said. He couldn't put his anger into words. But he sensed that Polly believed getting to the Pole was impossible.

"What are you guys talking about?" Andrew asked.

"Scott lost a couple of ponies to killer whales. Polly warned me before you left. I didn't want you to panic," Robert explained.

"It wouldn't have made any difference," Andrew said, and then wondered if he would have been more scared returning over that open water if he had thought about the fact that the killers were real, not props in a horror movie.

"See," Robert lectured Polly, "we have to be optimistic."

Polly almost laughed. If only Robert knew how hard that was. Besides everything else, it was cold, so cold here. She shivered. The shivers made her do a little dance in the soft light.

"We need to go," Robert said. With the morning gone, they'd be lucky if they made ten miles instead of the fifteen he had counted on.

18

When Steve woke up, he immediately sensed that something was wrong. He glanced at his clock on the table beside him. It said 7 P.M. He was over an hour late for work, and it was the day that the kids were setting out for the Pole. He hadn't watched that afternoon's episode of *Historical Survivor*. He felt completely out of touch. Anything could have happened to the kids!

I must have forgotten to set my alarm, he thought as he threw on a T-shirt and pants. He grabbed a few slices of bread and ran out the door.

Steve started jogging down the narrow path through Shanty Town. The homes were a hodgepodge of corrugated metal, plasterboard, plastic, wood, and other recycled materials. There were no sidewalks, but every so often a huge orange trash can with CLEAN STREETS, CLEAN MINDS written on it in bold black letters dominated a front yard. Laundry flapped in the breeze, and everywhere he looked he saw a maze of antennas and the blue glow of television screens.

Steve left Shanty Town behind and started through the high-end district, full of expensive town houses and restaurants. Since most businesses were open twenty-four hours, the street was full of people coming from and going to work, shopping, and running errands.

As he passed a row of fancy town houses, a loudspeaker blared out a Fair Society commercial: *"Life's a game. Each person gets a Toss. Winners are winners. Losers are losers. But it's not like the old days, when life wasn't fair. Now everybody gets a chance."*

A light went off in a window of one of the elegant homes. A coworker had told him that the Secretary lived somewhere on this street, in a luxury town house with a mood room, three fireplaces, and a heart-shaped Jacuzzi in her bathroom.

The Secretary was going to sleep in a bed with silk sheets while five kids were facing their first day trekking in subzero weather. Steve didn't care what the government wanted him to believe. Life wasn't fair.

When Steve finally made it through the door of the production room, several members of the night shift were standing around in front of the screens. "What happened?" he cried.

Chad turned around and looked at him. "Why are you late?" he said.

Steve felt himself flush. "I forgot to set my alarm."

"Did you watch the program today?" Chad asked.

"No."

"The ponies got caught on an ice floe, and Andrew tried to rescue them," Chad said.

"Andrew was a hero," John Matthews said.

"Andrew got Cookie back," Jacob explained. "But Milky didn't make it."

"He took a horrible risk," Chad said, looking into Steve's eyes.

Steve hung his head. "I should have been here."

"It happened this morning. The Secretary broadcast the scene live," Chad said. "You couldn't have helped anyway."

"We watched the episode earlier tonight than usual. We just got back from the screening room," Raymond Chiles explained.

"You'll be so proud of the kids," Jacob said.

Steve felt the eyes of the whole crew on him.

"Is he the Voice?" Raymond muttered.

"Yes," Chad said.

"But we barely know him," John objected.

"I knew his father," Chad explained. "We can trust him."

"Excitement's over." John turned toward the basement.

"He better keep our secret." Raymond's tone was stern.

But Steve hardly heard Raymond's warning, because he had just noticed that the screens weren't all dark. The kids were still traveling. He hadn't missed the whole day!

"Let's go play cards!" John called to the group.

"So tell me exactly what happened," Steve said to Jacob, but his eyes were on the live screens.

Robert, riding one snowcycle, with Billy and Polly on the other, blazed the trail. Andrew followed, riding Cookie. Driving the dogsled, Grace brought up the rear. The sun, still hanging unnaturally low in the sky, looked as discouraged as Grace felt.

Although Grace's grandfather had a house in Alaska, he spent hunting season moving from place to place. He had felt stuck in Arizona and had hated living on a reservation. "Life should be lived on the move," he used to say.

But so far dogsledding hadn't been the smooth ride across ice that her grandfather had so lovingly described. It had been a series of jerky lurches. And Grace didn't feel like a fearless Eskimo on a hunt, but like a frustrated American on a vacation gone wrong.

Even the analogies that popped into her head were American, not Iñupiat. Dogsledding was like riding in a car that was alive. What was the car going to do next? Which way was it going to turn? She had to stay attuned to every twitch of dog muscle, every howl and every growl.

Apatosaurus nipped Diplodocus; Diplodocus halted. The dogs in the back line toppled over those in the front line. Grace got out of the dogsled, straightened the traces, cuffed Apatosaurus and Diplodocus, and then climbed back into the sled. Her dogs didn't understand that they needed to maintain a steady pace on the trail. What was she doing wrong?

They had been traveling for a while, but the mountains appeared no closer. After spending the morning rescuing the ponies, they had spent the afternoon adjusting the sled contents and hooking up the sleds. Robert seemed determined to make up the lost time.

The other kids were so far ahead now that they were only specks, but Grace wanted the dogs to move slowly. They made fewer mistakes that way. She let the whip dip beside her and watched the swirling pattern it made in the snow.

Grace could no longer hear the roar of the motors, only the growling of the dogs. The warmth of the sun on her face re-affirmed her sense of the timelessness of this land. For the moment, the dogs were moving forward in rhythm. She wondered if any foot, either human or dog, had ever touched the ground that she was crossing now. If Grace got her wish, she and her dogs would experience the seasons on this plain, more expansive than any she had ever imagined.

Looking around her, Grace compared Antarctica to her home at Pueblo Village. Life on the snow was so different. For one thing, she had never gone so many hours without seeing trash. For another, if she moved her family to Antarctica, their home would be an igloo.

Her grandfather had told her how to fashion a home out of blocks of ice. How to cut the ice into smaller and smaller blocks, how to lay the largest blocks in a circle and step inside it to put the rest of the blocks up, how to fashion a low arch for an entrance and build a long passageway to break the wind, and how to leave a hole in the top block to let the warm air escape.

She realized that her grandfather had told her many times how to build an igloo, but except for his description of the smell, she had no idea what it was like to stay in one. During hunting season, no one bathed, and together with the grease and smoke, the smell was unique in this world. It was up to her to build her own igloo and find out what it was like to live in one.

T-Rex jerked to the right, and Polacanthus tripped over his traces. The forward motion of the sled dragged him along until Grace stopped it and scolded him. Would she ever get these dogs to run smoothly? She cracked the whip over the dogs until they cringed. She was ashamed of herself as the team started off slowly again. Frustrated as a dog driver, she felt like crying. Grandfather, if you didn't mean for me to live here, why did you tell me stories about the woman who adopted a seal and the hunter who became a bear? Why did you describe the taste of seal ribs? Why did you show me how to hunt a whale with a harpoon? Why did you bother to make me want to be part of a tradition six thousand years old? If I'll never be able to manage the dogs, why did you tease me with a vision of the northern life?

The wind changed, and Brontosaurus howled.

Suddenly the right runner caught in deep snow. The sled edged sideways, and Grace frantically shifted her weight to steady it. But she wasn't quick enough, because the dogs in the rear stampeded into another pile. You need to pay more attention, she lectured herself as she hopped off.

T-Rex stood there with his ears pinned back, as if to say that something was wrong.

Maybe this pile-up wasn't her fault after all.

Triceratops was dangling over a shallow crevasse. Only the traces held her up.

Grace stepped away from the crevasse, and using her most serious tone, she called to T-Rex. He ran toward her, eager to obey. The team easily pulled the little one out. She thanked T-Rex before turning to Triceratops. The little dog whined as Grace checked her for injuries and found none. She walked over to the crevasse, pulled off her goggles, and stared bare-eyed at the shimmering ice. Even though the crevasse was only five feet deep or so, it seemed to hint at another world she couldn't know. Her grandfather had once told her a story about ice tunnels that extended for miles under the snow. She looked at the horizon. The tracks that the others had made stood out like a frosty highway. But her team was wider than their tracks. This crevasse was just a few feet from where Billy and Robert had ridden so confidently, so unaware.

"Danger is one with life on ice. It sharpens your senses, clears your mind. Lets you know that you're alive," she heard her grandfather say.

He had been right. She could still feel her heart pumping in her chest as she settled back into the sled and cracked the whip. "Let's go," she cried.

The dogs bounded forward in one wild, uncoordinated lurch. A box fell off the sled.

She stopped the team again. Would the sled steer better if she shifted most of the weight to the back? She repositioned the box before climbing back in.

Patience, Grace counseled herself. Grandfather never said that being an Iñupiat was easy. He had said that living on the ice was an impossible life, worthy of love. The dogs leaned into their harnesses and started along the trail. They passed a lone twisted ice sculpture.

How was that formed? Grace wondered. In subzero temperatures, the wind must have gusted, causing the snow to freeze in midair. Wind art. Only in Antarctica.

She, Grace Untoka, was driving a dogsled in Antarctica. She wasn't driving it like an Iñupiat yet, but on the first day of her new life, she held a whip ready in her hand.

19

A small object that Polly hadn't noticed before stood in the distance. Or maybe it was a large object right next to her? Or perhaps an Antarctic mirage? She squinted at the object again. Could it be a plain metal pole that she and Billy were approaching? She had ridden quietly behind him on the snowcycle for several hours. The roar of the motor discouraged conversation.

Billy pulled up to the metal pole.

"Is that the meteorological stand?" Billy shouted, pointing at the pole.

"I think so, " Polly said.

Their map said that the stand was nine miles from Safety Hut. Although time was largely irrelevant here, Billy checked his watch. It was almost ten o'clock. Robert had slowed to keep pace with the dogs, but he had told Billy that he wanted him to stop after four hours. That meant that they would camp near the stand on their first night.

Starting in the 1950s scientists had monitored Antarctic temperatures. But after the Big Bust, when the government no longer had the funds for scientific exploration, the stands were abandoned. Polly couldn't help remembering that on the Scott expedition, Birdie Bowers had recorded most of the weather data. Since gloved hands would be too clumsy to do the work, Polly imagined Birdie touching his thermometer with his bare hands. Even though Birdie had been the man on Scott's team most impervious to cold, the daily temperature readings must have been agony.

Billy turned off the cycle. The plan was to set up camp before the others arrived.

Polly hopped off and tumbled into the snow. Her left foot was dead; it had no feeling at all. How had she failed to realize what was happening? She looked down at her green parka, now dusted with snow, and tears filled her eyes.

Billy stared at her.

"Billy," she cried, pulling off her goggles.

"What's wrong?"

"My foot."

"What?"

"I've lost the feeling in my left foot. Can you boil some water quickly? I need to drink something hot."

"Sure."

Polly tried to get her boot off, but her hands were cold, and she found even this small task daunting.

Billy went to the sled and rummaged around in the bags. It felt like a long time to Polly, but eventually he pulled out the Primus, just as she slipped her foot out of her boot.

Polly couldn't feel her foot, but that didn't necessarily mean it was frostbitten, she reminded herself. But what if it was?

Billy fumbled, trying to light the stove.

"Take your time," Polly said. This cold made accomplishing even the smallest tasks difficult. She kneaded her toes until they began to feel the way Polly did on being awakened by her mother too early.

"Darn!" Billy said as he tried to light a match. He blew on his fingers to warm them and tried again.

Polly pounded her foot with her fist.

On Scott's expedition, Titus Oates's foot had gotten frostbitten. It was clear that the remaining four men couldn't carry Oates and still survive. Polly wished that for once the Memory would fail her and that she couldn't remember word for word Scott's description of Oates's terrible decision:

> *He slept through the night before last, hoping not to wake; but he woke in the morning—yesterday. It was blowing a blizzard. He said, "I am just going outside and may be some time." He went out into the blizzard and we have not seen him since.*
>
> *. . . We knew that poor Oates was walking to his death, but though we tried to dissuade him, we knew it was the act of a brave man and an English gentleman.*

Would Polly be brave enough to crawl off into the snow and let the others go on without her? The books said that dying of cold was pleasant, almost dreamy. That you felt hot. She would love to feel hot right now.

Billy finally succeeded in lighting the match, and he loaded heaps of snow into the outer ring of the Primus. It seemed to take longer for the water to boil than for a glacier to form, but the stove gave off a little warmth, and Polly snuggled as close as possible to it.

Finally little bubbles appeared on top of the water.

Scott's men had described the large white blisters that appeared on frostbitten skin. The men had popped them. Sometimes the pus inside was frozen into hard white balls.

Billy poured hot chocolate mix into the water and stirred it. When it was ready, he handed her a cup.

Polly pressed it against her face. She breathed in the delicious smell of the chocolate. It was ironic that in these miserable conditions she could have all the chocolate that she wanted. What she would have given for a cup of hot chocolate each night in their hut in New York!

Polly didn't mind that her first sip burned her tongue, because her mouth filled with warmth. She swallowed. The bullet of warmth sped down her throat into her stomach. She took another sip, forgetting to savor it, just craving its life-giving warmth.

The warmth crawled farther this time, through her limbs, into her fingers—and yes, she felt a trickle travel to her feet, and through her feet to her toes. She took another big swallow and resisted the impulse to unbutton her jacket. For she was feeling warmer—even hot—and she tried once again to wiggle her toes.

This time the command reached them and they woke up. All five of them began to move. Now, instead of being drowsy and insensible, they screamed in pain. She yelped.

First little piggy, second little piggy. Ignoring their protests, she made them do exercises: sit-ups and stretches, a regular army drill.

"How do you feel, Polly?" Billy asked.

"Better," Polly said. "But I should stand up and get moving."

"Okay," Billy said. "We can get started on the tent." He walked over to the snowcycle and lifted off a heavy black bag.

Polly painfully tried to stand.

"I can do this. Just rest," Billy said.

"I can't!" Polly snapped, and then immediately felt bad. For once, Billy was trying to be nice. She hadn't shared Oates's story with the other kids. During his last few nights Oates had slept with his frostbitten foot out of the warmth of the sleeping bag so he wouldn't have to go through the painful agony of a partial thawing. The pain that she was experiencing was good. It was her friend. Giving up was not yet an option.

Billy looked at her curiously.

"I just have to use my feet, that's all," Polly explained. He didn't understand how serious frostbite was. Billy, Robert, Grace, and Andrew knew only what she had told them about Robert F. Scott and his men. They didn't hear the voices of Scott, Oates, Bowers, Evans, and Wilson in their heads. They couldn't feel these explorers' suffering. She wondered if the kids would be so relaxed if they knew what the Antarctic had done to those five brave, strong adults. She hobbled over to where Billy had dropped the bag with the tent. She started back toward the snowcycle. She limped to the spot where Billy was setting up the tent and back to the snowcycle, again and again and again. She was so worried about her foot that she barely noticed that the tent didn't look big or high enough to house five kids. But then what did she really know about camping in frigid conditions? Nothing, she despaired.

While Polly took care of her foot, Billy set up the tent by himself. It was hard in the cold, and when he finally stretched the last piece of canvas over the pole, he felt very hungry. Polly was still busy, so he unloaded his sleeping bag and crawled into the tent with it. He unrolled the fur bag, which had started shedding hairs. He quickly transferred his food from his back-pack to the bottom of his sleeping bag. Then he grabbed a bag of nuts.

It seemed impossible, but what if there were cameras in this small tent in the middle of nowhere? Or what if Polly looked in?

Just in case, he crawled inside the sleeping bag and pulled it over his head. He popped a delicious nut into his mouth.

"Billy, what are you doing?" Polly called a few minutes later.

"Just resting," Billy answered. But he felt panicky as she passed through the tent flap. What if she could smell the nut? He snapped at the air in front of him, trying to swallow the smell.

"What's that sound?" Polly asked.

"Nothing." Billy swallowed air again. "Is your foot okay?"

"It's better," Polly said.

Billy put the rest of the nuts into his pocket and peeked out. Polly was looking at him strangely. "Don't just stand there," he said. "Let's get the stove inside and the rest of the sled unloaded." He crawled out of his sleeping bag.

"This tastes great," Grace said as she took a second bite of hoosh. It was warm in the tent, maybe as warm as an igloo would be.

"Billy, you did a good job finding your way here," Robert said.

Billy blushed at the praise.

Robert nodded at Billy. "Useful guy. You're our snow-and-ice man, and"—he paused—"our navigator." Robert was impressed. Billy seemed to navigate effortlessly.

Billy didn't say anything.

Robert frowned. "We would have been here much sooner except for the dogs."

"They're getting better, Robert," Grace said simply.

Of course, they had had a late start because of the ponies, but in four hours they had made only nine miles. Robert knew that if they abandoned the dogs, they could travel faster.

Andrew sat down next to Polly, who was tending the stove. "How does your foot feel?"

"Okay," Polly said hesitantly. By the time the others had arrived, she was certain that her circulation was restored, but she still felt shaky.

"Take off your socks and let me see," Robert said.

Polly didn't want to cry, but somehow she felt as if she had done something wrong. She slowly, painfully, peeled off her layers of socks. Were her toes whiter than usual, or was that only her imagination?

"Robert, I've got an idea," Andrew said. "I used to do it for my little brother." He began unbuttoning his shirt.

"What are you doing?" Robert said angrily. "I don't want *two* people with frostbite."

"No, she can put her foot on my chest. It'll be like a heater. It'll warm up good."

Robert didn't stop him when Andrew grabbed Polly's foot and pulled it toward him.

Polly put her foot against Andrew's bare chest and felt its warmth. The warmth of the sun, she thought as she closed her eyes.

"Thank you, Andrew," Polly said.

"No problem," he replied.

"Is your whole family like you?" Grace asked.

"How do you mean?" Andrew said.

"Furnaces," Grace said.

Polly laughed.

"Not my little brother. He can't even go outside when it's snowing. My mother wears a bathrobe all the time." He pictured the heavy gray woolen bathrobe that his mother wore even in summer, and he felt homesick. "But my dad and I are. In fact . . ." He stopped. Should he tell them? It was just a silly old family story. Probably wrong.

"What?"

"My aunt always claimed that we were related to someone on Scott's expedition." He shrugged. "A man named Bowers. He's my great-great-great uncle. . . ." Andrew's voice trailed off, because he had no idea how many greats to string together. "Or something like that," he finished lamely.

"Oh!" Polly clapped her hands in delight. "He's one of my favorite men. So unselfish and kind, and so much like you. Even in this awful weather he hardly ever bothered to cover his neck."

"Did he . . . ?" Andrew started to ask a question, but Robert turned to him with a disapproving gaze.

"Did he what?" Polly said, but she knew what Andrew wanted to ask.

"Survive?" Andrew choked out.

"No," Polly said.

Robert glared at her.

Polly glared back. "You want me to lie to him?"

Robert shook his head. He wondered if Polly knew how depressing she was.

"Did he die of frostbite?" Andrew asked.

"Not exactly," Polly said. "He was one of the four men Scott took with him to the Pole. Three of the men—Bowers, Wilson, and Scott—died in their tent." On the ship, Polly had read several books about the expedition, but the cause of the last three men's deaths was still a mystery to her. She had a theory, though, that she wanted to explain to Andrew.

"Enough already!" Robert snapped.

Polly felt like ignoring him. "They called him Birdie—Birdie Bowers—and even Scott thought that he could do anything." She smiled at Andrew.

20

Andrew had never had a pet of any kind. Not even a pet rat. Now, to get to ride this great pony, to get to take care of her, to get to be her master—even though he was tired after a long day riding, it was almost too much happiness.

Cookie stumbled in a snowdrift.

"Come on, girl. You can do it," Andrew said.

There was only one drawback to his pony ride. Andrew understood, as clearly as if Cookie could talk, that she didn't like the snow or the cold. Andrew had never had this idea before, the idea that each animal had a personality. But it was true.

Cookie was a pony who liked the hot sun. He wondered what country she had been sweating in when someone told her that she had to go to the coldest place on the globe. What chain of bad luck had led her here?

Thud, slosh, snap, thud. If only Cookie could talk!

They had made better time on this, their second day. Against the backdrop of the mountains, the snowcycles looked like ants on spilled milk. He wasn't used to land looking like this. It had a weird quality to it. No one had ever messed it up.

But maybe it was the way he was looking at things that was

different. When he looked out the window of a bus, even if he stuck out his finger to let the wind bend it back, he felt as if he were watching the houses, fences, grass, and trees on television as they passed by. His view had always been framed by a window.

Here he felt he was actually somewhere.

He knew that the snow Cookie was plodding through was the real thing. The way the steel-gray sky blurred into the land at the horizon was real. The faint whirr of the snowcycles, the thud of Cookie's hooves, and the distant barking of the dogs were all real.

He pictured the kids at home who might be watching him. They would see Andrew and Cookie traveling in this big white land on a square television. He felt sorry for them.

Here there was no frame.

But wait a minute. *He* was the one everyone felt sorry for.

Cookie slipped again.

The audience might feel sorry for him, but he felt sorry for Cookie. She was a pony who longed for a beach. Andrew leaned down and nuzzled his face into her mane. "You can do it, Cookie," he said.

Steve stood in front of all five screens, but his eyes were drawn to Robert's. Robert was surveying the progress of the kids behind him, and his eyes had settled on Andrew. Riding that pony, Andrew looked like the king of the world. It took so little to make some kids happy. Like his little brother, Sam.

It made Steve sad that his memories of Sam had faded. Sam had died at the age of six, so he'd be fourteen years old if he were alive today.

Fourteen years old—the exact age of the *Antarctic Historical Survivor* kids.

Chad interrupted his thoughts. "How's the footage for today's episode?"

Steve started. "Great," he said. "An uneventful day."

"Well, after yesterday that shouldn't make the Secretary too mad," Chad commented.

"My guess is that they're about to stop and set up camp," Steve said.

Chad clapped Steve on the back. "Then what do you say? Let's go downstairs with the others and break for dinner."

"Not until the kids are safe inside their tent," Steve said.

"Have you spoken to Andrew again?" Chad asked.

"Not since the ship." Steve paused. "Do you think I should?"

"No rush, but it might not be a bad idea to check in with him. He needs to get to trust your voice."

Steve decided that he would try to contact Andrew that night.

"You sure you don't want to take a break in the basement for a minute?"

Steve shook his head.

Chad sighed. "All right, but you're missing some fun. Jacob baked us some cookies."

Steve watched Chad head toward the tile in the floor. Cookies sounded good. He couldn't explain the way he felt. He couldn't do much, but how often had he longed for someone to be with him when he was scared or in pain? The least he could do was watch the screens.

On Robert's screen, Steve saw Billy staring in Robert's direction and pointing at his watch.

Robert nodded.

Billy stopped his cycle, and Polly hopped off. Her legs looked stiff.

Robert shaded his eyes with his hand and scanned the horizon for Andrew and Cookie, and Grace and the dogs.

Andrew and Cookie would make camp soon, but Grace and the dogs were specks on Robert's screen.

It looked as if the kids were going to make it through a second day traveling in Antarctica. Steve pulled up a chair and sat down.

He could start to relax.

The low-hanging sun still watched over Grace as she knelt by T-Rex. She held his paw in her hand and slowly checked each of his toes for the little balls of ice that seemed to collect there.

He licked her.

She howled. Her breath was a white cloud in the gray sky.

He howled back.

She laughed and put his paw down on the ground. He turned around and around before settling down in the snow for his night's rest. As he turned, he kept his eyes fixed on her.

She turned to Dryosaurus next.

"Grace, the food is ready!" Polly called from the tent.

"Are you sure we can't help you?" Andrew shouted.

"Be there in a minute!" She'd take care of her dogs, then she'd eat. She wished that she had something to feed them besides moldy food.

Inside the tent, Polly was stirring the hoosh. The tang of fuel was in the air. She was grateful that the sun circled them without setting, because she was able to cook by its faded light.

Andrew was holding Robert's feet against his chest to warm them.

Billy was examining the map. "We made a little under eleven and a half miles today."

The short distance didn't surprise Robert. With the heavily loaded sleds, the snowcycles had had to work to plow through the soft drifts. At times Robert, Billy, and Polly had gotten off and pushed the sleds. Besides that, the dogs had gone so slowly that Grace had pulled into camp long after the rest of them. Yet there had been no surprises, and on balance Robert was content. It had been a fair day.

"So how far to the depot?" Andrew asked.

"About thirty miles," Billy said triumphantly. "We—by that I mean the cycles and the pony—averaged about three miles an hour today. Grace arrived later, of course, but if we can keep up the pace tomorrow, we'll easily make it to the depot in three days."

"This is not that hard," Robert said.

Robert sounds so cocky, Polly thought. They had been incredibly lucky so far. "We're riding," Polly said. "Scott and his crew had to man-haul a lot."

"What's man-hauling?" Andrew asked.

"They pulled the sleds themselves," Polly said.

"That would be miserable," Andrew said.

"How many miles did they have to man-haul?" Robert asked, curious despite himself.

Polly searched her memory for the answer. "The plan was for them to man-haul seven hundred forty miles, and each sled started out weighing around eight hundred pounds."

Billy was sick of Polly's books. It had been a long day, and he wished that she would shut up. "They were losers," he said.

"They *weren't* losers," Polly said angrily.

"Another explorer beat them," Robert countered wearily. They'd died on their journey back. It was obvious that they had lost.

"Against incredible odds, they made it to the Pole," Polly said. She didn't understand Billy's and Robert's obsession with being first.

"Who was it again who beat them?" Andrew asked.

"This guy Roald Amundsen," Polly said. "He was known as a North Pole explorer. When Scott was in Australia on his final stop before sailing to Antarctica, he got a surprise telegram from Amundsen saying, '. . . Proceeding Antarctic. Amundsen.'"

"My dad said Scott's considered a bumbler," Billy said.

Andrew hated that word. It had been applied to him once too often.

"That's because Scott liked ponies more than dogs," Polly said. "And Amundsen used only dogs." Why couldn't she make them understand that these men were heroes?

Billy yawned. Arguing with Polly was a waste of time.

"Did Scott know that Amundsen won?" Andrew asked.

"You guys about ready to turn in?" Robert said. Maybe Polly would take the hint and shut up.

Billy crawled to the front of the tent and yelled, "Grace, we're going to sleep!"

"Be there in a minute!" Grace called.

"Are you sure you don't want any help?" Andrew yelled.

"No!" Grace replied.

"Amundsen set up a tent at the Pole and left Scott a note in it," Polly said as she crawled to her sleeping bag. "Scott's diary entry for the day he reached the Pole reads: *Great God! This is an awful place and terrible enough for us to have laboured to it without the reward of priority.*"

She paused. "But the next day, Bowers wrote a cheery note to his sister, telling her, *Captain Scott . . . has taken the blow very well indeed.*"

"What's your point, Polly?" Robert said.

"Scott had spent his whole life dreaming of this one goal, but when Amundsen beat him, he didn't waste any time feeling sorry for himself," Polly said. "He and his men weren't losers."

"Have it your way, Polly," Robert said. "But shut up."

"Could you recite another page from the diary, Polly?" Andrew said when they were in their sleeping bags.

"A bedtime story?" Billy mocked him.

Robert groaned but didn't protest.

Polly ignored Robert and Billy and scanned her memory for something fun. "Okay, I'll tell you Scott's diary entry on Christmas day: *We had four courses,* Scott wrote."

"Four courses!" Robert yelped. "I thought the Secretary was supposed to be authentic. Why can't *we* have four courses?"

"The first, pemmican ..." Polly continued.

"Yuk," Billy said.

"...full whack, with slices of horse meat ..."

Billy sighed.

"...flavoured with onion and curry powder and thickened with biscuit; ..."

"Nothing that they had sounds good," Billy complained.

"...then an arrowroot, cocoa and biscuit hoosh sweetened; then a plum-pudding; then cocoa with raisins, and finally a dessert of caramels and ginger."

"Even though I don't know exactly what caramels and ginger are," Andrew said, "they sound delicious."

"After the feast, it was difficult to move. Wilson and I couldn't finish our share of plum-pudding. We have all slept splendidly and feel thoroughly warm—such is the effect of full feeding," Polly finished. She was glad that for once Robert and Billy didn't jeer.

"I would give anything for some candy," Andrew said.

"What kind do you like?" Polly asked.

"My favorite is Chocobombs," Andrew said. "I especially like the grape and the cherry."

Billy thought guiltily about the stash in his sleeping bag. He could feel the packages with his toes.

"I don't like them," Robert said. "Too gooey."

"I love them," Polly said. "My mother used to buy them on holidays."

"You guys won't admit it, but you're sick of pemmican," Billy said, glad that he only had to pretend to eat the miserable stuff.

"What does pemmican have in it, Polly?" Andrew asked.

"You sure you want to know?" Polly replied.

"Yeah," Andrew said.

"No," Billy said.

"Dried meat and lard," Polly said.

"I knew something tasted awful in that stuff," Billy said. "Scott probably invented it."

"He didn't," Polly said, tired of their disrespect for Scott. "Good night."

"I'm going to turn in, too," said Robert.

"Good night," Andrew said. He hadn't bumbled anything today, had he?

"Lard," Billy said. How could the others stand that stuff? He bent over and pulled up a bag of cherry Chocobombs, Andrew's favorite.

Polly closed her eyes. She remembered another passage from Wilson's diary. He was one of the four men who had died along with Scott during his attempt to return from the Pole. She wouldn't share Wilson's quote with the group:

Very hungry always, our allowance being a very bare one. Dreams as a rule of splendid food, ball suppers, sirloins of beef, caldrons of steaming vegetables. But one spends all one's time shouting at waiters who won't bring one a plate of anything, or else one finds the beef is only ashes when one gets it. . . . One very rarely gets a feed in one's sleep.

I'm going to prove Wilson wrong, Polly decided. She tried to glue a picture of a bag of strawberry chips on the inside of her eyelids. She challenged herself to eat the whole bag in her dreams.

Billy listened until he heard the kids begin to breathe regularly. Grace would be outside half the night with the dumb dogs. He ripped open the candy bag as quietly as he could and took that first bite. It was delicious. There were five in a bag. Maybe he should wake the others and share a Chocobomb with each of them.

He popped another one into his mouth.

Naw, they needed their sleep.

Next Billy ate two at once. Robert didn't even like them. He had one left. Maybe he should wake Andrew.

He popped the last Chocobomb into his mouth. There weren't that many in a bag. Sharing with the other kids was impossible. Besides, they weren't as good as he remembered. The kids hadn't missed that much.

Then Billy heard the thud of footsteps in the snow. His mouth full of cherry and chocolate, he froze.

Grace crawled inside.

Billy swallowed the whole mess in one gulp. It was impossibly sticky and gooey, and he coughed.

"Billy?" Grace whispered. She started peeling off her layers.

"Hmm," he mumbled.

"What's that smell?"

"I dunno," Billy said, feeling his heart start to race.

"Is there such a thing as a smell hallucination?" Grace said.

"I dunno," Billy said again.

"Because I'm having one," Grace said.

"Shh," Billy said. "Don't be so inconsiderate. The others are sleeping."

Grace slipped into her sleeping bag. She was too tired to eat her hoosh, but not too tired to wonder.

"What's he doing?" Chad asked. He had just returned from working on his summary of the kids' day.

The screens were dark and quiet except for Billy's. The scene on his screen flashed with silver.

Steve turned up the volume on Billy's screen. They heard some loud cracks and rustlings, then a soft, muffled "One, two, three . . ."

"Billy's got some junk food hidden in his sleeping bag," Steve explained. "It sounds like he's counting it."

"How do you know?"

"I saw him do the same thing on the ship."

"He's put one over on the Secretary, hasn't he?" Chad said.

"Yeah, and on his teammates," Steve said.

"You're right," Chad said. "You want to intervene on this one?"

Steve smiled, thinking of how outraged Robert would be if he learned about the candy. "I'm going to let Billy answer to his conscience."

"Probably the toughest voice there is," Chad said.

Steve nodded.

"Ready to go back and make our last set of edits?" Chad asked.

"Sure," Steve said. All the screens were dark now. "But if you don't mind, I'm going to help Billy hide his candy from the Secretary."

"Go right ahead," Chad said.

While Steve double deleted the scene, Chad was giving him advice: "I think the best drama is still Grace and the dogs. So let's send the Secretary at least an hour of footage showing Grace's struggle to get them under control."

"Good idea," Steve said.

"I'll work on the dogs," Chad said. "Why don't you go through and see if you can find some scary shots of that sky?"

"What do you mean?" Steve asked, his heart in his throat.

"You didn't notice it?"

Steve shook his head.

Chad met Steve's eyes. "I'm afraid bad weather is on the way."

21

"So, what are we likely to see today, Billy?" Robert asked after breakfast on the morning of the third day of their trek. They were all huddled around the Primus stove, even though Billy had turned it off to save fuel.

Once again Polly felt relieved that she wasn't the navigator.

"Five or six miles from here this old map says that the ice is full of crevasses," Billy said.

"Triceratops fell into one the other day. I didn't see it because those darn goggles that we have to wear are tinted," Grace said.

"Why didn't you tell us about that sooner? What happened?" Robert said.

"It was shallow. The dogs pulled her out," Grace said.

"And you didn't even see it?" Billy asked. He wouldn't have ridden in the lead so confidently if he had known that they might hit an early crevasse.

Grace shook her head.

"We all need to wear goggles to prevent snow blindness," Polly said.

"What's snow blindness?" asked Andrew.

"The snow reflects the sun's rays, and your eyes are burned by the light." Polly paused. "In Scott's expedition the men got snow-blind a lot."

Robert held up his hand. "No history lessons. We don't have time." He looked at Grace. "But wear the goggles."

"I thought I saw some crevasses, but they were shadows," Andrew said.

"What if we let the dogs lead?" Polly said.

Billy snorted.

"The dogs are too slow to lead," Robert said.

"But the dog team is long and wide. If the dogs' weight makes a snow bridge collapse, chances are some will get across. The others will dangle in their traces over the crevasse. But"—Polly sounded like a schoolteacher even to herself—"if one of us falls into a crevasse, we'll fall all the way down."

Grace wanted to tell Polly not to argue with Robert. The snow would be his teacher. But she started crawling toward the tent flap instead. Time to harness the dogs.

After thirty minutes on his cycle, Robert could feel the tiredness easing out of him. The sun had gotten stronger, and the wind, which had been a torment when he had been colder, seemed friendly now.

But Robert was watching something that made him nervous. Something that he guessed the others didn't see. Between the mountains, a thin, dark line sliced the northwest sky near the horizon. A storm was coming toward them, getting ready to spoil their third day out.

Robert hit a slight rise and the drone of the motor became louder, but not so loud as to drown out his worries.

All morning something had been bugging him while he drank the hot chocolate that Billy had made, and while he loaded the tent and the other supplies onto the sled attached to the back of the cycle. He hadn't seen the line yet. But without knowing it, he had picked up on the wind and humidity that made bad weather more likely. A thin black line without any clouds meant a cold front.

That line linked this world of ice and snow to the world he knew. It told him that though they were different, in many ways they were the same.

Just like this snowcycle's engine and the one in his dad's motorboat.

He had worked on his dad's motorboat since he was a little boy; he knew its exact clatter. It sounded like a disposal grinding away at a spoon, sort of alarming and brittle until you realized that the sound was good.

He didn't know the snowcycle's engine well, but the vibrations against his legs were even. He checked the engine's temperature with his hand. Neither hot nor cold. Reassuringly warm.

The engine was in good shape.

But the line hadn't moved, and that was bad. When fronts moved fast, they passed over quickly.

In Houston cold fronts could be violent. On the bayou it was best to hole up for a few days and get out of the way.

He settled in for a short ride.

Grace noticed that she was gaining on Andrew again. She braked the sled to keep the dogs from catching up to him. They had been on the trail for only an hour, but she had had to hold the dogs back the whole time. To avoid crevasses, she was following the path already taken by the others. But soon she'd have to pass Andrew.

She had harnessed the dogs the same way as before. They looked the same in their traces, but overnight so much had changed. The constant nipping and feuding, slipping and sliding, and bumping into one another had all but stopped.

The dogs were finally working as a team.

For the first time, she was riding trancelike, trusting the dogs. "Iñupiat Eskimos have great powers of observation and a fantastic memory for the landscape," her grandfather had bragged. "I can draw a map of the cove where we fished, with every inlet, although I haven't been there for many years." Her grandfather had never lied, but it was hard to believe that even he would have been able to remember the slight valleys and low hills of this white desert.

Desert. She would never have believed it, but Polly had sworn that it was so. According to Polly, a desert didn't have to be hot, only dry. Polly claimed that Antarctica was one of the largest and driest deserts in the world.

So what was the sky doing? She shot the black clouds the evil eye. Not now, she wanted to command them. But she knew better than to try to control the weather.

"Accept what you cannot change," her grandfather had always said.

One of her dogs growled. Then another. Their ears stood up. Fur bristled on their backs. Grace tensed, waiting for a fight, but then noticed that the animals weren't focused on one another.

She scanned the dark horizon and spotted a speck of black against the white snow. Could it be moving?

Grace squinted. She yanked off her fogged goggles, and the vast whiteness seemed to collapse on top of her. She struggled to focus again. Unmistakably, a spot of black was crawling across the snow.

About half a mile ahead of Grace, Robert and Billy stopped their snowcycles and stared in the direction of the seal. Robert got off his cycle and began searching for his rifle.

Grace kept her eyes on the animal.

Ears back, T-Rex lunged forward.

As Grace sped past Andrew and Cookie, she gripped the handles to keep from falling. Why hadn't Robert shot the animal yet? He must be having trouble finding the rifle.

Polly got off the cycle and began searching through Billy's sled.

What was a seal doing so far from the coast? Grace wondered. Had it gotten lost during a storm? She wished that her grandfather were with her so she could ask him. Grace dragged the paddle in the soft snow as a brake and whipped the air over the dogs' heads to slow her team down, but the animals were racing. She couldn't help feeling proud of her dogs. She was going faster now than the snowcycles could. Why, she would bet she was going over five miles an hour!

Robert pulled the rifle off the sled and aimed.

A shot rang out, and Grace winced. It had been a long time since she had heard a loud noise, she thought as she desperately whipped the air again to slow the dogs. They kept up their pace, oblivious.

"Stop those dogs!" Billy called.

Grace hated to do it, but she lashed their backs. The whip licked brown fur. Once, twice. Instead of slowing, the dogs moved forward in a frenzy, past Robert and Billy. Their eyes trained on the bleeding seal, they tumbled down an incline. The seal appeared to be small, maybe a youngster lost from its family. Grace stuck the paddle in the snow as hard as she could, but the paddle popped out, worthless.

"Get those dogs!" Robert shouted at her.

Billy was jumping up and down. "Stop them!"

T-Rex, Brontosaurus, and Dryosaurus were in front, so they pounced on the seal first. Bits of black fur and blood popped out from the jumble of animals. The other dogs, maddened by the smell of blood, rushed to join them. The pack seethed with squirming, climbing, snarling bodies.

Grace jumped off the sled. "T-Rex! Dryosaurus!"she cried. She whacked T-Rex on the head with the paddle, but he didn't seem to notice. There was no other way: She pushed through the ring of frenzied dogs and barred their way to the seal.

T-Rex, Dryosaurus, and the others pulled back. They snarled and growled, but they didn't attack her. She raised the paddle, ready to smash any offender's head.

Brontosaurus alone ignored her. He thrust his teeth into the seal's side. She whacked him, then bent down and shoved his face away from the seal's body. She stood up, careful to stay between the dead seal and the dogs. The dogs fidgeted and whined but backed away.

"Wow!" Robert said.

Until Robert spoke, Grace hadn't noticed that the others had run over to her.

"Those dogs looked like they were going to eat you alive," Billy added.

"Are you all right, Grace?" Polly asked.

Out of breath, Andrew arrived on the pony.

"Yeah," Grace said, but her heart was pounding. She led the

dogs a few paces away from the seal's bloodied corpse.

"Good shot," Andrew said.

"Thanks." Robert examined the dead seal. "I don't want to stop and skin it now," he said, cupping his hand over his eyes and reexamining the sky. "But I think we should take what's left of its carcass with us. It'll give us a few days' extra food."

"Where did you learn to shoot like that, Robert?" Polly asked.

"Around," Robert said. On the bayou, sometimes, if he didn't shoot dinner he went hungry.

"Fresh meat will protect us from scurvy," Polly said.

"What's scurvy?" Andrew asked.

"It's a vitamin C deficiency," Polly said.

"I've never taken a vitamin in my life," Robert said.

"Robert, I'm tired of you not taking what I have to say seriously. Scurvy can kill you." Polly said sharply.

Grace's grandfather had told her about scurvy. People didn't get it unless they had had no vitamin C for months, but she didn't want to contradict Polly. What was the point?

"Okay," Robert said. "So we also need the meat to prevent scurvy. But"—he looked around carefully—"I'm worried about where we're going to load it."

"Why?" Grace asked.

"The cycles are already loaded. The pony can't pull any more," Robert replied.

"The dogs could," Grace said. "They're moving faster than the pony now."

"I'll say!" Robert said.

Robert's dark eyes were fixed on Grace. She wondered if he had noticed that the dogs were faster than the cycles, too.

"Okay," Robert said, though he didn't know how much

longer they could risk traveling. Twenty minutes? Thirty minutes? An hour? It was important that they cover as much distance as they could, but getting caught in a storm could mean death.

Billy and Andrew began dragging the seal's body over to the dogsled.

"I have an extra rope," Grace said.

Grace stood over the carcass while Billy lashed it onto the sled. He couldn't help hoping that the TV audience was watching him right now. He was good with knots. He had represented his Scout troop in a national knot-a-thon. He stood back and surveyed his work. The seal was tied tightly to the sled.

Even though Grace wanted to eat the seal, she felt sorry for it. "There's a special prayer that you're supposed to say when you kill a seal," she said.

"How do you know?" Billy asked.

"I'm an Iñupiat," Grace said.

Robert sighed. "So what is it?"

"I don't remember," Grace admitted. But she wanted to honor the memory of her ancestors at her first kill. "My grandfather used to sing it to me. But I'll make one up." She pitched her voice low. *"Oh, seal, oh great black one,"* she sang. It was almost scary how much she sounded like her grandfather. *"Thank you for giving your life that we may live."*

"Amen," Robert said. It was kind of strange. Grace was singing songs. Billy, his snow-and-ice man, looked unconcerned. None of these kids understood the weather. But he warned himself not to worry them yet. He wanted them to concentrate on making the best time they could in the short time they had before the front moved in.

"Amen," Polly, Andrew, and Billy said.

Robert stared at the sky. "Can't you go a little faster?" he asked Andrew.

"I don't think so," Andrew said. "But Grace, you flew by me."

Grace climbed into the sled. The seal's purplish tongue brushed her jacket. The steam from its body warmed hers, but she was already warm, almost overheated.

I'm an Iñupiat coming home from a good hunt, she thought. She flicked the whip.

The dogs started moving gracefully across the white wilderness. If only the sky weren't getting so dark, the day would be magical.

"A storm's coming." Robert stopped his cycle.

Billy pulled up next to him. "But we're just starting to make good time," he protested. Ever since they had killed the seal, the snow had been soft. Ahead of them, he saw a stretch of blue ice that his machine would fly across.

Robert glared at him. He was tempted to ask Billy where he had gotten his snow-and-ice experience, but Billy was so prickly. He understood in his gut that it was better to praise Billy than to risk making him feel ignorant. "We've got to stop." They had traveled for thirty minutes since shooting the seal. He didn't want to push their luck.

Polly stared at the clouds overhead. "It doesn't look good," she said to Robert, "but Billy knows about snow, don't you, Billy?"

"I guess we shouldn't risk it," Billy said quickly.

"Right here?" Polly said.

"Here—and fast!" Robert said as he climbed off his snowcycle. "Let's set up the tent before the others get here."

Polly climbed off Billy's snowcycle. A gust of wind came up

and blew against her. She stared toward the south and wondered how long this strange monotonous landscape went on.

"Snap to!" Robert shouted at her.

"Yes, sir," Polly said sarcastically, but she turned toward the sled attached to Billy's cycle. Billy had already started unloading.

"We don't have much time," Robert repeated. He heard his breath crackle as it froze in midair. The temperature was dropping fast.

22

Ever since Steve had missed Andrew's rescue of the pony, he had slept very little. He watched *Antarctic Historical Survivor* during the day, together with the accompanying educational documentaries and family interviews. Then he went to work and watched the day's episode again along with the real-time footage. He was using so much electricity at home, that soon he wouldn't be able to afford his small luxuries like new comic books. As the Secretary of Entertainment intended, his twelve-inch television, which sat in the middle of his tiny hut, was becoming the focal point of his life.

"Although the weather looks ominous, the contestants are still heading for the Pole," Johnny Sparks's oily voice was saying. "Earlier, Robert fired an incredible shot that killed a seal. Grace's dogs showed their stuff in a mad dash toward the dead animal. Only when the dogs were on the verge of devouring the seal did Grace succeed in getting them under control. Now let's break and interview family members."

The scene shifted to an immaculate living room. "Mrs. Pritchard," Johnny Sparks asked a small, demure-looking woman sitting in a wheelchair, "how do you think your daughter is doing so far?"

"I have to say well, Johnny. Polly's no outdoors girl, but she's certainly making her contribution."

"Are you aware that over thirty-three percent of the viewers are voting for her as Most Valuable Player?"

"I had heard that figure."

"You know that award means an extra ninety thousand dollars."

The woman nodded, her lips pressed tightly together. "Johnny, I don't care about the money. I just want my little girl back."

Johnny smiled. "We can certainly understand that. It's been easy to guess what her super talent is."

"Yes," Mrs. Pritchard said. "She's had the Memory since she was a little girl. Her father, rest his soul, had it."

"Do you think Robert is treating her as well as he should?"

"I think Robert would be better off if he listened more to Polly."

"Do you think Polly should lead the group instead?"

Steve hated how Johnny Sparks would never quit until he had gotten the contestants' parents to say something ugly.

Mrs. Pritchard hesitated. "I wouldn't say that. I just think each member of the team has strengths, and Robert undervalues Polly's contribution."

"But you would say that Robert doesn't listen, wouldn't you?"

"He's not a great listener, but he seems to do many things well."

"Robert's mother said that Polly is a prissy little girl who shouldn't be a contestant at all."

"How I wish that Polly weren't a contestant!" Mrs. Pritchard's bottom lip trembled as if she were about to cry. She reminded Steve of his own sweet mom, and Steve wanted to reach out and hug her.

"So you don't like television." Johnny Spark smirked.

Criticizing EduTV was a crime.

"I didn't say that. You're putting words in my mouth. I think television serves a useful purpose in calming people." She grimaced. "After all, I lost the use of my legs in the first Urban Trash War."

Steve pushed the MUTE button. He couldn't stand listening to Johnny Sparks anymore. He picked up his favorite long-sleeved T-shirt from the mat on his floor and slipped it over his head. He opened a bag of tomato, spinach, and cheese chips and began eating breakfast.

The sound of his neighbor's television penetrated the thin walls. "Mr. Morton . . ." he heard Johnny Sparks say, beginning his interview with Andrew's dad. Then silence.

"Mom, what are you doing?" a child's voice objected.

"I'm turning this off." His next-door neighbor's voice came through the walls. Her name was Mrs. Poppers, and she had two kids. "You guys have watched enough. Our government jails us if we trash the streets, but they trash your minds."

"Mom, we have to watch this. It's teleschool."

"You can earn an F on this, for all I care. I can't stand to hear any more about those poor kids or their poor families. It's too sad and depressing."

Steve had never paid much attention to Mrs. Poppers before; she seemed like just a typical overworked mother. But now her words filled him with hope.

"You're crazy, Mom!" a kid shouted at her.

"She's not crazy!" Steve said in a loud voice.

The Poppers' shanty fell silent. Then Steve heard Johnny Sparks's voice again. "If Andrew wins, what will you buy?"

"A new television. Ours is falling apart," Mr. Morton said.

"I told you, turn that thing off!" Mrs. Poppers yelled.

Mrs. Poppers must have won the argument this time, because the next-door shanty grew quiet again.

If Mrs. Poppers didn't like *Antarctic Historical Survivor*, then maybe, just maybe, the Secretary's latest series was backfiring. Steve decided to leave early for work, hang around a street or two, and see what he could find out.

Near the DOE a man wearing a Planet Hollywood cap was hawking *Survivor* souvenirs. Steve looked at the Polly and Grace dolls and the Andrew, Billy, and Robert T-shirts. "How are they selling?"

"Like hotcakes," the vendor said. "The Secretary, she's really good for business."

Steve bent toward the man and said in a whisper, "I'm just curious. Do you watch the series? What do you think of it?" They could both go to jail if the telepolice heard him.

"Who are you?" The man's eyes darted around anxiously.

"I'm not the telepolice. I just want to know."

The man stared hard at Steve and then pulled open the bottom drawer of his cart. He lifted a T-shirt and spread it out. On the front, images of the five kids were frozen inside blue, green, purple, red, and pink Popsicles. The Secretary, her red lips open, was just about to eat the frozen bar with Andrew inside. The caption was "POPSICKLES."

"Why did you show me that shirt?" Steve asked.

The man chewed his lip and shrugged. "Thought you might be interested."

"You don't like her, either," Steve exulted.

The man only arched his eyebrow.

23

Billy knelt by the Primus. In the middle of the day, Robert had insisted that they stop and set up the tent. As Billy stirred the seal-leg soup they were going to try for dessert, he hoped that Robert had panicked about the weather and that their fearless leader would end up looking like a fool. Sure, it was growing darker outside, but it seemed equally likely to Billy that the storm would blow over.

Billy took a sip of the soup. He had become the group's cook. Of course he had eaten his own crackers and peanuts instead of the pemmican concoction that he had served the others, but he did love the hot chocolate.

Polly was taking a last bite of her luncheon ration of pemmican when she heard the wind rise. "Robert was right. A storm . . ." Polly began to say, then realized that she needed to shout to make herself heard over the wind. No, a blizzard, she thought, remembering the definition in one of her books. *An Antarctic blizzard is a period of strong winds sufficient to whip existing snow up off the surface and change the landscape to a formless wall of swirling white powder—a world in which it would be difficult if not impossible to find one's way.* A blizzard outside, and Andrew was taking care of the pony!

How could Robert predict the weather so accurately? Billy wondered. He stirred the soup faster in frustration.

"Did we forget anything?" Robert shouted.

"I'll check the dogs!" Grace yelled. She hadn't taken off her parka.

Robert pulled on his gear. "The supplies!" he shouted.

Polly stuck her arms into her parka and her hands into her gloves. She put her cap on her head and followed Grace outside to see if she could find Andrew. Her breath looked like puffs of smoke. She took one step away from the tent, then another. After her third step, she was lost in a great white blur. Her cheeks felt numb. She knew that she was close to the tent, but terror rose in her throat. She looked for the ground but saw only rivers of snow. She looked up and found herself floating in a stinging white cloud.

"Help! Help!" Polly cried. The men in Scott's expedition had felt their way through blizzards in the remotest part of Antarctica. How had they managed?

Someone reached for her. She buried her head in his shaggy parka. She could tell by the open zipper that it was Andrew.

Polly felt her tears freeze. "I got lost," she tried to say.

Andrew pushed her toward the tent.

"Where's Grace?" Polly cried, but the wind ripped the words out of her mouth. She stumbled into the tent.

Billy was still squatting next to the Primus. Polly crawled next to him. She slipped off her gloves. The frozen tears bit her skin as she knocked them off her face.

Andrew waved at her from the open tent flap.

"Don't go back out," Polly begged him.

Andrew shook his head before disappearing.

"How long do Antarctic blizzards last?" Billy asked.

Polly bent toward him so she could hear his question.

He repeated himself.

It was curious. Billy was the only one with experience of ice and snow, yet he didn't seem to feel at all bad about staying inside the tent while the others braved the weather. "It depends. It could last a few days," Polly answered. Then she paused. The raging white winds outside terrified her, but she tried to think of something positive to say. "Thank goodness for the seal. Do you like the soup?"

Billy nodded. He had convinced himself that seal meat wouldn't be bad.

"If we're stuck here for a few days, at least we have extra food," Polly said.

"You're right," Billy agreed. "You ready to try it?"

"Sure," Polly said.

Billy handed her a cup. She held it against her nose for warmth, then took a sip. It tasted like flavored water, but she loved it anyway because it wasn't pemmican.

Andrew pushed Grace into the tent.

"And Robert! Where's Robert?" Polly shouted. But the wind was howling, and she couldn't hear Andrew's answer.

Grace crawled next to them. Billy handed her a cup of soup, and Grace peeled off her gloves.

Polly raised her voice above the sound of the wind. "Did you see Robert, Grace?"

Grace shook her head. She had seen a whole continent turn into a ghost.

"How about the dogs? Are the dogs okay?" Polly asked.

Grace nodded. "They dig holes in the snow. They stay warm. But the pony . . ." She shrugged.

"Don't worry. We have the snowcycles," Billy said loudly.

Over their cups of hot seal-leg soup, Polly and Grace exchanged glances.

A few minutes later, Robert and Andrew pushed their way inside. Snow blew in through the tent flap.

Robert quickly closed it.

Andrew took a few deep breaths after joining them at the Primus. "The pony!" he shouted. "Cookie's getting lashed by the snow!"

"Scott built snow walls for his ponies," Polly suggested.

"Polly, if you want to tell me how, in that blinding mess, we can build a snow wall, then great. Otherwise, keep your suggestions to yourself!" Robert yelled.

Polly took a sip of seal-leg soup. Even though new ideas seemed to frustrate Robert, he had been right about the storm, and she was grateful, oh so grateful, that they were inside right now.

Andrew sat down beside her. In a tight circle around the Primus, they all enjoyed the slight heat of the stove. The snow continued to beat on the tent, but as they sipped their soup, the wind grew quieter.

Andrew crawled over to the tent flap and peeked out. "It's still snowing, but the wind's died down."

"It feels warmer," Grace agreed.

"You're right," Polly said.

Andrew crawled back to Polly.

"Weird weather," Billy said.

"The best thing we could do would be to sleep," Robert said. "Anybody sleepy?"

"Sort of," Grace said.

"I want to hear more about Scott sometime, Polly," Andrew said.

"That's a real upbeat topic, Andrew," Robert said. "Let's hear about it after we collect our prize money."

Again Polly reminded herself that they owed their escape from the storm to Robert. "What are you going to do with your money, Robert?" Polly asked in what she hoped was a pleasant voice.

"I'm going to buy me a boat with my name written on the back of it in big red-and-silver letters," Robert said.

"You should invest it," Billy said.

"Heck, I don't know anything about finances. But I know everything about bayous," Robert said.

Polly smiled. "You'll probably buy a bank, Billy."

"I'm going to go to high school and college," Billy boasted. "I bet Grace will use it to buy dogs." He laughed.

Polly thought his laugh sounded mean.

Grace looked down at her cup. "I've thought about starting an animal shelter. With so many starving people, no one pays attention to animals." Grace didn't want to tell the kids about her real dream. They might laugh at her. She planned to use the money to move her family to Antarctica. They would eat seal soup and seal steaks every night.

"And you, Polly?" Grace looked at her.

"I'm like Billy. I want an education," Polly said.

Robert laughed. "Why? You're already an encyclopedia."

"Do you want to teach, Polly?" Andrew asked.

"Maybe." Polly wanted to do something that would make a difference in the world, but that sounded too grand. She turned to Andrew. "What about you?"

Andrew panicked. He hated big broad questions like that. He had no idea what he wanted to do. Before this trip, all he had wanted to do was watch more television and do fewer chores. But now he wasn't sure what he would want to do. He just knew he couldn't go back to the soft spot on the couch.

Billy watched Andrew's discomfort with pleasure. There was no way that the viewers would vote for such a dumb person to be MVP. Andrew was out of the running. And Robert was too bossy, Polly too cerebral. He was sure the winner would be either him or Grace. And if the dogs were losers, then Grace was, too.

"I say that we take a nap," Robert said. "If it's still calm when we wake up, I'll go out and finish cutting up the seal."

"Good idea," Polly mumbled, suddenly tired.

Andrew struggled to keep his eyes open. The wind must have stopped completely, because he could hear the sounds of the other kids' breathing. Even after two nights in the tent, it still felt strange to be so close together. After all, they hadn't even known one another two weeks ago.

He had set out his sleeping bag as far from the others as possible in the small tent, because even though they had left the ship, he hoped his friend could still talk to him.

Billy was snoring.

Would his friend talk to him again? Andrew wondered. The tent was strong and sturdy, and he was almost dry and very warm. He felt his eyelids growing heavier.

Some nine thousand miles away, Steve, who had just checked into work, was wondering the same thing. Except for Andrew's, the other kids' eyes were closed; their cameras were shut down. This was his chance.

Steve watched the steam from the kids' exhalations rise to the center of the tent. He listened to the sounds of the children sleeping, and from behind him the slow *swish, swish, swish* of Pearl's broom. At least there were no soldiers with muskets ready to shoot the kids, as in the *Civil War Historical Survivor* series, or wild beasts outside waiting to tear the kids up, as in the *African Explorers Historical Survivor* series. These kids weren't going to catch any dread disease, the way the contestants in the Black Plague contest had. There were no pyramids to build, as in the Egyptian contest. Yet a storm raged outside their tent. It was minus fifteen degrees. The weather could be bad for a long time, and the kids probably had only five days' worth of food. He didn't believe that five kids could actually survive without help.

And he doubted whether the advice that he would be able to offer would be enough. He hung his head. If he was honest with himself, he had to admit that he really didn't think that the kids were going to survive.

The audience rating for the past two days had been higher than for any survival show in history. It had climbed to 97.8 percent.

Hourly, the production department received e-mails from the Secretary of Entertainment:

> Who are those subversive 2.2%? How dare they ignore this show? Before this is over, we want 100% viewer ratings.

> Production room: It is your job to see that we attain 100% ratings. It is your job to see that everyone in America is having fun.

Steve hoped the ratings didn't mean that viewers were having fun. But he wasn't sure of anything except that the situation was hopeless.

Andrew's screen blinked on, then off. He was fighting sleep.

Could he be waiting for Steve?

Why not? Why not be kind to the kid? It was the least that he could do. Steve reached under the screen and pulled out the mike. Holding it, he felt that Andrew was closer to him. He hesitated, almost hypnotized by the steady swish of Pearl's broom.

When he was young, Steve had put his little brother to sleep with rhymes. Before he had a chance to change his mind, he flipped on the switch: "Good night. Sleep tight. Don't let the nuclear monster bite."

"Ahh . . ." Andrew gave a long sigh of satisfaction and closed his eyes.

Steve faced five dark screens in the empty room. The other members of the night crew were in the basement, playing cards. While Steve liked Chad and the rest of them, he was much younger than they were, and he didn't care about the things they talked about: their kids, their taxes, and their bills.

On his way to the water fountain, he caught sight of Chad's briefcase sitting on a stool. He was drawn to its shiny blackness. If the top hadn't been open, he might have been able to resist. He walked over to it.

He cast a glance at Pearl. As usual, she was paying attention only to a spot on the floor. He riffled through Chad's papers and found what he was looking for almost immediately. ANTARCTIC SCRIPT, he read.

CONFIDENTIAL
CALAMITIES:

Calamity One: The Glacier. On day one, the ship's
   motor shuts off, but it turns back on in the middle

of the night, setting the stage for calamity number one. The ship will ram into the glacier and knock some ice loose. Of course, nothing can be predicted with certainty, but it is highly unlikely that the kids will have safely stowed all their foodstuffs.

Calamity Two: The Motor Sledges. The motor sledge engines are programmed to fail quickly. If the kids have placed too much reliance on these motor sledges, they will have to man-haul at least some of the supplies to the Pole.

Calamity Three: The Heating Oil. Scott and his men had placed heating oil at the depots, but because of faulty containers, some of the oil evaporated. As a consequence, they had much less heating oil than needed, and when the terrible weather hit . . .

Steve looked away from the script. At the moment he couldn't read any more of it; he was too angry. The calamity on the ship had been bad enough, but he held in his hand written proof that the Secretary planned five more calamities. The contest wasn't fair anyway, and here the Secretary had gone out of her way to create more problems for the kids. How could she do this? Why did America view the troubles and almost certain death of its poor as entertainment?

He had a vague recollection of an EduTV series about Roman gladiators. Men placed in the middle of a coliseum to fight lions and tigers while Roman crowds cheered. Didn't the

Romans' love of gladiatorial combat predict the fall of their civilization?

How were the gladiators different from these kids?

"This series is wrong," he said out loud. *Historical Survivor*'s rules prohibited acts of kindness like Pearl's. Its aim was to torture people—even kids. He stared at the five blank screens on the wall. The Secretary's treachery just made him want to fight harder to protect the kids.

He reminded himself that nothing was hopeless. His whole family had died, but he had survived the Superpox, hadn't he?

He still didn't know how much he could do, but he leaned toward the screens and promised the kids, "You're not alone."

If he was to help them, he couldn't let himself get too worked up; he needed to use his head. He picked up the script again from the floor where he had dropped it.

> Calamity Four: The Weather. Although blizzards cannot be predicted, they used to be prevalent at the South Pole during November. . . .

Steve skipped ahead.

> Calamity Five: The Crevasses. The route marked for the contestants is full of crevasses. Even experienced polar travelers find crevasses difficult to maneuver around.
>
> Calamity Six: Frostbite. One of Scott's men died because he got frostbitten. It will be a miracle if one or more of the kids don't get it. After gangrene

sets in, there is no cure but amputation of the limb. It could make for an interesting episode if one of them needs an amputation. Grace Untoka has considerable experience operating on animals. She will surely be the one to attempt this. . . .

Steve, feeling tears sting his eyes, closed the script. He sat down in a nearby chair and cried as Pearl swept. He wasn't sure who he was crying for—himself or the kids or Pearl or the millions of viewers.

All of us, he decided through his tears.

24

In his sleep, Billy heard a noise and tried to wake himself. He felt as if he were at the bottom of a deep well. No, a crevasse. He tried to climb out, but he kept slipping down the icy slope.

The noise grew louder. Billy opened his eyes. He heard the sound of wild animals. Was he in Africa, in some jungle somewhere?

He stuck his head out of his sleeping bag and noticed the blue walls, a wool cap sticking out of the sleeping bag next to him, and the Primus stove. Then he remembered. He was in a tent in Antarctica in the middle of a blizzard. But Antarctica didn't have any wild animals, except for seals and penguins. He listened some more. Apart from the animal noises, it was quiet outside. The blizzard was over. He glanced at his watch. It was three A.M. or three P.M. in D.C. There was no way for him to know. All he knew for sure was that he had been asleep for hours.

The growling, snarling sound was loud. It was coming from more than one animal, and they were crazed and howling with excitement. They sounded like fierce wolves. Was this another calamity, another event in the stupid game? Had the Secretary transported wolves to Antarctica? There was something about this cold, forbidding terrain that made wolves seem appropriate.

He listened closely to the howls.

It was the idiot dogs. Who were like wolves, they were so fierce.

The dogs had gotten loose and were destroying the camp. Maybe the best thing he could do was to go back to sleep. The dogs would make a huge mess, and Andrew and Polly would vote to get rid of them in the morning. They had traveled seven miles yesterday before the bad weather hit. They had only twenty-three miles to go to get to the first depot. Pulling the loaded sleds, the cycles were slower than Billy and Robert had hoped, but on a normal surface they could make four miles an hour. Driving the cycles, Robert and Billy could make it to the depot in six hours.

Billy slipped his head back into his sleeping bag, pleased that they were not about to get attacked by wolves. Besides, he felt like he was closer to depositing one hundred thousand dollars in his bank account. With Grace out of the way, he'd have a better shot at being MVP.

Then Billy remembered the seal. That's what had excited the dogs.

The dogs were chowing down. Billy had tolerated the seal-leg soup, and seal steaks were bound to be even better. The dogs were eating his food. Billy reached over and shook Robert.

Robert groaned in his sleep.

Billy shook him again. "Listen."

Robert shot up. "What?"

"The dogs."

Robert paused and listened. "Why are they making so much noise?"

"They've gotten loose," Billy told him. "Now we have to

risk frostbite to catch them."

Billy shook Grace. She sat up quickly, too. "What's up?"

"The dogs," Billy said simply.

"You must not have tied them up," Robert said, completely alert now.

"I tied them, all right," Grace said as she scooted out of her sleeping bag.

"Then how could they get loose?" Billy asked.

"They probably ate through their harnesses," Grace said. "Their food is moldy, and they're hungry."

"Well, come on," Robert said.

Billy started groping around in his sleeping bag for his fur gloves. He felt his bags of nuts and candy, packages of crackers and health food bars before finally touching his gloves. He'd help Grace. Score points with the audience and Robert. He wouldn't complain. Maybe tomorrow Robert would get rid of those stupid dogs. Didn't Robert realize that he was setting Grace up as MVP?

Billy climbed out of his sleeping bag and, to keep his stash safe, carefully rolled it up. "Do you want to wake the others?" he asked Robert.

Robert was pulling on his parka. "I think we can handle it."

Grace opened the tent flap and walked outside. The blizzard had stopped. They must have been asleep for a while, she thought, because the landscape had changed. The light from the sun and both moons reflected off the blanket of new snow. The air seemed full of dazzling light. The mountains glowed in the distance. The temperature actually felt warmer, but Grace couldn't enjoy the snowy wonderland because of the dogs.

Brontosaurus, Diplodocus, and Apatosaurus were loose.

The tethered dogs were standing and panting in frustration as they watched the feast in progress.

Not only had the loose dogs attacked the seal, one of them had ripped open a box of pemmican. The loose pemmican littered the white snow like dog droppings. The seal's blood splattered the snow with pink polka dots.

Grace cracked the whip over Brontosaurus. He was undoubtedly the ringleader.

"You're just hitting the air. Hit them!" Billy yelled. "They're eating our food!"

What Billy said was true. The three dogs, large enough to be wolves, were devouring the seal. When Grace cracked the whip again, Brontosaurus turned back and looked at her, his fangs drenched in blood. Grace moved in quickly and pulled him off the carcass. He snarled and bit the air.

Grabbing his collar, Grace yanked him toward Robert. "Here," she said. "Tie him up."

Robert pulled a rope out of his pocket and tied the dog to the sled.

Billy tried to shrink away. Surely Grace wouldn't ask him to hold a dog.

Luckily, Grace had a rope in her pocket. She used it to tie Apatosaurus's mouth shut.

She pushed the muzzled dog toward Billy. "Take Apatosaurus."

Billy held on to the collar of this dog, who managed to snarl even with his stupid mouth roped shut.

Grace struggled with Diplodocus, trying to pull him away from the feast.

Apatosaurus was a big dog, and strong. He fought to get free. Billy held his collar. He wished that he had the whip. *He'd* get this dog to calm down.

Grace examined Diplodocus. "Just as I thought—they ate through their harnesses."

Billy wrestled Apatosaurus onto the snow and squatted on his back.

Robert examined the seal's body. "Not much left," he called.

So much for seal steaks, Billy thought bitterly. Apatosaurus tried to twist away from him, but Billy only held him tighter. The dog stank of blood.

But Billy wasn't unhappy. The dog was muzzled and couldn't bite him. Yesterday Grace had had a good day with the dogs, but now, once again, they had proved that they were more trouble than they were worth. After this, Robert would have to get rid of them. Without the dogs, Grace didn't have a chance to be MVP. Not a chance.

"You ready to go?" Chad said to Steve. "The day crew will be here soon."

"The Secretary overlooked a calamity," Steve said. "The script didn't mention the dogs eating the kids' food."

Chad looked serious. "You read the script?"

"Yeah." Steve waited for Chad to get angry.

The lock on Chad's briefcase clicked loudly before he picked it up. But all he said was, "So you understand how bad the odds are?"

"I do." Steve grabbed his coat.

"I'm sorry," Chad said.

"Were you going to tell me?" Steve turned and faced Chad.

"Sometimes it's better not to know everything," Chad murmured.

Steve walked to the door. In a way, Chad was right. If he let it, that script could steal his hope, and then how could he face watching the kids?

"See you tomorrow," Chad called.

Steve didn't bother answering. I'll be here tomorrow and the day after and the day after that. No matter how bleak their chances, I will be there for those kids, Steve promised himself as he walked down the dark hallway.

25

Later that same morning, Polly examined Robert, Grace, and Billy. The trio had been up for half the night looking after the dogs, and Robert was in a particularly foul mood. In contrast, she and Andrew had been asleep since yesterday afternoon. She felt bleary-eyed from too much sleep, and Andrew was yawning.

"I've checked the supplies, and we're down to one day's worth of food," Robert said. "The dogs ate the rest." He glared at the group.

"I want to call another vote on the dogs," Billy said. "We could stake them here and pick them up in the helicopter on our way home."

Billy was cruel, Grace thought. Her dogs would starve before they returned.

"What's to keep them from eating through their harnesses tonight, Grace?" Polly asked.

"Nothing," Grace said. "They're tired of their moldy food. From now on, we'll have to store all our food in the tent."

"What do you think we should do, Polly?" Andrew said.

"We need the dogs," Polly said.

"You want to change your vote, Andrew?" Billy asked.

Andrew took a sip of hot chocolate, remembered the voice of his friend, and shook his head.

"Robert, what do you think?" Billy said.

"Even though Grace still has trouble controlling them, the dogs have been performing, Billy," Robert said firmly.

Polly was proud of Robert, but she didn't want to say anything. It would just make him mad.

Robert had noticed, Grace thought. Her dogs were a team. She wasn't perfect yet, but she was a dogsled driver.

Billy sighed in disappointment. Didn't Robert know that he was setting up Grace to win the game? Robert wasn't nearly as smart as he thought he was. Billy flattened one of the maps on the floor of the tent. No use arguing. He knew he was beaten.

"We have a straight shot. Only twenty-three miles and we're there," Billy said. "Before the blizzard, we were just about to cross a patch of blue ice."

"That's good and bad," Grace said, remembering her grandfather's tales of ice and snow.

"Why?" Robert asked.

"More crevasses," Grace explained.

"The map warns that the area is full of them," Billy agreed.

"How many crevasses are there supposed to be?" Andrew asked.

"No one can know," Grace said.

"We've been lucky so far," Polly moaned. At least they weren't dead.

"You call a drowned pony, a storm, loose dogs, and losing our food supply luck?" Billy stared incredulously at Polly.

"It could be so much worse," Polly said.

"We need to stay upbeat," Robert said sharply.

"Sure." Polly remembered Scott's words: *One can only say, 'God help us!' and plod on our weary way, cold and very miserable.*

Robert turned his attention away from Polly's dour expression.

"Billy, I'll lead today," Robert said in what Billy thought was a particularly bossy tone. "I'll carry an ice pick in my backpack and some rope. If I go down, with any luck I'll be able to climb my way out."

Grace thought of the icy sides of the crevasse that she had stared into on the first day of their trek. She wouldn't want to climb out of one of those.

"Robert," Polly objected, "some of the crevasses are hundreds of feet deep. Have you ever used an ice pick?"

Robert shook his head.

"I'll stay in the lead," Billy heard himself say.

"You're sure?" Robert asked.

Billy nodded. He wasn't going to let Robert win so easily. Billy was supposed to be the most experienced one in the group. People would expect him to be the leader, especially now. He'd just have to be very careful.

"Okay," Robert said. "Let's see if we can take down camp in under two hours." He looked at Billy. "Time us."

Grace was trying to mend a chewed-through harness with rope, but even in the relative warmth of the tent, her fingers were stupid and stiff, and it took a while. From time to time she had to stop and warm her hands by tucking them under her armpits.

When she finally went outside to feed the dogs, she spotted Brontosaurus trotting off toward the direction of the ship.

Trotting off toward his certain death. What did he think he was going to eat? Moldy food was better than none.

That morning she had put him in a makeshift rope harness. He must have eaten through it.

"What's wrong?" Andrew said.

Grace pointed at the dog.

"I'll go get him." Andrew took some skis off the sled and skied after him.

But Grace didn't have much hope. Bronty had had a head start, and he was fast.

She turned back to the other dogs, who were roped to the frozen gear on the sled. As she adjusted Diplodocus's harness, she noticed several bald spots in his fur. She examined T-Rex. He was fine, but little Triceratops had a bald spot on her neck. She wondered whether this was a skin disease or poor diet.

Grace hugged Triceratops. Although small, she was a perfectly built sled dog, with a broad chest, strong haunches, and a narrow waist. But if she lost her hair, she wouldn't last long in this frigid temperature. Grace hated the fact that the Antarctic posed dangers for dogs as well as kids. She wasn't planning to alarm the others, but Robert, who was walking by, stopped and stared.

"Are the dogs sick?" Robert pointed at little Triceratops's neck.

"I don't know," Grace answered.

"Great," Robert said.

"Their food is moldy. I think if we want to keep them healthy, we might need to feed them the pony soon."

Robert didn't say anything, but he was fuming inside. Cookie had been little trouble. Using her snowshoes, the pony had handled the snow just fine. Although for the last day and a half the dogs had worked together well, last night they had gotten loose and eaten the food. Robert was tempted to feed the dogs to Cookie, not the other way around.

The clock ticked loudly inside Robert's head. After last night's disaster, all they had was a day's worth of pemmican. They ought to get to the first depot in eight hours, but to be extra safe, he'd figure on a ten-hour journey to the depot. As long as nothing else went wrong, they would arrive at the depot a little hungry, but they would be fine.

Robert resumed loading his cycle's sled. Since Billy was going first, they were moving the critical gear to Robert's sled and Polly was going to ride with Robert. Robert wouldn't let himself worry about the crevasses they were likely to encounter. "Prepare for the negative, but don't dwell on it" was Robert Johnson's first rule of wilderness survival.

Two hours after breakfast, Billy, who was going to lead, gunned his silver-and-blue snowcycle. Even though it was early, the sun was polishing the surface of the ground, and it looked like a skating rink—so blue, so smooth.

They were starting off without Brontosaurus. Andrew had returned exhausted from a fruitless chase, and they had had to wait for him to load his gear. A dog had slowed them down again, Billy thought.

Robert surveyed the group. He'd been surprised when Billy had volunteered to stay in the lead on the blue ice. So far Billy had been handy with the maps and navigation, but he had been cautious. Until this morning Robert had thought that Billy was a bit of a coward.

Grace came next, on the dogsled. Would the dogs cause more trouble today?

Andrew was going to follow Grace. Since this surface was going to be particularly tough on the pony, they had decided that they needed to reduce her load. Andrew planned to lead her for the first few miles.

Polly was helping Andrew with some last-minute adjustments to Cookie's sled.

Polly and Andrew were sure a funny pair, Robert thought. In a way, she was one of the smartest girls that he had ever met, and Andrew was one of the dumbest boys. She was smart but impractical. Scott's expedition had taken place almost two hundred years ago. It had ended in his death. It seemed to Robert that the less said about Scott, the better. Yet if he let her, Polly would yammer on about Scott, Bowers, and Wilson—and who were those other guys? Anyway, she would yammer on until polar ghosts haunted all of them.

"Wait up!" Robert shouted at Billy, who had already started to pull ahead. He wanted them to stay together. Just in case . . .

Polly finished with the sled. Robert turned on his motor as she climbed behind him.

At least the sound of the engine would drown out Polly's chatter.

26

For the past two hours, Billy had been leading. The group had had some problems with the smooth, windswept ice. Cookie's hooves had broken through the crust many times. Once Andrew, who was on foot to reduce the weight on the pony, had stepped into a hole and sunk to his waist. The group had bypassed five or six cracks, as well as a field of fissured ice that looked like splintered glass. Andrew was walking more and more slowly but refused to trade off, saying that he wanted to stay with Cookie.

Robert had removed all the important stuff from Billy's sled in case he hit a crevasse, so Billy wasn't pulling much of a load. Billy could easily have gone ahead and set up camp, but Robert insisted that they all stay together. Although they hadn't made good time, Billy tried not to feel too frustrated; at least they hadn't hit anything serious yet.

Suddenly Billy spotted a gash in the ice a long way ahead of him. "Crevasse!" he yelled.

When he got close to it, he jumped off the cycle and peered down. This one was deep and wide and brutal.

Robert parked his cycle next to Billy's. The word *crevasse* had not meant anything to him, but now he saw that it was a canyon with icy, slippery sides. He would hate to have to climb his way out of one of those.

Death-traps in your path, opened by the pressure of slow-moving ice against the land, Polly remembered reading as she stared.

Looking into the depths, Billy made up his mind. He didn't care enough about being MVP to take the lead again.

"We need to find a way across," Robert said, pointing in the direction of the Pole. "Andrew, you hike along the crevasse and see if you can find a crossing. I'll hike the other way. Billy, why don't you see if you can boil us some hot chocolate?"

"Billy, are you all right?" Polly asked.

Billy looked into her worried face. "Oh, sure." He headed for the sled to unload the Primus. He was all right if you thought that being scared to death was all right. What would have happened if he hadn't seen the crevasse? If it had been covered with snow? How far would he have fallen before he hit the bottom?

Robert followed the long crack in the ice to a point where it disappeared and all he could see was snow. A few yards later, the crevasse appeared again. This snowy area looked like a snow bridge, all right. But would it hold? He put one foot on the snow, and it felt solid. Was it strong enough for the heavy snowcycles, pony, and dogs to make it over?

There was no way to test the bridge's strength except to cross it. For reassurance, he stuck his hand in his backpack and squeezed the wooden handle of his ice pick. He hoped he wouldn't ever have to use it. He put one foot on the snow bridge. It felt sturdy. He walked slowly and deliberately across the crevasse. The snow bridge held. He walked back and followed the crevasse to rejoin the group. He shouted at Andrew to return.

When he got back, the kids were all there staring wide-eyed at him. "I've found a snow bridge," he told them. "It took my weight, but I'm not sure what will happen if the animals and the cycles go over it." He hated to ask her, but he felt he had to for the good of the expedition. "Polly, what did Scott do?"

Polly thought about his question. From the books, she remembered a couple of incidents when the men, wearing harnesses, had been pulled up by ropes, but she had no idea what the harnesses looked like or what they were attached to. She knew that without all these details, her answer would only irritate Robert. "The men wore harnesses," she answered anyway. "That way if one fell, the group could pull him up."

Robert felt his temper rise. "I haven't seen any harnesses in our supplies. Have you?"

Polly shook her head. "But the dogs wear harnesses. We could let them go first. If the snow bridge collapses, the sled that the dogs are pulling would serve as an anchor, and the dogs would hang in their harnesses."

Robert considered this for a minute. He wished he could avoid taking Polly's advice, but it couldn't be helped. "Okay. Let's try that. Grace, are you willing?"

Grace nodded.

"You cross with the dogs," Robert said.

"What happens if the bridge collapses after Grace is on the other side?" Polly said.

"I don't know." Robert had to admit that Polly had asked a good question.

Polly thought out loud. "We'd have to unhook the pony sled. It's the longest one. We'd lay it over the crevasse. Then everyone could crawl over to the other side. We'd lose the cycles and the pony."

"You're right." Andrew looked at Polly in admiration.

"We don't have many choices. If we don't get to that first depot, we'll starve," Robert said. "Let's go."

The bridge was wide enough for the team and appeared solid.

"Okay, Grace," Robert said. "You ready?"

An Eskimo doesn't fear what she must accept, Grace thought. She stood behind her sled and flicked her whip at the dogs.

Together they rushed across the snow bridge. On the other side, Grace quieted her team: "Good dogs."

"You guys go next," Robert said to Andrew, Billy, and Polly.

"What about you, Robert?" Polly said.

"If you all cross, I'm going to try to take the pony."

"I want to take the pony," Andrew protested. Then he watched Polly take a few steps toward the bridge and stop.

Instead of remembering the details of how Scott and his men had handled crevasses, Polly was paralyzed by another quotation: *The light rippled snow bridge gives no hint or sign of the hidden danger, its position unguessable till man or beast is floundering, clawing, and struggling for foothold on the brink.*

Andrew had wanted to be last so he could cross with Cookie, but he could tell that Polly was scared. He made up his mind to help her. "Watch me," he said. He started confidently across the bridge. "It's easy, Polly!" he called back. He didn't feel like a bumbler at all.

Polly's heart thumped loudly as she shadowed him.

Billy crossed next, his body tense with fear. That crevasse had looked as deep as an ocean.

Robert pulled at Cookie's reins, but she refused to budge. He pulled again.

"Let me try!" Andrew yelled from the other side of the crevasse.

"I guess you're going to have to!" Robert shouted.

Andrew walked back across the bridge and took Cookie's reins. Cookie followed him over, but the sled that she was pulling caught on a rough patch of ice. The sled landed on the far side of the crevasse with a jerk, but heaps of snow fell off the bridge. Andrew tried not to notice that he hadn't heard the snow hit bottom.

Polly cheered and hugged Cookie. Her mane was freckled with bits of ice.

"Who said ponies weren't good on polar trips?" Andrew whispered into Cookie's ear. "You're doing great." He bent over and adjusted one of the pony's snowshoes.

"Now for the cycles," Robert said. Billy's was closest. Robert climbed on and turned the key.

The key twisted, but the engine made no sound.

"Come on, baby. Come on," Robert said. The ignition still didn't catch.

"Try to pump it!" Billy called. He wanted to try it himself, but not badly enough to cross that snow bridge. Quite a bit of snow had fallen off.

Robert turned the throttle again. The engine was dead. "Did you have any trouble with it this morning?" he yelled to Billy.

"No!" Billy replied. He was almost sure that if he were sitting on the cycle, it would start for him. But what could he do? It wasn't worth risking the crossing.

Robert turned the key again and again. He felt betrayed. It couldn't do this! It was the same old beautiful snowcycle that Billy had ridden that morning. His frustration made him feel hot and sweaty.

"Try the other one!" Polly called.

Robert reluctantly climbed off Billy's snowcycle and climbed onto his own. His good old engine started right away. As Robert roared over the snow bridge without incident, he wondered what he should do.

More snow dropped from the sides of the bridge. Safely across, Robert cut the motor.

Polly interrupted his thoughts. "Let's forget about the other snowcycle."

At that moment Polly's voice irritated Robert so much that he wanted to shout "Shut up!" But he took a deep breath.

"We can't just leave it. That would mean leaving gear behind." Even as he spoke, Robert reviewed the items on Billy's sled: skis, a plank to form the door of an igloo, a few extra blankets, and some additional tools. Billy's sled held nothing critical except the rifle.

"That last trip over knocked off more snow. Don't risk it, Robert," Polly warned him.

If Polly hadn't made him nervous, Robert would be tempted to man-haul the sled and gear across. But he warned himself to be cautious.

Robert walked over to the snow bridge. He put one foot on it. The bridge still felt solid. He put his other foot on it so that it was bearing his full weight. Still the bridge held. It still felt solid. He crossed the snow bridge and climbed onto Billy's silver-and-blue snowcycle.

"Wait a minute before trying it! The engine might be flooded!" Billy shouted. He would have sworn that the motor had been sound earlier that morning.

Robert decided to give it ten minutes.

Polly watched Robert tinkering with the motor. "What are

you doing?" she called. "Why aren't you trying it?"

"He's just giving it a little time," Billy chided her. The cycle would start. It had to.

Robert thought he could hear Polly sigh from the other side of the bridge.

"Robert, at the beginning of the trip you warned Grace that she couldn't get too attached to the dogs! You're too attached to the snowcycle!" Polly shouted.

"One more try!" Robert called back. If it didn't start, he would walk back over the snow bridge and they'd get going. He turned the key. Nothing.

Billy groaned.

Robert couldn't just leave the cycle here. He flipped it on its side and stared at the motor.

"Robert, you promised!" Polly cried. "We've got to go!"

"Maybe the carburetor's frozen! If you warm it with a blanket for a few minutes . . . !" Billy suggested.

Robert studied the engine.

Polly interrupted his thoughts. "I don't like the look of the sky!"

Robert looked up. Darn, she was right! He had been so absorbed that he had failed to notice the weather. Gray clouds now hid the sun. He slowly stood up. "Billy, after we make camp, let's hike back and see if we can get it started!"

"Okay," Billy replied. "Do you have a blanket?"

"Good idea!" Robert pulled a blanket out of a gear bag on the sled and threw it over the snowcycle. He grabbed the rifle from the back of the sled and turned to cross the snow bridge. He had taken only a few steps when he heard a crack. He lost his footing right before he began falling through an avalanche of ice and snow.

Polly's scream followed him as he smashed into the bottom of the crevasse. Only it wasn't the bottom, because his feet and legs crashed through it, and he was falling again, this time along-side another avalanche of ice and snow. His fingers lost their grip on the rifle. When he stopped, he couldn't breathe. The fall had knocked the air out of him. Icy debris pinned his upper body against a wall but left his legs dangling. He gasped to regain his breath and tried to take stock of his surroundings.

He kicked his legs but found that they didn't touch solid ground. Unbelievably, they swung in empty air. Luck had kept him from falling much deeper. The remains of the icy bridge wedged him against the crevasse wall.

He turned his face upward and saw Polly and Billy leaning over the edge. It was hard to judge the distance, but he guessed he had fallen about twenty or thirty feet. He looked down. To his right, the ice ledge below his arm extended for some distance, but to his left, the little ledge ended. He stared at the depths below.

"Can you hear me?" Polly called, but the crevasse seemed to stretch her words into a long thin wail.

"Yeah!" Robert shouted back.

"Are you hurt?" Polly asked.

"My shoulder," Robert said.

"Which one?"

"My left shoulder."

Polly turned to Billy. "Billy, what should we do?"

The crevasse was wide at the top but narrowed as it got deeper. Billy saw Robert's blue wool cap surrounded by ice. It appeared that Robert had fallen onto a ledge twenty or more feet below them. Over to his left, the crevasse revealed its true depth.

Perhaps a hundred feet. It was an impossible situation. "Robert, can you move?"

"No," Robert said.

One hundred feet. Billy gulped. If Robert hadn't gotten lucky, he would be lying on an icy bottom one hundred feet below them. They didn't have a rope that would reach that far.

"How are we going to get him out?" Polly asked.

"We'll rope him up," Billy said.

"I'll find some ropes." Andrew turned back toward the sleds, glad to be of use.

"But if he's wedged in?" Polly asked.

"Can you use the ice pick?" Billy asked.

"No!" Robert called.

"If we threw you a rope, could you pull it over your head?" Polly said.

"Yeah," Robert answered.

Grace could feel the wind rising. She looked over at the dogs. They appeared restless. She sensed a storm on its way.

Andrew returned with two ropes.

Billy took one and tied one end into a slipknot. He moved back to tie the other around Robert's snowcycle. He climbed on the snowcycle and turned the ignition. It didn't start.

"They were programmed," Polly said quietly.

Billy kicked the machine again and again as hard as he could. He wanted to punish it, just as he'd wanted to punish those dogs last night for eating his food.

Polly waited as patiently as she could. Didn't he understand Robert was trapped down there?

Finally Billy stopped. "We're in subzero weather in the middle of nowhere, and Hot Sauce has to make it harder for us!"

"It's a simulation. Scott's motors failed. Ours had to fail, too," Polly said.

Grace heard her grandfather sigh and say, "In the ice and snow, life goes quickly from terrible to worse." She looked up at the darkening sky.

"I can't believe how mean she is," Billy said.

"I know," said Polly.

Billy felt the anger boil inside him. He didn't know where the camera was, but he glared at it anyway. Secretary of Entertainment. Secretary of Torture. If she were here in Antarctica, he would kill her.

"Billy, come on," Polly said.

"I'll get Cookie," Andrew said.

Grace turned to unload the tent from the sled just in case the weather turned bad.

Andrew led Cookie to the crevasse. He fastened one end of the rope to Cookie.

"Robert, we're going to drop the rope!" Billy called.

Billy dropped the knotted end of the rope, watching it bounce against the crevasse wall as it fell.

"You got it?" Billy said.

"Yeah, I've got it."

"Pull it over your head, slip it under your arms, and tug it until it's good and tight!" Polly called.

"I will."

"Let us know when you're ready," Polly said.

In the few minutes that passed, Polly watched absent-mindedly as Grace set up the tent. She knew that she should help Grace, but she couldn't. All she was able to do was stare at the gray sky and crunch her finneskoe in the snow. She tried to think about anything but the crevasse. Or what would happen if they couldn't pull Robert out.

"Ready!" Robert finally called.

Polly turned and nodded at Andrew.

Andrew held the pony's lead and started walking her away from the crevasse. One step, two steps. Robert's life depended on her.

The slack rope dangling down the side of the crevasse tightened.

"Stop!" Robert screamed. "It's tearing me in two!"

"Back her up, Andrew!" Polly called. "He's crammed in there too tight," she said to Billy.

Andrew backed the pony toward the crevasse.

"One of us will have to go down," Polly said.

Billy felt cold fear constrict his throat. "That's really dangerous."

"What else can we do?" Polly said.

Billy shrugged.

"If we lowered you, you could hack at the ice around him," Polly suggested.

"You want to lower me down into that crevasse?" Billy shook his head. "No way."

"Well, then climb down."

"No way."

"Then what do you want to do, Billy?" Polly's voice rose.

Billy had only one idea: He wasn't going down there. "You need to loosen the ice that's got you packed in," he called to Robert.

"I can't!" Robert called back.

"What's pinning you?" Billy called.

"A solid block."

Polly looked at Billy. "You're the ice climber."

"I've done a little climbing," Billy explained. "Never anything like this."

"We don't have time to discuss this." Polly looked him in the eye.

For a moment before he looked away, Polly's face, with her wide, staring eyes, reminded Billy of a camera. He had wanted to be MVP, but what good was money if he didn't survive?

Billy was clearly terrified. "Andrew!" Polly called. "Do you think if we lowered you down the crevasse, you could chop away at enough ice to free Robert? I'd do it, but I wonder if I'm strong enough to hack the ice."

"Sure." Andrew grinned. He didn't know if he could do it, but he'd try.

Billy suddenly hated Andrew more than he had hated any other person in his whole life. More than Grace and the dogs. More than Tom Jenkins, his next-door neighbor, who had won the Toss and was going to college. Still, Andrew needed help managing the ropes, and Billy turned to help him.

"Here," Billy said. "You do it like this."

Andrew slipped the knotted rope over his head and under his arms.

Billy examined it. "That'll hold," he said. He reached for Cookie's halter.

Then Andrew had a frightening thought. Robert's rope was tied to Cookie. She wasn't heavy enough to bear two kids' weight. The dogs were still in harness. He'd feel much better relying on Cookie, but what could he do? He had to rely on the dogs. There was no sense worrying. "Grace, I need the dogs."

Andrew sat down in the snow and waited for Grace to get the dogs ready.

In the meantime, Polly comforted Robert: "Don't worry. We're coming."

Grace looped the rope around T-Rex's harness. If Andrew went down, he'd take all the dogs with him. But she knew the dogs could do this. She turned to her team and murmured, "Don't let me down."

"They're ready!" She called to Andrew.

Andrew yanked the rope. It held. He walked to the crevasse. "Okay, Grace," he said.

Grace stood next to T-Rex and nudged her knee into his chest. He backed up toward the crevasse. Thank goodness, Grace thought.

27

On his television at home, Steve watched Andrew trudging toward the crevasse and wished that he were at work. But he reminded himself that he couldn't have talked to Andrew anyway. Because the scene was tense and had "high viewer appeal," Hot Sauce was broadcasting live.

Steve was proud of Andrew. Although he was frustrated that he wasn't able to talk to him, what would he say except "good job"? Andrew had made the right decision on his own, without any help from Steve.

The screen went dark. Not another advertisement! Earlier, when Robert's motor had refused to start, the Secretary had abruptly interrupted the show with a commercial about cloning a new Fido. While the commercial droned on, Steve bet the kids had been badmouthing her for programming the motor to fail. In those three minutes before programming resumed, Steve had chewed off all his fingernails.

Johnny Sparks, the announcer, sat in front of a map of Antarctica. "Today's votes are in! The viewers have spoken out on who is our most valuable player. We'll have those scores for you in a moment, and as an extra bonus, we've been granted a special interview with Billy Kanalski's parents."

"Oh, no," Steve groaned. This interruption was horrible. What was happening to the kids? Occasionally, if a scene was particularly scary—"high drama," the Secretary called it—she previewed the scene before broadcasting it. Right now he guessed the Secretary was watching Andrew head into the icy crevasse rather than showing it live to the audience.

A chart flashed onto the screen.

"Yesterday afternoon, when we polled our viewers," Johnny Sparks's voice-over began, "this was the breakdown of votes for MVP—

Robert	28%
Grace	27%
Polly	25%
Billy	15%
Andrew	5%

"But today our audience's mood has shifted, and we have a new favorite for MVP—

Andrew	31%

"The other contestants' numbers are—

Robert	24%
Grace	23%
Polly	21%
Billy	1%

"As always, we have kicked the undecideds out of the polls for their un-American refusal to have an opinion. Now we go to our reporter in Andover, New Hampshire, to get the reaction of Billy's parents to the recent poll."

Steve wanted to throw his only chair at the screen. What was happening to Andrew? Who cared about Billy's position in the silly MVP game?

A reporter named Cathy Kress sat in the Kanalskis' modest hut. Billy's father was a small man with glasses. His mother was a large woman with silver hair partially covered by a green felt hat.

"Mr. and Mrs. Kanalski, thank you for letting us join you this morning."

"Yes, ma'am," Mr. Kanalski said.

Steve noticed that he spoke firmly but didn't meet the reporter's gaze.

"Just to give our viewers some background, Mr. Kanalski, you are a computer geek, correct?"

Mr. Kanalski grinned.

"And we are looking at one of your products?"

The camera panned the Compu-gametable.

"Yes, ma'am," Mr. Kanalski said proudly.

Cathy Kress stopped smiling. "If you have a big computer company, why would you allow your son to participate in this dangerous contest?" she asked.

Mr. Kanalski didn't immediately answer. Mrs. Kanalski's bottom lip trembled. She broke in. "My husband's company went bankrupt last year. Billy has no money for high school or college."

"So he needs the contest money?"

Mrs. Kanalski nodded.

"Then what happened? Why didn't your son rescue Robert?"

"Don't count Billy out yet," Mr. Kanalski said. "He's a survivor, a chip off the old block." The man chuckled. "And so far, he's the only contestant to have his own website. All of you interested viewers can click on BillyKanalskiAntarctic.com and see his EduTV grades, his photo, and a description of the Compu-gametable."

Cathy smirked. "I'm not sure you answered my question, Mr. Kanalski."

"I hate to admit it, but it's not a good day for Billy's percentage points," Mr. Kanalski said. "He's gone down quite a bit."

Mrs. Kanalski started sobbing.

Steve disagreed with Cathy Kress. Billy Kanalski's dad had answered the question, all right. It was clear that the Kanalskis hadn't bothered teaching Billy about right and wrong. All Billy knew were games. Rescuing Robert had looked too risky, and Billy had decided not to play.

But surviving in Antarctica wasn't a game.

In disgust, Steve clicked the TV off. He wasn't due at work for hours. Reluctantly he turned the set back on.

Andrew was sure there was a better way to travel than holding on to the rope and sliding his feet down the icy wall of the crevasse, but he didn't know what it was.

The ice passed quickly in front of him, and he marveled that close-up it looked light blue, not white. The crevasse narrowed quickly. Robert's blue cap and shoulders filled Andrew's view of the V-shaped bottom.

Andrew was glad to see that Robert had managed to get the rope under his arms.

Robert smiled weakly at him.

"I'm there!" Andrew called up to the surface as his feet touched the ice ledge. He braced himself in case the makeshift ledge collapsed under his weight, but it held. Standing over Robert, who was wedged tightly against the wall by the ledge, Andrew had hardly any room to maneuver. He felt as though he and Robert were shut in a small white closet. Then Andrew glanced to one side, and his eyes traveled to the bottom of the deep crevasse. He promised himself that he wouldn't look down again.

"Thanks, man," Andrew thought he heard Robert say, but the words were muffled by a groan.

"We'll have you out of here in a minute." Andrew pulled the ice pick out of his backpack.

"I lost the rifle," Robert said.

"Don't worry," Andrew replied.

"See if you can chip near my left arm," Robert suggested.

Andrew tried leaning over, but his head knocked against the side of the crevasse. He squatted on the ledge. He was almost sitting on Robert's head. "Sorry about this," he said. He could smell Robert's sweat, and something else that he had never smelled before: He could smell Robert's fear. He raised the ice pick and chipped at the ice near Robert's arm.

"How'd you get wedged in this?" Andrew asked.

"I busted through, and part of the snow bridge must have caught me."

"Lucky." Little chips of ice flew from Andrew's pick.

"Yeah." Robert watched Andrew's slow progress.

Andrew knew he could chip at this stuff all day. What he needed to do was dislodge the ledge entirely, but that would leave them both dangling by ropes over the icy crevasse.

"I know what you're thinking," Robert said slowly. "Go ahead."

"I'm going to let them know." Andrew straightened up and called, "Keep our lines tight. I have to . . ." He didn't have time now to explain the problem. "Do something!" he concluded. "Do you understand?"

Polly's "Yes!" bounced off both sides of the crevasse.

Andrew was glad that Polly and Grace were overseeing the ropes. He trusted them. He was a little nervous about the dogs, but he wouldn't think about them now. "I'm going to jump up and down," he said to Robert. "Keep our ropes tight!" he yelled up to Polly.

"Okay!" Polly called down to him.

Andrew looked into Robert's eyes.

Robert nodded.

Andrew stood on the ledge and jumped up and down. Being a little heavy was good for something after all. He felt the ice plank tilt. He jumped on the weak side with both feet. As the ice cracked, he tasted his own sweat.

"You okay?" Andrew asked.

"You're getting it," Robert said.

The hope in Robert's voice helped Andrew muster all his strength and jump hard on the crack. One foot broke through and dangled into nothingness. He pulled his foot back up and jumped again. A piece of ice clattered down. He waited for an instant but didn't hear it hit bottom. He had knocked a hole in the ledge and could now see the void directly below him. Still, Robert remained pinned.

Andrew jumped again. This time he could feel the whole platform tip sideways.

Robert's rope tightened.

Andrew stared for a second into Robert's dark eyes. He

sensed that he needed to be brave for both of them.

"Keep Robert's line tight!" he called.

Andrew jumped once more and the ledge popped loose. Immediately the rope cut into his underarms.

"Aah!" Robert grunted in pain.

Andrew twirled around in the air. Only their ropes supported them now.

With ice still clinging to Robert's body, the rope pulled Robert upward, but Andrew's body blocked him.

"Pull me up first!" Andrew yelled. He let the rope drag him up a few feet before he looked down. Robert was still below him, but he could now clearly see the bottom of the crevasse. It seemed to go on and on in icy splendor until at its greatest depth it became a bottomless blue.

Robert lay on the ground. Polly, Grace, and Andrew were bending over him.

Robert's left shoulder looked collapsed and weird. They had no painkillers. No slings. No doctors. And they were only fourteen years old. Polly didn't allow herself to lapse into bitterness; her mother said it did no good. But she hoped the viewing public was enjoying this. She hoped *someone* was enjoying this. At least Robert was safe.

Grace touched Robert's shoulder softly.

Robert flinched.

"It may be dislocated," Grace said.

Robert gritted his teeth.

He's a brave guy, Polly thought.

"Before I try to fix it, you're going to have to take off some of those clothes," Grace said.

"Can you walk to the tent?" Polly asked.

Robert groaned as he slowly stood. He leaned against Andrew.

Polly walked alongside them.

"I lost the rifle," Robert said.

"You're alive," Polly said, "and that's what counts."

"Where's Billy?" Robert asked.

"In the tent," Polly said as Robert limped toward it. She wasn't going to be the one to tell Robert that Billy had refused to help him.

28

Inside the tent, Grace popped Robert's shoulder back into place.

Robert screamed.

Grace felt bad that she had hurt him. She had been as gentle as she could.

Outside, working with the dogs, Andrew covered his ears.

"Ah," Robert sighed. "That feels better."

"I wish I had something to give you," Grace said.

"Scott had some opium on his trip," said Polly. "I'll bet we have some here."

"I'm okay," Robert said. "Thank you, Grace."

Grace smiled.

"Here," Polly said, handing him a rolled-up sweater. "You can use this as a pillow."

"And Polly, I want to thank you. You were"—Robert searched for the right word—"strong." He smiled feebly at her.

Grace felt Robert's ribs. "I don't think any are broken."

"That's a miracle," Polly said.

"And Andrew? Where's Andrew? I want to thank him." Robert lifted his head up.

"He's feeding the dogs," Polly told him.

Robert's gaze fell on Billy.

Billy's face reddened. He needed to face the facts. This morning had been a disaster for him. Probably everyone watching television hated him, just as every kid he had ever known ended up hating him. He needed desperately to do something to save his image. He felt his face grow even redder. "Robert, I . . ."

"What happened, Billy?" Robert looked into his eyes. Was this guy a coward, or did he just not know what he was doing? "Why did Andrew come for me and not you?"

Polly admired the way Robert faced things.

"I panicked," Billy said.

You sure did, Polly thought.

"I've done some climbing, but never with a big drop," Billy explained.

Polly believed that.

Billy hung his head. "I'm sorry."

"No problem," Robert said, deciding that Billy was both scared and inexperienced. But he knew shaming Billy wouldn't help. "We're all in this together."

Robert's forgiveness made Billy feel better, but he'd never forget Polly's look when he had refused to rescue Robert. "I'm not a coward, just practical," he wanted to tell her now. But he never wanted to talk about that killer crevasse again.

Andrew stuck his head into the tent. "It's snowing."

The flap closed and Andrew was gone again.

Robert tried to sit up. "We've got to secure camp."

"You're not going anywhere," Polly said.

Robert touched his hurt shoulder. "You're right." It was funny, but Robert didn't mind that Polly seemed to be taking over as leader. He had always been the leader in every situation that he'd been in. But he was injured and shouldn't move, and that was that. He felt relaxed. Let her take the burden for a while; she'll do a good job, Robert thought. Polly, that geeky girl, was a natural leader. Weird.

Robert turned his attention to Grace, who was adjusting the rolled-up sweater under his head. "Thanks," he said.

Fine flakes fell lightly on Polly's shoulders, but there was no wind. This was more of a snowstorm than a blizzard, Polly thought. Still, travel would be difficult. Oh, well, they weren't going any farther today, anyway.

Polly found Andrew standing next to the pony.

"Cookie hates this cold," Andrew said as he pulled a blanket up near Cookie's head. He patted her. "Poor Cookie. This is all I can do for you."

"I bet it's way below zero," Polly said. "Let's go."

"I guess I could get out the thermometer." As Andrew turned toward the blue tent, Polly linked her arm in his.

"Bowers took most of the temperature readings for Scott's group," Polly said. "Imagine. He took off his gloves, picked up a metal thermometer that stuck to his skin, and held it out in the cold air long enough to get a reading."

"You really like him, don't you?" Andrew said.

"Yeah," Polly said.

"Why?"

"He was unselfish." Polly knew what she wanted to say but felt embarrassed. She felt her face grow red. "Like you're unselfish, Andrew."

Andrew stopped and stared at her. Snowflakes dusted her cap and the shoulders of her parka. She smiled at him.

"I mean it. That's really your special gift. Oh, I know that you can bear the cold. But everyone else here has done just fine with that. Only you were brave enough to risk your life for Robert this afternoon."

"I couldn't just let him die." As he said these words, Andrew thought of himself just a few months ago. Heroic words like these never came out of his mouth then. Thinking about his past, he felt something else strange. It was as if he had awakened from a long sleep. That old pudgy Andrew who had a special place on the soft couch seemed like a dream.

Suddenly they heard Grace shout, "Get him!"

Andrew saw the large shape of a dog trot past.

"It's Brontosaurus," Grace called.

The dog that Andrew had chased this morning had returned to camp.

Grace guessed that the dog had run off to find more food. When he couldn't find any, he had come back.

Polly lunged for him, and Andrew turned to run after him, too.

"No!" Grace screamed. "I forgot! There might be more crevasses."

Polly shuddered, remembering Robert's narrow escape. "You're right. Chasing him is too risky."

Brontosaurus skipped to the outer edges of camp, next to Robert's abandoned snowcycle, and sat there licking ice off his paw.

Grace held out her hand. "Bronty! Come here, boy!"

A gust of wind scared Polly. "Grace," she said, "in case it starts snowing hard again, we need to get inside." She turned toward the tent.

"Bronty! Come here, boy!" Grace repeated.

Brontosaurus dashed away from her and rolled on his back in the snow. He was having a great time.

Grace turned away from the dog and followed Polly. Each life form must make its own choice about whether to live or die. Maybe Bronty would stick around camp until tomorrow. Then again, maybe not.

Polly carefully checked the sleds to make sure that they had brought all the food inside. They couldn't take a chance that a loose dog would eat their meager supplies.

Grace crawled into the tent. Polly and Andrew followed her.

Robert was snoring in his sleeping bag. Usually he was a light sleeper, but now he slept as though nothing would wake him.

Billy was leaning over a pot of boiling water, about to drop some pemmican into the pot for a late lunch.

"Billy," Polly said, "we can take a vote on this if you want, but I think we should save the pemmican for later. We don't know how long this storm will last."

Billy didn't say anything, but he rolled the pemmican up in foil. He couldn't care less if he cooked the pemmican or not. He wasn't going to eat it.

After taking off her gear, Polly squatted next to the stove.

"We just had one," said Billy. "Why is it storming again?"

An Iñupiat would never ask that question, Grace thought.

Polly shook her head in despair. "We have a little food. If the snow quits soon, we'll still be in good shape."

"Where will we put all the gear without the snowcycles?" Andrew asked.

In her mind, Polly reviewed the collection of things on Robert's sled. "Grace, do you think that the dogs could carry the stuff from Robert's cycle, too?"

It would be hard. The dogs' load was already heavy. But Grace felt proud as she answered simply, "Yes."

"Great." Polly stared at the water boiling in the pot. She felt thankful but exhausted. It was hard to believe that this game had barely begun.

"I can't believe that Scott's crew lived in Antarctica for two years," Andrew said.

"Yeah," Polly agreed.

"How many blizzards did they live through?" Andrew asked.

"Lots," Polly said.

"I don't see how they did it," Andrew said.

"Me either," Polly said.

"And we've been here only five days," Andrew said.

"Yeah, five days," Polly said. Five long days. Scott's men had endured two years of temperatures like this and much colder. She knew that adults were a lot tougher than kids, but she wondered if people in the twentieth century had been tougher than the people of the twenty-first century. "The time would go faster if we napped," she finally said. "Maybe, when we wake up, the storm will have quit."

"I'm not sleepy," Andrew said.

"I know," Polly said. She was too hungry to sleep.

Every time Billy looked at the watch, he thought about D.C. "It's four o'clock." Some people were getting ready to go home from work and watch the five-o'clock news. What he wouldn't give to be in D.C. or any city now!

"What else can we do in this small tent but sleep?" Polly asked.

"That's a good idea, Polly," Billy said. He climbed into his sleeping bag and fingered a package of peanuts. He shut his eyes.

After the kids went to sleep, he'd comfort himself by eating a health-food bar or a bag of peanuts.

Billy heard Andrew's stomach growl, and suddenly he felt ashamed. If his friends couldn't eat, neither would he. But he clenched the peanuts in his fist, grateful to know that he wouldn't starve. Not for a while, anyway.

29

Steve was out of breath from his sprint to the office.

"The ratings went crazy again today," Chad said when Steve walked into the production room.

Pearl was sweeping quietly in a corner.

"Did you see Robert and Andrew make it out of the crevasse?" Chad asked.

"Yep," Steve panted. He had spent his afternoon watching the live broadcast.

"What are the kids doing now?" Steve asked.

"Napping," Chad said. "We got a 99.1 percent rating." He paused. "Do you realize what that means? This afternoon, almost every single home in the United States had its television tuned to *Historical Survivor*." He shook his head and grinned. "First time ever in the show's twelve-year history!"

Steve looked sadly at the dark screens. He must have been dreaming to think that the viewers didn't approve of the program.

"You don't get it," said Chad. "The great thing is that the questions and the mail are not positive."

"What?" Steve said.

"People don't like this series. They're calling the Secretary a bully. They're angry." Chad turned to his computer and clicked it on. "Here's a random e-mail. 'Dear Mrs. Secretary: If life is a game, why don't people like you play? A viewer in Cincinnati.'"

Chad turned back to Steve. "Want to hear what our Secretary had to say to him?"

Steve shrugged.

"Here it is: 'I did play. I played the Toss and won. Stop whining, loser.'"

"Her toughness has shut people up before," Steve said.

"Not this time," Chad said. "I think that people feel bad for the kids."

"They should," Steve said. He walked over to the five dark screens on the wall.

Just in case Andrew could hear him, Steve picked up the microphone and whispered, "Good job!" But Andrew's screen stayed black.

The five kids sat in a circle in the middle of the small tent. Following a long nap, they had had a small portion of pemmican for dinner. Robert's arm was supported in a makeshift sling. His shoulder still ached, but by immobilizing it, Grace had stopped the sharp stabs of pain.

"We'll run out of pemmican after breakfast tomorrow," Polly said.

Billy looked at one of the maps. He was really glad that he had his secret cache of food. "Remember, we covered six miles before we hit the crevasse," he said. "The good news is that the next depot is only seventeen miles away. If we really push, we could almost make it all in one day."

"But we can't travel in this weather," Polly objected. It was still snowing outside. Not to mention that without the motors, most of them would have to walk, and the dogs would need to carry a heavier load. She looked at Andrew's kind face and decided to say what she had been dreading. "Andrew, I'm sorry to say this, but I think we may need to butcher the pony soon."

Andrew couldn't meet Polly's eyes. He had known this was coming. "Cookie's weak. I don't know how long she can keep going, anyway."

"But then we have the problem of what to do with the gear Cookie's pulling," Robert said.

"True," Polly said. The dogs couldn't carry everything. Each of them would have to wear heavy backpacks. They could take turns pulling a sled. She was sure that their task would seem easier if they weren't so hungry.

Robert interrupted Polly's thoughts. "I bet that I can get the cycle working again." He turned to Billy. "Did you cover the motor?"

"Why?" Billy asked. He wished that Robert hadn't mentioned the cycle. He had loved his silver-and-blue machine. Remembering that Hot Sauce had programmed the motors to fail made him angry all over again.

"I haven't given up on the cycle," Robert said. "If it worked, you or I could ride to the depot and bring food back."

Billy shook his head. He no longer believed in the cycle. "Good luck."

The wind howled.

"I'll go cover it," Andrew offered.

"No," Polly said. "It's not that important."

"I want to see how Cookie's doing, anyway," Andrew said softly, pulling on his parka and gloves.

"Polly's probably right, Andrew," Robert said. The snowcycle had already been uncovered for almost six hours. What did a night matter? But then again, it was warmer after blizzards. Maybe, if the carburetor wasn't frozen, he could get it running.

Andrew crawled toward the tent flap. "Covering the cycle won't take me a minute."

"Please, Andrew," Polly begged. "Forget the motor."

Robert allowed himself to imagine the motor's purr. If he could fix it, it would be so sweet.

"Polly, I really don't mind." Andrew closed the tent flap quickly to avoid having too much snow fly into the tent.

Snow stung Andrew's face; his ears burned. He wouldn't bother to zip up his coat, but he realized that he should have worn his goggles.

The scene inside the tent was serene, but on Andrew's screen snow danced in the wind, forming and re-forming into crazy patterns.

"I'm worried," Steve said.

"Me, too," said Chad. "He shouldn't be outside." He nodded at the mike.

But Steve hesitated. "I hate to order him around. He was a hero earlier today, without me." In his mind's eye he could picture Andrew's bullying father.

Chad shrugged. "You're the boss."

The sleds lay on their sides near Cookie to protect her from the weather. She stood behind them, her flanks glistening with frost and quivering from the piercing snow. Andrew knocked a big icicle off her nose. "I wish there was something

I could do for you, girl."

The mounds of snow marking the sleeping dogs were bumps on the otherwise flat terrain. Poor Cookie. Unlike the dogs, her coat wasn't thick.

Dogs were better suited for Antarctic exploration, Andrew decided sadly. "You didn't ask to be here," he murmured into her ear. Andrew straightened her blanket and pulled out a piece of pemmican that he had saved from breakfast. But when he tried to feed her, she gritted her teeth and refused to eat.

A few feet beyond Cookie, Robert's snowcycle stood in the swirling snow. Its shiny blueness looked out of place. As Andrew trudged through the snow toward it, he sensed that the wind had picked up. To take the last few steps, he turned his back to the wind. With difficulty he removed the cycle's plastic cover from its case and threw it over the machine. He searched for the hook to secure the cover. But just then the wind gusted, and the plastic cover flew into the air like an ungainly kite before landing fifteen feet from where Andrew stood.

Steve couldn't restrain himself anymore. "Let it go!" he commanded, speaking urgently into his mike.

Chad nodded approvingly.

"What did you say?" Andrew said.

"Forget about the cover!" Steve repeated.

"Who are you, really?" Andrew asked.

"We'll talk later. Go back to your tent."

Andrew took one more step into the fuzzy nothingness and then the snow on his screen stopped falling. Steve and Chad were staring at white ice.

* * *

Andrew fell straight down the narrow crevasse and landed on his feet. Hunks of snow from the surface of the crevasse fell on his head. He stamped his feet and shook the snow from his clothes. He had lost his cap in the fall, and he could feel the chill of bits of ice in his hair, on his face, and down his back.

He needed to find a way to climb out. He searched the icy walls for handholds. But the sides of the crevasse appeared silky smooth. He peered upward. At least the crevasse wasn't as deep as the one Robert had fallen into. The ground was only about fifteen feet above him. And a few feet from where he stood, a sheet of ice covered the crevasse like a frozen roof. He walked to the enclosed part and immediately felt warmer.

But wait, Andrew reminded himself. He needed to stay in one place so when the others came looking for him, they could find him. When they came looking for him . . . When would that be?

More than anything, he needed to stay calm. He didn't have an ice pick or any other tools besides the pocketknife he always carried. Could he carve steps in the ice and climb out? He fumbled in his pocket for the knife and took it out. Then he took off his glove and stuck the pocketknife into the wall. A tiny chunk of ice fell off.

He struck the wall again. Another chip lay at his feet.

At this rate, making stairs would take hours. But what else could he do?

Steve drew close to the mike.

Chad nodded slowly.

"Andrew, you're not alone," Steve said.

"Who are you?" Andrew asked again.

Steve didn't know what made him say the name. It just came to him. "I'm your ancestor Birdie Bowers."

"Oh," Andrew said. "You died in this stuff, too."

"You're not going to die," Steve said. "You're going to make it."

"How?" Andrew asked.

"You're not hurt, are you?"

"No," Andrew said. "I'm fine."

"First, let's try to figure out if there's anything else you can do to stay warm."

"I'm not that cold," Andrew said.

"Incredible," Chad whispered to Steve.

"Great. But you may have to be there for a while. So zip up your parka, button up all your buttons, and pull the flap down on your cap."

Steve heard Andrew fumbling around in the narrow crevasse.

"I can't find my cap," Andrew said after a while.

"That's bad," Chad murmured to Steve.

"What happened?"

"I must have lost it in the fall."

"Do you have anything that you could cover your head with?" Steve asked.

"No."

"Do you have anything to eat in your pockets?" Steve asked.

Again Steve heard a rustling as Andrew checked his pockets.

"A little pemmican," Andrew said.

"Good," Steve said. He looked at the other screens. Polly

and Robert had opened the tent flap and were staring at the storm.

Billy and Grace sat huddled around the Primus stove.

"I can't see him," Polly said.

"The storm has gotten much worse," Robert said.

"Andrew!" Polly called. But the wind carried her words away, and Steve could hardly hear her.

"I'll go look for him," said Robert. "He saved my life this morning."

"No," Polly said. "You've got a hurt shoulder. I'll go."

"You get cold the easiest," Robert pointed out.

"I won't stay out there too long," Polly promised. She pulled on her gloves, her neck warmer, and her parka.

"Tie yourself to a rope," Robert directed.

"You're right. We should have never let him go outside without a rope," Polly said.

"It wasn't that windy when he left."

"Life becomes death in an instant," Grace heard her grandfather say.

Polly and Robert stared into each other's eyes as Polly handed Robert one end of the guide rope.

Steve and Chad watched Polly slip the rope around her waist and lift the tent flap.

Steve waited anxiously to view the storm through Polly's eyes.

As Robert held the flap open for Polly, she pushed away the heaps of snow that had piled up at the entrance to the tent. On her knees, she entered a swirling white world.

The morning's snow had been fine and powdery. This snow was wet. After crawling only a few feet, Polly lost her sense of direction. She wiped the snow off her goggles with her gloves. Her knees sank into the deep, soft powder.

Cookie's white body would be hidden in the snow, but if she got closer, she might be able to make out the outlines of the sleds.

The wind howled, and from every direction the snow pounded her. Polly fought it off as she would a raging white beast and crawled a few more steps. The wind gusted again and lashed her face. She struggled to lift her head. "Andrew!" she tried to yell, but she couldn't hear herself over the roar of the wind. When the burst of wind died, she held her hand in front of her face but still couldn't see it. Both her mind and her body felt numb. She tugged on the rope. She felt Robert's answering tug and then the rope tighten before she began tumbling, tripping, and crawling her way back to the tent.

Steve went back to Andrew's screen. He was chipping away at the wall of ice. "You're really lucky you have that roof. The blizzard has picked up. Polly tried to reach you, but it looks like she won't be able to rescue you for a while."

Neither Steve nor Andrew spoke for a moment.

"Was it colder when you were here, Birdie?" Andrew asked.

Steve would have to try to remember everything he had heard on EduTV. "Yes," he said. "It was seventy below, night after night."

"Tell me about it."

"When we woke up in the morning and tried to put on our clothes, they were frozen into boards."

"So you know what it's like to be cold?" Andrew said, trying to ignore the growing numbness of his hands and feet. I never want to be cold again, he thought.

"Poor kid," Steve muttered to Chad.

"How long do blizzards last?" Andrew asked.

"Not too long," Steve said. He wished that he knew.

30

"Polly, it's impossible to rescue him right now," Robert argued. "Go to sleep so you can be fresh when we try again." Even though they were all huddled around the Primus, he had to raise his voice to make himself heard over the wind.

"No," Polly said.

"Don't get emotional on me," Robert said.

"I *am* emotional," Polly said. "I'm mad and scared."

"Who are you mad at?" Billy asked.

"What?" Polly said.

Billy repeated his question. Ever since he had failed to help Robert, he had felt guilty.

"I'm not mad at you, Billy," Polly said. "Or at you, Robert, for caring about a broken-down motor."

"Then who?" Robert asked.

"I'm mad at the Secretary of Entertainment. I'm mad at any-one watching this stupid television show. I'm mad at America. A sweet boy may die so the viewers at home can be amused. It's sad. It's sick. I don't care what the Secretary does to me, I am never, ever watching one of her sick shows again."

"The viewers," Billy said.

"Oh, she'll cut this scene from the program," Polly said with disgust. "I'm sure other contestants have felt like me, but no one has ever heard them complain on television."

"I agree with you," Robert surprised Polly by saying. "But we can't let our anger get in the way of our survival," he continued. "We're running out of food. The best thing we can do is sleep."

"But we just woke up," Grace said.

"Does anybody have a better suggestion?" Robert said.

As if in answer, the wind howled.

"I can't sleep, thinking of Andrew lost out there," Polly wailed.

"If anybody can make it, Andrew can," Robert said.

Billy planned to eat a health-food bar for his dinner tonight. But it was his last one, and he was worried. He had lots of Chocobombs, but the sugar wasn't filling. He hoped that everyone would fall asleep, because he wanted to count the bags of peanuts and crackers. He was scared that if the blizzard didn't stop soon, he was going to be hungry. It was frustrating to realize that more supplies were only seventeen miles away.

"What happened, Polly?" Billy asked suddenly. "Why did Scott and his men die?"

"I thought we were going to try to get some sleep," Robert said.

"You were," Grace answered.

"Sounds like an essay question for EduTV," Robert said.

Billy didn't laugh. "I want to know."

"Well," Polly began, "the mystery about Scott's death is that he and his men died in their tent eleven miles from a depot of food. Scott's diary suggests that the polar party had a run of unusually bad weather, a blizzard of ten days' duration."

"Ten days?" Billy said. This blizzard couldn't last that long. They would run out of food for sure.

"So just bad luck?" Robert said, interested in spite of himself.

Polly shook her head. "On the ship, I read some modern books about the expedition. Research proves that on Scott's polar trek the weather was colder than usual, but it also proves something else."

"What?" Billy said.

"In all the years that scientists tracked temperatures here, they never once recorded a ten-day blizzard."

That's better, Billy thought. "So why didn't Scott hike to the food?"

"Scott wrote this: *My right foot has gone, nearly all the toes—two days ago I was proud possessor of best feet. These are the steps of my downfall. Like an ass I mixed a small spoonful of curry powder with my melted pemmican—it gave me violent indigestion. I lay awake and in pain all night; woke and felt done on the march; foot went and I didn't know it.*"

"So Scott had frostbite?" Robert asked.

"Yes," Polly said.

"But what about Bowers and Wilson?" Grace said.

Polly was surprised that Grace knew their names. She hadn't realized that Grace listened to her stories.

"So Scott ordered Bowers and Wilson to stay?" Robert said.

"No," Polly said. How could Robert think that Scott was a man who would order his friends to starve to death?

"Don't make us guess," Robert said. "You said that Scott had frostbite and that's why he didn't go for food. Why did Bowers and Wilson stay in the tent instead of trying to get to the depot?

257

They could have brought food back to Scott. At least two of the explorers could have survived. Why didn't they?"

"Wilson and Bowers could have made it to the depot eleven miles away. Their feet weren't frostbitten. But they couldn't have carried Scott the hundred miles back to camp."

"You're not making any sense," Billy said. "You just said that blizzards don't last for ten days. Why did Scott lie about the ten-day blizzard?"

"Scott would never lie. Remember, Scott couldn't walk. He couldn't leave the tent," Polly said. "He had to depend on what Bowers and Wilson told him about the weather."

"I don't understand. Stop talking in riddles," Billy said.

"This was one of his last diary entries: *Since the 21st we have had a continuous gale. . . . We had fuel to make two cups of tea apiece and bare food for two days on the 20th. Every day we have been ready to start for our depot 11 miles away, but outside the door of the tent it remains a scene of whirling drift.*"

"So they all starved." Billy had made his decision. He would rather freeze to death than starve.

"Probably," Polly said.

"Was that his last entry?" Billy said.

Polly shook her head. "No. His last entry was undated: *For God's sake look after our people.*"

"But what about Wilson and Bowers?" Robert asked.

"Wilson and Bowers gave up," Billy said. "It was easier for them to stay inside a warm tent than to brave the cold."

"Those two would never have given up!" Polly shot back. The insult to her heroes filled her eyes with tears.

Suddenly Grace understood: Bowers and Wilson had stayed in the tent because they didn't want Scott to die alone. She heard the pounding of the wind outside and found herself strangely grateful for the two men's kindness to the long-dead explorer.

"There wasn't a blizzard, but Scott believed there was." Robert thought out loud. "Wilson and Bowers must have lied to Scott. Why would they lie?"

"Otherwise Scott would have ordered them to save themselves," Polly said, reciting the theory of an expert on polar exploration. "That was the kind of man he was. The kind of man whose last words were *For God's sake look after our people.*" After everything he'd gone through, Scott thought of their families at the end.

"So Bowers and Wilson chose to stay?" Billy asked, amazed.

"Who knows what really happened?" Polly nodded her head and wiped her tears with her sleeve. "But somewhere out there in that snow and ice Andrew is dying alone," she choked out. She couldn't talk anymore. She crawled toward her sleeping bag and stuffed her head inside it to muffle her sobs.

Bowers and Wilson were good guys, Robert thought.

Bowers and Wilson died because they were loyal. Andrew went down into that crevasse to save Robert. Polly wanted to go out in the snow to look for Andrew. The snow teaches people to take care of one another, Grace thought.

I miss my home, Billy thought. I miss my Compu-gametable. I want to survive. I don't care if I win. I want to go home. More than anything else, I don't want to starve.

When Polly lifted her head up, she heard Robert's and Billy's loud snores.

"Grace, are you awake?" Polly asked.

"Yeah," Grace said.

"Can I talk to you some more?"

Grace didn't say anything, but Polly didn't sense her silence to be unfriendly.

"Scott headed to the Pole with only four men. The rest of the expedition waited at different camps. Around the time Scott was expected to return to the main camp, Cherry-Garrard, one of Scott's crew members, drove a dog team to try to find Scott and make his journey back easier. When Cherry-Garrard was about to run out of dog food, he returned to the main camp. That's what Scott had told him to do. He was just following orders. Months later, Cherry-Garrard was one of the men who found the explorers' bodies. He read their diaries. He figured out that he had been only a two- or three-day march away from the Scott team as the men lay dying.

"Cherry-Garrard was a rich man. He had an estate in England. But he was never happy after he learned that he might have saved Scott. He always wished that he had ignored Scott's orders and gone on and looked for his friends."

"Horrible," Grace said.

"Yet Cherry-Garrard shouldn't have gone on searching," Polly said. She paused to gather strength to recount the haunting story. "His trip to find Scott was the first time that he had managed a dogsled. Cherry-Garrard wore glasses that constantly fogged up, but he was blind without them. He probably wouldn't have survived if he had ignored his orders and continued looking for Scott."

"Just like you and the wind," Grace said.

"Yeah," Polly said. "The fact that Cherry-Garrard didn't attempt that impossible task ruined his life." She started crying. "And that's what I'm afraid of."

"Polly," Grace crooned, as she did to her animals.

"I'll hate myself," Polly mumbled.

What could Grace say? What could anyone say? Blizzards froze comforting words into ice.

31

"How can I leave him?" Steve said to Chad.

"You must," Chad said. His hand lay heavily on Steve's shoulder. "The day shift will be here any minute."

Steve sighed. Some nights the sound of Pearl's sweeping was reassuring, but now its clocklike regularity was eerie, and Steve wanted to yell at her to stop.

"What you've done is a crime," Chad reminded him. "Do you want to get us all on *Court TV?*"

Steve didn't say anything. They stared at each other. Chad's face was white, his mouth tight. Steve knew his father would not have wanted him to repay Chad's kindness with disobedience.

Chad leaned close to Steve. "I trust you." He gestured toward the empty basement. "We all trust you. I just don't want us all to become Pearls." Chad's eyes were big and dark. Steve had never seen a grown man so scared.

"Okay." Steve turned to Andrew's screen. "Andrew, buddy, this is Birdie."

"Yeah," Andrew answered groggily.

Andrew might not be alive when Steve returned.

"I've got to go for a while." Steve struggled to think of an explanation. "I've got duties in heaven."

"Okay."

"You've got to promise me something," Steve said.

"Yeah."

"Hang on till I get back."

Andrew moaned.

"I mean it. I'll be back."

"Soon?"

"Yeah. You'll be fine," Steve said, and wished that he believed it. He turned away from the screen.

"You did what you could." Chad clapped Steve on the back.

"That's supposed to make me feel better?" Steve muttered.

"Yeah. It is," Chad said. He walked over to the corner of the room. "Let's go, Pearl." He took her broom.

The three of them were walking out the door just as Blair Provenzano and a few of the day-shift guys burst in.

"I've skimmed your summary," Blair said. "So we've had a great night."

Chad nodded sadly.

Steve turned away. He couldn't bear to watch the day shift's excitement.

Steve hurried home and turned on the television.

Except for a white slit, the screen was black. Andrew's eyes must be almost closed. He imagined Andrew huddled in that tiny crevasse, his small store of hope dwindling.

Steve stood up. He couldn't watch television anymore. He didn't know how or when he had changed, but he had. In his heart, he knew that he was no longer a viewer.

The Secretary appeared on the screen. "History exam day. We have now covered the land . . ." A photo of Antarctica appeared on the screen, captioned LAND.

Steve barely paid attention as the Secretary reviewed the other topics: the explorers, the journey, the diaries, and the weather. How could the Secretary interrupt the program to give an exam? Andrew was in the crevasse. Polly was still stuck in the tent.

"I quit!" Steve yelled at the image of the Secretary on the screen. "Not only that . . ."

Steve's heart was racing from his daring decision. But he would go back to the DOE and do what he could, regardless of the consequences.

His father would probably have said that he had lost his temper again, but the decision to act made him feel calmer than he had felt since Andrew had fallen into the crevasse.

But what could he do?

He started thinking through his options. It was unlikely that he could get past Security and talk to the Secretary. Even if he did and she agreed to help—a highly unlikely proposition—what could she do at this point? Dropping food supplies wouldn't save Andrew's life.

In fact, the more he thought about it, the clearer the solution became.

The only person who could save Andrew was Polly.

He had to go to the production room and get hold of the mikes.

With a little luck, the weather would have cleared. Then all he would need was ten minutes or so to guide Polly to Andrew.

He felt excited until he remembered that he still needed to

figure out how to take over the mikes.

Steve looked around the apartment for something that resembled a gun—or better, a bomb. He pulled a piece of string out of his drawer. That could be his fuse. His bowling ball was under his bed, but he couldn't risk trying to get anything that big through Security. A pizza crust, a bag of chips, and an empty box of Fried Flying Shrimp, the Crispiest Grasshoppers Around, lay on his kitchen counter. Think, he commanded himself.

Steve poured the crumbs out of the box, punched a hole in the bottom, and pushed the string through the hole.

He held up his amateur bomb and examined it. The string hung out of the bottom of the pink box like a droopy tail. The bomb looked pitiful, and not at all scary. This wouldn't work.

He paced around the small hut. There was no point in getting frustrated with himself. It wasn't as if he knew how to be a terrorist.

Wait a minute.

Steve knew something that the Secretary was afraid of. She didn't want anyone to know about the corneal implants. If he cleared everyone out of the production room, he could threaten to broadcast some footage about the corneal implants. He wasn't sure what Chad had saved in the P.B. (possible blackmail) file, but at least he could broadcast the scene on the ship when the kids had discussed the operation.

I still need a bomb to clear the room, Steve reasoned. He forced himself to think. A dangerous-looking bomb. Not a bomb with a picture of a grasshopper on the front.

What kind of bombs were there?

Atomic bombs.

Nuclear bombs.

Pipe bombs . . .

A pipe bomb!

"Questions for ages eight through ten. First: Scott liked ponies better than dogs. True or false?" The television was still blaring as Steve rushed out the door.

Steve headed for the DOE. His stomach was churning, but his goal was clear. Polly needed to save Andrew, and Steve was going to help her.

Although it was almost winter, the air outside was hot and muggy. The weather was totally unlike a polar day.

How was Andrew holding up in the cold? Steve wondered.

Steve didn't have to imagine how Andrew was feeling, because he knew.

Andrew felt all alone.

As Steve rounded the corner of K Street, he heard shouts and cries. He quickened his pace. A mob was demonstrating in front of the Department of Entertainment.

Steve scanned the signs. "SAVE ANDREW" "SURVIVAL ISN'T A GAME" "SECRETARY OF ENTER-TROCITIES" "GET ANDREW OUT OF THE FREEZER" One man held an effigy of the Secretary. Her body dangled at the end of a rope. Her neck was bent. Fake blood oozed out of her mouth.

Steve elbowed his way to the DOE. This crowd was huge, and angry. All around him, men, women, and children were chanting, "Child murderer! Child murderer! The Secretary is a child murderer!"

Steve was glad that this crowd was here, but demonstrations wouldn't save Andrew. He followed the path to the employee entrance at the back and flashed his credentials. The guard glanced at Steve's ID before waving him through.

Steve put his package on a bench, collected his gear from his locker on the back wall, and sat down. He dutifully tied his heavy shoes, but he slipped the tooth mike into his pocket. He passed through the metal detector without a problem. His weapon was waiting for him inside the DOE.

At the entrance to the production corridor, he stepped on the foot pad and pressed his thumb on the fingerprint detector. He waited for the computer to recognize his weight and thumbprint.

Come on. Come on.

The door opened, and Steve started down the familiar hall. He was breaking all the rules, but the Secretary had left him no alternative.

The production room was packed. He snaked his way through the crowd toward the entrance to the basement.

"Hey," Toby Kyle, his old friend on the day shift, exclaimed. "You're not supposed to be here!"

Steve pushed past him. He didn't have time to argue. He popped the tile in the floor, only vaguely aware that he had just given away one of the night shift's biggest secrets, and rushed down the dark stairway. He didn't have time to worry about what the night shift or Chad would think. He had run out of time even to be afraid for himself.

There were a bunch of old cans of liquid ice, a few flashlights, and a card game set up in the middle of the room. He picked up a piece of loose pipe in each hand. After he began beating the pipes on the walls and the ceiling, the room above him grew quiet.

He ran up the narrow stairs and stuck his head into the production room.

Blair Provenzano stared him. "What are *you* doing here?"

Steve squeezed the piece of pipe in his hand. Could he really go through with this?

"What's happening with Andrew?"

"On behalf of the Secretary, I'm ordering you to explain yourself," Blair said. His tone was clipped. His mustache twitched.

To hell with the Secretary's orders! "What's happening with Andrew?" Steve repeated.

"He's taking off his clothes, saying he's hot," Blair said, in a tone that let Steve know that Blair didn't consider Andrew's impending death to be his problem.

God. He was going to get hypothermia.

It was only an empty piece of pipe, but Steve lifted it over his head. "I have a bomb!" he shouted. "Get out of here, or I'm going to blow us all up!"

He heard Blair's quick intake of breath.

Someone screamed and ran out the door. Several other crew members slipped out, too.

"He's bluffing," a voice muttered.

"Let's not take any risks," Blair counseled the others in a soft voice. He turned and faced Steve. "We'll leave, but you're making a huge mistake."

Steve watched the day shift start to shuffle out. Some were wide-eyed. All his former colleagues moved in a stiff, unnatural way that meant they were scared.

Blair was taking too long to get to the door.

Steve brandished his bomb at Blair. "Leave, or I promise you I'll use this!" he shouted.

The last day-shift crew member walked out.

Blair stood in the open doorway. "This is outrageous."

Steve forced himself to use his toughest voice. "Shut the door."

The door slammed shut. Steve ran over to the door and locked it. He had just a few minutes before the security guards arrived. He doubted whether they would buy his bluff about the bomb for long. He only hoped that he had enough time. He hurried to the screens.

Steve reached under Andrew's screen for the mike. He twisted it up and turned it on. "Andrew! Andrew!" he shouted. "This is Birdie. Do you hear me?"

"I thought you'd never come back," Andrew said.

"Put on your parka. Your mind is tricking you."

"But I'm so hot." Andrew moaned.

"Put your parka back on," Steve insisted.

On Grace's screen, he found Polly, who was staring out the tent at a scene of gusting snow.

Steve dropped Andrew's mike and found the one to Polly's receiver. He spoke quickly into it. "Polly, this is Birdie Bowers, Andrew's distant uncle. I'm going to lead you to Andrew."

"What?" Polly heard a voice in her head. She looked wildly around the tent.

"I didn't say anything," Grace said.

"No time for questions now," Steve interrupted. "Andrew's not that far away. Carry a rope, because he's in a crevasse."

"Grace, I'm going to look for Andrew," Polly said.

Robert sat up and rubbed his eyes. "It's not going to do us any good to have two people dead."

"Don't argue. Help," Polly said. "Grace, get me the big rope."

"Polly, you can barely carry that rope. Let *me* go," Robert said.

"No, I'm going," Polly said. She threw the guide rope over her head. She didn't have time to explain.

Grace handed her the heavy coiled rope needed to pull Andrew up.

Polly pushed open the flap of the tent and crawled outside.

Billy sat quietly, hoping that no one would notice him.

Steve heard the sound of men outside the production-room door. Security had arrived. He flicked the mike off. "I've got a bomb!" he shouted at the door. "But if you give me ten more minutes, I'll give myself up."

"Son, we don't think that you have a bomb," a woman's voice said. "But we'll know for sure in just a minute."

It was almost time to put into effect his backup plan, Steve thought.

"Birdie! Birdie!" Polly called to Steve. "Am I headed the right way?"

Steve picked up her screen's mike and spoke into it. "Yes. Keep crawling with your eyes on the ground. You should be able to see the crevasse soon."

Polly's screen was a blur of snow. She was a brave girl, all right. She crawled a few more steps, dragging the rope, and Steve could make out the sleds. "He's just past the sleds."

Steve heard the crackle of a walkie-talkie. "Negative," a stern voice said.

"Let me talk to him." Steve recognized Blair's voice. "Stephen Michael. Be reasonable. Give yourself up."

"I will. Give me a few more minutes," Steve pleaded. Polly was so close!

"Okay," he said into Polly's mike. "Start looking very carefully on the ground." He couldn't ignore the muffled sound of a conversation behind the door.

"Oh," Polly said. "I think I see something dark."

Steve squinted at her screen. "That's it." He glanced at Andrew's screen. Andrew's eyes were barely open. Steve picked up Andrew's mike. "Polly's here. Don't give up. She's going to drop the rope in a minute."

"You got there just in time," Steve said into Polly's mike. "Now crawl along the crevasse until you see him."

"We've X-rayed the room! We know you don't have a bomb!" a man shouted.

Security had called Steve's first bluff. "I have something worse!" he yelled. "I have the footage of the kids in the clinic!" he lied. "The footage that shows the corneal implant operation. If you don't give me another ten minutes alone with the kids, I'll broadcast that."

"Steve, you're crazy!" Blair shouted at him.

The walkie-talkie crackled again. Given the secrecy surrounding the corneal implants, Steve guessed that security wouldn't dare break into the room without checking first with the Secretary. He wouldn't let himself worry about the fact that he was running out of time.

Steve turned to Andrew's screen. "Andrew, do you hear me?"

"Yes." Andrew's voice was faint.

"I need you to try to stand up. Polly's looking for you."

Steve heard a rustle. Andrew had been able to stand. "Now let me hear you shout."

"Hello!" Andrew called.

"Louder!" Steve said to Andrew.

Steve turned to Polly's mike. "Polly, Andrew is shouting. Listen carefully."

"I don't hear anything," Polly said.

"You're still not above him. Keep crawling," Steve said to Polly. Then, to Andrew, he said, "Shout louder. She's almost there."

"Hello!" Andrew shouted now.

The effort must have been hard for him. "Did you hear anything, Polly?"

"No," Polly moaned.

"Don't give up," Steve said to Polly. "Andrew, shout louder!"

"Hello!" Andrew shouted, louder this time, but not by much. It was clear to Steve that Andrew was reaching the end of his strength.

"I hear him," Polly said. "Andrew!" she yelled.

"Polly!" Steve heard Andrew call.

"You're a few steps from him," Steve said into Polly's mike. "Keep going and drop the rope." Then he spoke into Andrew's mike: "Andrew, she's going to drop the rope."

"Rope?" Andrew sounded befuddled.

"Yeah, rope. You're being rescued," Steve said.

"I can see him," Polly said.

Behind him, Steve heard a lot of scuffling and yelling outside the door.

"Drop the rope!" Steve said to Polly. Then, into Andrew's mike, he said, "Look up."

"I can't see it. I can't see anything," Andrew mumbled.

"Feel for a rope," Steve said.

"I tripped on something," Andrew said.

"It's the rope. Now slip it on over your head," Steve said.

"My fingers . . . I can't."

"Try again," Steve said into Andrew's mike. He switched to Polly's. "He's got it. He just needs to slip it on."

"I've got it. I'm pulling it over my head but I can't do anything more . . ." Andrew's voice trailed off.

"Five more minutes!" Steve shouted at the door. "Then I'll turn myself in!"

But this time, the men behind the door didn't bother to answer.

Steve surveyed the other screens. Because of Robert's injured shoulder, Steve should ask Billy to pull Andrew up, but he hesitated. Injured or not, Robert was more prone to quick action.

"Don't ask questions, Robert," Steve said urgently into Robert's mike. "Andrew has the rope around his waist. Go outside and pull him up."

On Grace's television screen, Steve watched Robert look wildly around the tent. None of this Birdie Bowers nonsense for Robert. This kid needed to hear the truth. "I'm a DOE guy, but I'm on your side. You've got to believe me."

Steve heard the pop of gunfire. The guards were shooting the lock off the door. He turned around.

The door burst open, and a crowd of men dressed in uniforms rushed toward him.

"Grace, Billy!" Robert said. "Andrew's on the rope!"

"How do you know?" Billy said.

"It tightened," Robert lied. "Now quickly, we don't have time for questions. Get your parkas on and let's go!"

Four men surrounded Steve. He felt the cold metal of pistols against his temple.

"Okay, okay," Steve said. He tried to pull Andrew's mike

toward him to say good-bye but felt a tremendous blow on the back of the head. In his last seconds of consciousness, he stared at the glowing green LIVE button. As he crumpled into a heap, he was able to fall on it. His last thought was, Andrew is safe.

32

Andrew was propped against a sleeping bag. He had heard of people's teeth chattering, but his whole body seemed to be chattering.

"His feet are the worst," Grace said, touching Andrew's bare left foot. "Can you feel this?"

Andrew shook his head.

His face, including the tip of his nose, was chalk white. He had only one eye open, and it looked dull. Polly massaged his arms. She couldn't bear to look at his lips. They had cracked into bloody crevasses.

"Did the books say anything about frostbite, Polly?" Grace asked. "I don't know anything about it."

Polly searched her memory. *"If the frostbite is deep-seated then the blood vessels do not recover and the last stage is gangrene and the only hope ..."* she recited. Then she stopped.

"I know," Andrew said.

Robert tried to give Andrew a sip of hot chocolate but he turned away as though Robert had hit him.

"The only hope is amputation." Andrew wasn't a genius like Polly, but even he could finish Polly's quote.

Polly's face flushed from embarrassment. She searched for a way to distract Andrew from her gloomy words. "You want to hear what Scott said about your great-great-great-uncle?" she asked.

"What?" Andrew mumbled.

"Scott wrote in his diary that Birdie Bowers was *the hardest traveller that ever undertook a Polar journey, as well as one of the most undaunted.... Never was such a sturdy, active, undefeatable little man.*"

"I met him," Andrew said.

Grace patted Andrew on the shoulder. Poor boy.

"He talked to me, too," Polly said to Grace.

Grace's eyes opened wide. *She* was the one who talked to spirits, not them.

"What are you talking about?" Billy stirred the hot chocolate. They had hardly any left. He wondered if boiling a couple of Chocobombs in a pot of water would make hot chocolate. Then he remembered that the candy was his secret.

"It was a cameraman who talked to me," Robert said.

"Hey, guys, I don't understand," Billy said.

"Birdie Bowers helped us," Polly explained.

"What do you mean?" Grace asked.

"No, he was a cameraman," Robert repeated.

"My great-great-great-uncle's ghost." Andrew sighed.

"Cameraman!" Robert cried, suddenly realizing what that meant. "Where are they?"

"We've known all along that they must be here," Billy said.

"If you're watching, help us!" Polly shouted. "We need food! Andrew needs a doctor!"

Polly listened. Only a dog's growl broke the polar silence.

Robert held the cup to Andrew's lips again. "It's okay. If we have to, we can get out of this alone."

As he swallowed, Andrew slowly, painfully opened his closed eye.

No one had a chance to think about its inflamed redness because a clear disk jumped out of it on a transparent spring.

"Ahh!" Andrew cried.

Grace pulled back, horror-struck.

Andrew looks like a monster, Robert thought.

"What's wrong?" Andrew said. But involuntarily his hand moved to his face. His left eye felt very strange. He blinked, and a disk fell on the floor of the tent.

Robert held the disk up for all to see. It was smaller than a button, and clear. But in the center, unmistakably, a lens stared out at them.

The mystery was solved. Robert closed his fist around the disk and shook it at the ceiling. "Hot Sauce, you are sick!" he shouted.

"Some kind of device popped out of your eye," Polly told Andrew.

Andrew blinked his injured eye. The white part had turned bloodred.

"Sick!" Grace spat out the word as though she had bitten into a piece of bone.

Billy rubbed his eyes. "Implants!"

"What else did they stick in our bodies?" Grace said.

"Calm down," Polly said. "We all need to concentrate on Andrew."

"What should we do with the little camera?" Billy asked.

"I'm going to stick it up my butt," Robert said. "Let her watch that for the rest of the television show!"

"We hate you, Hot Sauce!" Billy yelled. He had been cheated out of high school and college. He would be lucky if he even found a crummy job. She had programmed his snowcycle to fail. Those things were bad enough. But nobody—nobody!—had a right to put equipment in his eyes.

Robert laughed. "Remember, Billy, at the beginning of this game, I warned you not to suck up."

"Andrew, can you feel this?" Grace asked as she touched his foot with a cloth.

Andrew shook his head. "No."

"I'm going to rub your feet now. It's probably going to hurt, but I have to," Grace said.

Andrew nodded.

Grace watched Andrew's face. He didn't flinch as she rubbed. Even though she knew little about frostbite, she was sure that it was a terrible sign that he didn't feel any pain.

"So each of us is a walking digital camcorder," Billy said slowly. Thank goodness he had eaten his candy inside his sleeping bag. He doubted if anyone could have seen him do that. But could they have heard him?

Andrew groaned as Grace massaged his calf.

Polly looked into Grace's dark eyes for reassurance but found only worry.

"Maybe there's a cameraman named Birdie Bowers on *Historical Survivor*," Robert suggested.

"Birdie told me some stories," Andrew said. His good eye was half closed.

He needs to sleep, Polly thought. "Did I ever tell you about the time Birdie, Wilson, and Cherry-Garrard went in the dead of winter to collect emperor penguin eggs?" she asked.

"No," Andrew mumbled.

"They got caught in a blizzard and their tent blew away," Polly continued.

"Can you imagine if we didn't have a tent?" Billy said, looking around at the blue tarp that covered them. Maybe Polly was right. Things could be worse.

"Luckily, the men found the tent after the blizzard ended. When they got back to camp, Scott asked Wilson what he would have done if they hadn't recovered it. Wilson said, with an unforgettable expression on his face, '*I would have trusted Birdie to have got us out of anything.*'"

"He got me out of the crevasse," Andrew said.

"He sure did," Polly agreed.

"Birdie!" Andrew called wildly. "Where are you now?"

"Only his toes are really bad," Grace said to herself.

But Polly heard her.

"He's doing angel work," Andrew said, and closed his good eye.

"He's delirious," Billy whispered.

"He's not delirious," Polly said. "There was an angel out there."

After Andrew was asleep, Polly examined the pemmican. There was enough for one small meal for each of them. They had given Andrew all the hot chocolate. She looked around at the drawn faces of the other kids. One of Cherry-Garrard's quotes floated through her mind: *I watched my companions' faces with their eyes and necks falling in. . . . One day I got a piece of looking-glass and found I looked just the same.*

Polly was glad that she didn't have a mirror. "Guys, I think we should skip dinner tonight," she said. When the snow stopped, they'd have to butcher the pony.

No one said anything, but as if they had protested, Polly shared her reasons. "I don't know how long the blizzard will last or how much meat will be on the pony."

Grace was kneading Andrew's toes. Polly sat next to her.

Billy watched them from his sleeping bag. He felt for his candy with his toes.

"What are we going to do if Andrew can't walk, Polly?" Billy asked.

"I'm going to stay with him," Polly said firmly. As she spoke those words, she thought of Bowers's and Wilson's decision to stay with Scott after his feet had gone bad. Even though Bowers wasn't talking to her, he was helping her again.

"If that was me over there, would you stay with me?" Billy asked.

Polly didn't like Billy much, but would she let him die alone in the middle of nowhere? "I'd stay with you," she said without hesitation.

Billy believed Polly meant it. She would stay with him if he had frostbite. Of course, Billy was too smart and careful to get it, but you could never be too sure. Billy looked at Andrew, who was slumped against the tent wall; at Robert, whose arm was in a sling; and at Grace, who was now kneading Andrew's feet. He saw the worried look on Polly's face, and he felt bad.

He was the snow-and-ice man, but what had he done? He'd read a few maps. Tied a few knots.

Then he had a crazy thought. What if he spread out his food on the floor of the tent? He was sick of eating his candy with his head stuck in his sleeping bag. He toed his food, considering the idea.

Polly had saved Andrew, Robert thought admiringly. If she had waited, as Robert had told her to, Andrew wouldn't have made it.

"What more do you know about gangrene?" Grace whispered to Polly.

"Nothing," Polly said. "Besides that quote . . ."

"So you don't know how fast it sets in?"

"No idea," Polly admitted. "Do you?"

Grace shook her head.

Polly had intended to read the medical encyclopedia that was on the ship; she just hadn't gotten around to it.

Billy interrupted Polly's concentration. "Have you ever noticed that I don't eat much, Polly?"

"Yeah," Polly said. Billy was small. Besides, some people didn't need much food.

"I'm the world's most picky eater. I won't eat carrot chips, or strawberry chips, even. The only flavors I like are beef, chicken, and broccoli." He felt amazed that this was Billy Kanalski talking—the same person who had once gotten kicked out of his Sunday school class for refusing to share food.

Polly repeated a line of her mother's: "Well, each pack of chips has all the nutrients we need."

"I know," Billy said, sitting up in his sleeping bag. "I just wanted you all to understand why I did this."

"Did what?" Robert broke in.

"Brought junk food," Billy said.

"Candy?" Robert asked.

So that was what she had smelled from time to time, Grace thought.

Before he could have second thoughts, Billy began shoveling

his store of Chocobombs and nuts out of the sleeping bag.

Polly, Grace, and Robert stared at the gleaming pile.

"Go ahead," Billy said. The sight of the food made him feel wonderfully generous.

"You've had this candy all along?" Robert said sharply to Billy as he grabbed for a pack of Chocobombs.

Billy braced himself for the kids' anger.

Robert tore open the wrapping. "Cheater!" He tossed a handful of chocolate into his open mouth: "Jerk! Psychopath! How could you have held out on us for this long?"

Billy winced.

"Why are you giving this to us now?" Polly asked. She wanted to understand the part of Billy that she had always sensed was secretive and dishonest.

"I don't know." Billy tossed Polly and Grace packages of Chocobombs.

Polly opened her package and popped one in her mouth. It was the most delicious morsel she had ever eaten in her whole life.

"Thank you, Billy," Polly said.

"I can't believe you've been feasting while we've been choking down pemmican," Robert said with his mouth full.

Billy shrugged.

"I ought to beat you up . . ." Robert paused.

Billy hung his head. No matter what he did, Billy always seemed to get other kids mad at him.

". . . but this tastes so incredibly good." Robert reached for another pack.

"I bet if he'd given them to us earlier, they wouldn't taste as good as they taste right now," Polly said.

Robert almost said "Thanks, Pollyanna." Then, remembering her heroism, he stopped himself.

"This is good," Grace said with her mouth full. She felt like waking Andrew up and giving him some candy, but the deep lines in his sleeping face stopped her.

"What are you going to do when you run out?" Polly asked Billy.

"Eat pemmican, I guess," Billy said, although he hoped he wouldn't have to.

"If we have any," Polly said.

"I counted the Chocobombs," Billy said. "There are five to a pack, and I have fifteen packs. And I have two hundred seventy-nine peanuts . . ."

"Who knows?" Robert mused. "The audience may vote you MVP after all. None of the rest of us had the sense to bring any food."

Billy laughed in relief. Robert had calmed down. Billy ate a Chocobomb. It would be great if the audience voted him MVP. But whatever happened, the Chocobomb tasted much better than all the Chocobombs he had eaten alone.

33

The snow had stopped during the night. Grace was anxious to go outside to check on the dogs, but the other kids insisted that they all talk and plan. They didn't understand yet that in this land, plans were made to be changed.

"It's just as well that Andrew slept through breakfast," Polly said. Their meal had consisted of hot water and twenty of Billy's peanuts for each of them.

"So what are we going to do?" Robert asked the question before he remembered that he always told people what to do.

"We need to slaughter the pony," Grace said.

"Yes," Polly agreed. "We should eat a big stew, and then . . ." She looked at Robert and Billy. "Robert, do you think you feel well enough to hike to the depot with Billy?"

Robert nodded. "Sure." His shoulder still hurt, but he could do it.

"We need all the food we can get." Polly bit her lip and looked over at Andrew's sleeping figure. She reminded herself that she would do whatever she could to help Andrew survive. But she wasn't ready yet to talk to the others about their long-term options.

"If we don't make it back in one day, we can always sleep under the sled," Robert said.

"You could make it there and back if you used the dogs," Grace suggested.

"If we take the dogs, you need to come with us," said Billy.

"We don't know how fast gangrene sets in," Polly explained.

"Oh," Billy said.

They all looked over at Andrew.

Grace had wrapped Andrew's feet in the warmest blankets, but this morning, when she had checked his toes, they had been blistered and lifeless.

"Billy, let's hook up one dog to the sled," Robert said. "We can put him in a simple harness."

"Good idea," said Grace. She felt sick, thinking of the operation that she might have to perform.

"Robert," Polly said, "in Scott's diaries, he said that they had some opium but refused to take it. Do you remember seeing any little white pills?"

"Yeah. Check the first-aid kit," Robert said.

Polly crawled to the pile where they kept the kit. She sifted through its contents. Sure enough, she saw a little brown bottle with ten white pills in it. The bottle was unmarked, but Polly guessed that she had found her painkiller.

If Andrew's toes turned black, what choice would they have then but for Grace to amputate them? Polly held the bottle tightly in her hand. It would make things a lot easier. She turned to the other kids. "Don't think I'm crazy, but I'm going to try talking to Birdie."

Robert looked curiously at her.

Polly turned to the ceiling. "So, Birdie!" she called. "If you can hear me, please let me know what we should do."

Silence can be earsplitting, Grace thought.

Grace stuck a knife in her pants before exiting the tent. The new snow shimmered in the sunlight. In some places, it was deep.

Polly peeked out of the tent and watched Robert, Grace, and Billy push through the powdery snow toward the pony. *There was a grace about us when we staggered on and kept our tempers—even with God.*

They had taken only a few steps when Robert realized that something was wrong.

"What happened?" Billy said. Big patches of blood had reddened the snow.

"The dogs couldn't have gotten loose. They couldn't have," Grace said. And then she saw Brontosaurus sitting on his haunches behind the sleds. She had forgotten about him. His tongue was lolling out of his mouth. With his blood-spattered fur and snout, he looked pleased with himself.

Where is Cookie? Robert thought.

"Oh no," Grace groaned.

Robert stared down at the bloody carcass partly hidden by snow. The stupid dog had killed the pony sometime during the storm.

"Now what are we going to do?" Billy said.

"Let's get that dog," Robert said.

"What do you think Brontosaurus stew would taste like?" Billy would have loved to eat a big bowl out of spite.

Grace scraped snow off the carcass of the pony. She saw bloody bones, but also meat on the legs and the head.

Billy and Robert gazed at the unappetizing spectacle.

"We can make a stew," Grace said.

"I want to kill that dog," Billy said through gritted teeth.

"Let's take the legs back to the tent and feed the head and guts to the dogs," Robert said.

Billy swallowed to keep from getting sick.

Grace turned and noticed Brontosaurus again. "Bronty!" She kept her voice light and happy.

For once, the runaway sat still. Grace grabbed the dog by the scruff of his neck.

Was there ever such a contrary dog? Billy thought.

34

"The only good thing is that it's so warm," Grace said. Except for Andrew, who was sleeping, they had all stripped to their long underwear. The inside of the tent felt steamy, and moisture that had collected on the tent ceiling dropped down in a light rain. Billy had cooked a quick pot of pony stew. They each held a cup.

"It's always warmer after a blizzard," Polly said.

"Life is not without its small mercies," Grace said, repeating what her grandfather used to say.

"It's almost noon. We need to go," Billy said. He had managed a few bites of the stew. He guessed that it tasted like watered-down dog food. But he'd never eaten dog food, so he couldn't say for sure.

"I agree." Robert put his cup down. "Can we leave you guys with the dishes?"

Polly smiled. "Sure."

Andrew groaned in his sleep. His forehead felt hot, as if he might be running a fever.

Robert pulled on his parka, gloves, hat, and goggles. When he had finished, he looked at Polly. "If anything happens to us, Polly, will you tell my mom and dad?" He stopped and thought for a moment. How could he convey to his parents how hard he had tried, how much he loved them? "You'll know what to say."

Polly nodded. Robert was really quite sweet.

"You're still on TV," Billy reminded him.

"Oh, yeah." Robert involuntarily reached his hand to his eye. "I forgot about that."

"Hi, dad." Billy stared at a spot on the tent wall. "The Compu-gametable is going to be a great success someday. Mom, you shouldn't cry too much, and . . ." He looked at Polly. "I feel dumb saying good-bye on television. Will you talk to them in person?"

Polly nodded solemnly.

Robert opened the tent flap. "Good luck," he said before crawling outside. Billy followed him.

Grace's and Polly's eyes met. They didn't want to talk about it, but each understood what they might need to do. "Should we do anything to get ready?" Polly asked. She felt so ignorant.

"Boil the knife," Grace said. It felt strange to pretend that she was knowledgeable. But hadn't she acted as if she knew how to handle the dogs, and hadn't she turned into a dogsled driver? She was positive that the first thing that a surgeon did before an operation was to sterilize her equipment. But even if she was wrong, staying busy was better than nervously hovering.

"What knife are you going to use?" Polly asked.

"The seal knife will do," Grace said.

"Have you ever done anything like this before, Grace?" Polly turned on the Primus stove. On top of everything else, they were low on fuel.

"I've cut off a few dogs' legs before," Grace said. One dog had gotten into a fight with a coyote. His leg hung off him, a shred-ded thing. She had operated on him in her refrigerator carton, by candlelight. Once he got better, the poor dog had followed her around everywhere until he was killed by a hunter's stray bullet.

"These are only toes," Polly said.

"Toes," Grace repeated dully.

"Grace," Polly said gently. "If his toes turn black, we've got to do this."

Usually it seemed to take forever for the water to boil, but not today. Polly stared at the pot for a few seconds before calling out, "It's ready!"

Grace gripped the long, sharp knife as she crawled toward the boiling water.

Robert trudged next to Billy. He could feel the soft mounds of snow through his finneskoe. It was like wearing gloves on your feet, he thought. Now that more snow had covered up the crevasses, Robert sensed that they were even more dangerous. The deep steps jarred his shoulder, but he tried to concentrate on the crunching and crackling of the snow.

Sometimes, when Billy took a step, his foot never reached a firm base. He would never have had the courage to make this march without Brontosaurus, who bounded through the soft snow ahead of them, pulling the sled. Brontosaurus would fall into a bottomless pit, not Billy.

Since the wind was at their backs, Billy worried whether they would make decent time on their return. "Another day, we could rig some canvas as a sail and make this sled fly."

"You learned how in a survival course?" Robert asked, although he doubted that Billy had ever taken one.

"No," Billy said slowly. If he got a chance, he would lie to the Secretary again. He didn't feel bad about that, but he did feel bad about lying to Robert. "I want to tell you something, Robert."

"Go ahead."

"I lied on my application," Billy said. "I've never taken snow-and-ice survival courses. I've skied a bit. Been active in Scouting. That's it."

"Why?" Robert asked. The junk food had been a surprise. Billy's lack of snow-and-ice experience wasn't.

"Why did I lie, or why am I telling you?"

"Both," Robert said.

"I don't know why I'm telling you," Billy said. "But I wanted to go to college. That's the reason I lied on the application."

"We could have used a great snow-and-ice man, but you're amazing with directions and knots." Robert smiled. "And you're the king of junk food."

"Thanks," Billy said. He felt that he'd been forgiven.

"Have you ever been lost?" Robert asked.

"Not for very long." Billy said. "It's a game I play. I keep track of my longitude and latitude in my head. If there's no sun, I guess."

"It's funny. When I first saw you guys, I never guessed how important each kid would be to the team." How much I would need every person on the team, Robert thought. He wasn't used to needing anyone.

"I still can't believe that Andrew—the human freezer—is the one with frostbite. I mean, I was expecting skinny Polly . . ." Billy said.

"No one else would have survived so long in that crevasse but Andrew."

"You're right," Billy said.

"With only some dead toes," Robert said glumly.

"Do you think that Grace will have the guts to . . ." Billy couldn't finish the sentence.

"If she needs to," Robert said. "It's either that or watch him die."

"He can't die," Billy said.

Robert didn't answer. To take his mind off his aching shoulder and Andrew's toes, he looked around. The sky was a light gray, and the mountains were a purplish hue. He had gotten used to the fact that the snow hardly ever looked white. Today it was a paler gray than the sky. These were soft colors for such a tough land.

Brontosaurus barked, and Billy watched the hackles rise on his neck. Oh, no—the dog had used up his good behavior for the day and was going to start giving them trouble!

The dog barked again.

"Idiot dog," Billy said.

"No, I think he's trying to tell us something."

Billy examined the dog carefully. Maybe Robert was right. Bronty's ears were flat against his head. Instead of bouncing, he was picking his way warily, with his eyes stuck on the horizon.

Billy spotted something moving. A black dot came toward them. Polly had warned them of Antarctic hallucinations. According to her, the Scott party had experienced lots of them. But this black dot didn't go away. In fact, it kept growing larger until Robert punched Billy in the shoulder and asked, "What can that be?"

Billy shook his head. But before long, he could make out a man.

"Who in the world?" Billy said.

"I thought no one lived here," Robert said.

"No one used to live here," Billy said. "But maybe now that it's warmer?"

"What if he's lived here for a long time and doesn't even know about the Big Bust or . . . ?" Robert searched for a recent technological innovation.

"Or instant trees. Or the human fax," Billy said.

"Or the Nuclear Accident?" Robert added.

"Good boy." Robert held on to Bronty's harness. The dog's fur bristled along his backbone.

Why, the darn dog would attack that stranger if he tried to hurt us! Billy realized with amazement and pride.

A big, burly man in a parka walked up to Robert. Bronty lunged at him, but Robert held the harness tightly.

The man removed his headphones. Robert could hear the faint strains of "The Hologram Blues."

"Captain Scott, I presume?" the man said.

"What?" Robert said.

"I'm *Historical Survivor*'s Amundsen," the man said. His face was long, as Cookie's had been. The color of his eyes matched the gray stubble on his face.

"Amundsen?" Billy said.

"I'm rescuing you," the man said.

Robert felt sadness and relief all rolled up into one.

"What if we don't want to be rescued?" Billy surprised himself by saying. He wanted to go home more than he had ever wanted anything in his whole life, but in a way he was sorry to see an adult. He had gotten used to kids making the decisions.

"Orders of the President," the man said. "Viewers don't want to watch kids die."

"But what about the prize money?" Billy said.

"The President has instructed me to tell you that you each get the ten thousand dollars."

I wasn't going to be voted MVP anyway, Billy thought. *At least the ten thousand dollars will pay for my freshman year of high school.*

Robert pictured his new red boat with silver trim for a moment before his thoughts shifted to Andrew. "Do you have food?" he asked

The man nodded.

"Let's hurry back, then," Robert said. *Maybe it wouldn't be too late. Maybe this man could help Andrew before Grace . . .*

Robert and Billy looked at each other. Neither wanted to put into words the situation in the tent. "One of us . . ." Billy started to explain. But he gave up.

"Well, let's go," Robert said. It felt strange to turn around. Each step into the wind was doubly hard. Bronty's sled flapped like a metal kite behind him.

"Did you get caught in the blizzard?" Billy asked.

The big man shook his head. "No. I parachuted in afterward, but the blizzard must have messed up our bearings because I was supposed to land next to you."

"So you just landed?" Billy asked. All of a sudden, the man appeared soft to him; this man didn't know how tough the Antarctic could be.

"Yeah," the man said. "See, my partner and I have been on alert at a secret location. The plan was to drop me off at the Pole a few hours before you guys arrived. It was supposed to be a simulation of how Amundsen beat Scott to the Pole."

Billy shook his head. "Sick."

"But the viewers were too upset," the man continued.

"What about?" Robert said.

"I haven't been able to watch television. But my boss tells me there are riots in front of the Department of Entertainment."

"Why?" Billy asked.

"People are angry about your situation," the man said.

"About us?" Robert wondered.

"About the boy who was trapped in that crevasse, and about the whole thing. People are mad about the whole *Historical Survivor* series."

"What do you know!" Robert said. "Maybe the viewers aren't so sick after all."

"Maybe not," Billy said.

"So you're . . . ?" The man pointed at Robert.

"I'm Robert."

"And I'm Billy," Billy said.

"You can call me Harry," the man said. "You're supposed to call me Roald, but I can't pronounce it." He looked around. "Besides, who cares if we stick to the story? Where could the cameras be out here, anyway?"

Billy and Robert looked at each other. This man had a lot to learn.

35

Robert pushed open the tent flap and painfully began crawling into the tent. What he saw made him stop. A bloodred towel lay next to the Primus. Oh, no! The rescue had come too late.

Grace and Polly turned to him. They both looked worried and tired. Grace's face was especially white and pinched.

Andrew was awake, and smiled at him.

"Are you okay?" Robert asked as he entered.

"I had a nosebleed," Andrew said.

Polly nodded.

Robert sighed with relief.

Billy stuck his head in and crawled toward them. "You won't believe this. We've been rescued."

"Rescued?" Grace said in a tone of disbelief.

"By Amundsen." Robert sat down and rubbed his shoulder. "Not really by Amundsen. I mean, by the guy who's playing Amundsen. His name is Harry."

Harry stuck his head into the tent. "What happened?" he asked, looking at the bloody towel.

"I almost froze," Andrew said. "It messed up my nose."

Billy looked at Polly with a question in his eyes. Polly shook her head. So Andrew's toes were still intact. Thank goodness.

The man wagged his finger at the girls. "Where are the smiles? Ol' Harry has rescued you."

"We thought we were in this game alone," Polly said, irritated at this man's silliness.

"Not anymore." Harry grinned broadly. "I'm here."

Polly and Grace exchanged glances. Both disliked this big man, but what were their alternatives? Andrew needed a doctor and lots of warm food to get well.

Harry held up his radio locator. "The military transport helicopter will be here before you know it." He chuckled. "If I didn't know better, I would think you guys didn't want to be rescued."

"I don't," Grace piped up. "I'd like to stay."

Harry scowled at her. "What does a little girl like you know about her own good? You're coming with me."

Grace set her teeth and glared at him.

How could Grace want to stay? Polly couldn't wait to leave this cramped tent. "Could you leave us alone for a minute?" she asked Harry.

Harry doffed his cap at her and backed out of the tent.

Polly turned to Grace. "So what's going on?"

"I don't expect you guys to understand, but my whole life I've wanted to live somewhere like this. I don't want to go back yet." Grace looked at the kids' solemn faces. It felt good to have shared her dream and to realize that no one was laughing.

"But you'll die," Polly said finally. "We can't leave you."

"There's plenty of food at the depots for me to stay awhile," Grace said. She was starting to admit to herself that she wouldn't be able to live here, that she needed to rethink her dream. The time that she got to spend here on account of this game might be all she'd ever have.

Robert eyed Grace. The trip had been hard, but he was beginning to figure out ice and snow. If he left now, he'd be turning away from a challenge. "I'd like to go with you to the Pole," he said. It was strange to realize that he probably couldn't make it without her.

"But Robert, your shoulder," Polly said.

"I hiked through the thick snow today, and it hardly hurt at all," Robert lied.

"We could take turns riding the dogsled," Grace said to Robert.

Robert grinned at Polly. "You could watch us on television."

Polly wasn't convinced. But what could she do? Grace and Robert had a right to make their own decisions. "I guess the government could send the rescue team back for you," she said.

Robert and Grace looked at each other and smiled.

"Billy, you don't want to stay, do you?" Polly asked playfully.

Billy shook his head. He had eaten enough seal and pony meat to last a lifetime.

Polly laughed. "I didn't think so." Then there was a loud noise. "What's that?" she said.

Everyone's head turned in the direction of the noise.

"The helicopter," Robert said. "Polly, make sure they pick us up in a military transport helicopter." He was tempted to leave just for the ride. But it would be so cool to be the first kid to make it to the Pole unassisted by an adult.

Harry stuck his head back in. "My orders are to take you back. All of you. Now come on."

"Andrew, Billy, and I will come," Polly said cheerfully. "But Grace likes it here. This is her home."

"Nobody lives here," Harry argued.

"And Robert wants to be a record setter," Polly added.

"You kids are crazy," Harry said. "If I have to get out my gun, I will."

Robert hated threats, but while he was feeling tongue-tied, Polly responded in her brisk, confident way.

"There are cameras here, and I can assure you that the President would not want the viewers to see us taken out at gunpoint," Polly said.

"Cameras? Where?" Harry looked around the small tent.

"In our eyes," Polly said.

"What?"

"We're freaks," Polly said. "We have cameras in our eyes, and I'm filming you right now."

Harry backed off.

Then the kids heard someone calling. "Harry?" It was the helicopter pilot.

Antarctic Historical Survivor was over for Polly. She was going home. "Are you sure you want to stay?" she asked Grace.

Grace nodded.

Polly turned to Robert.

Robert beamed at her. "We'll make it."

Polly thought about Robert's silly grin. Optimism was his brand of courage.

"You guys can have my whole stash of peanuts and Chocobombs," Billy said gravely.

Robert laughed. "Thanks, Billy." Even though Billy was going back to America and they were staying, Robert knew that it was hard for Billy to give them his stash of food.

Andrew grinned. "I don't have anything to give you unless you want my parka."

"You never buttoned it anyway," Robert said.

"I don't have anything to give you but this," Polly said to Robert. She crawled over and kissed him.

"Thank you, Polly," Robert said.

Billy stuck out his hand to shake Grace's.

Grace pulled him to her and hugged him.

"Hug me, too," Andrew said.

Grace crawled to Andrew and hugged him.

"I would have trusted you with my toes, Grace," he whispered into her ear. "Thank you for taking care of me."

Robert overheard him. "Thank you, Andrew, for all you did for me." He leaned down next to Andrew. "I'm sorry if I treated you badly at the beginning of the trip."

"It's not important. I was a different person then," Andrew said.

"Can we do anything else for you?" Polly asked Robert.

"Yeah." Robert grinned. "Make sure they send someone back for us after we reach the Pole!"

Polly nodded.

"It's time," Billy said. He was excited.

"Let's help Andrew out," Polly said.

Billy and Robert each grabbed one of Andrew's arms and pulled him.

Grace held the tent flap open.

Polly crawled toward the open tent flap for the last time. She felt as if she were leaving her death behind. She had never believed that she would make it home.

Billy and Robert helped Andrew toward the helicopter.

Grace stood in front of the tent and looked at the shiny helicopter. She felt a stab of joy that she didn't have to go back to the modern world yet.

"Good-bye!" Polly grabbed Grace's hand before she climbed in. Grace squeezed it. "Good-bye."

They stared at each other for a few seconds before the pilot shouted, "Let's get out of here while we can! You never know when bad weather will blow in down here."

"Everybody buckle up!" the pilot called.

Polly grabbed Andrew's hand and looked out the window.

Billy, who was sitting up front with Harry, waved at Robert.

Polly waved, too.

With its propellers whirring, the helicopter lifted off.

Polly pressed her forehead against the icy glass. She remembered what Wilson had written in his diary: *These days are with one for all time—they are never to be forgotten—and they are to be found nowhere else in the world but at the poles.... One only wishes one could bring a glimpse of it away with one with all its unimaginable beauty.*

Polly stared out the window. Robert and Grace were standing next to the blue tent below. She watched them until they, the tent, and even the mountains had disappeared and all she could see was a great expanse of white.

36

For seventy-two hours Steve had been locked up in a small, windowless room. His head still ached. No one spoke to him. Every once in a while he heard the dry metallic sound of a plate of chips being pushed under the door, and once, in the middle of the night, he thought he heard the swish of Pearl's broom. Occasionally he heard voices. He was so lonely that his heart leaped whenever this happened, but he quickly grew afraid. Were they coming for him?

Mostly he worried about the kids. Was Andrew still alive? Or any of the kids, for that matter? He wondered if Chad had gotten into trouble. He had a million questions and no answers. But every time he asked himself whether it had been wise to intervene, he pushed aside his doubts. Maybe trying to rescue Andrew had been a reckless act, but it was the only shot he had had to try to keep Andrew alive. The more he thought about it, the more he believed that his dad would understand. A boy's life had been at stake, and the rigged *Survivor* show didn't leave him any other choice. He wouldn't waste any time on regrets.

Suddenly keys rattled in the lock.

Steve felt sick. Was it time? Were the guards coming to beat him senseless? Or was it the bailiff for *Court TV*?

When the door opened, Chad stepped in.

The flood of light hurt Steve's eyes and gave Chad a sort of halo. Steve stood up on shaky legs.

Chad beamed. "You're a national hero."

Steve's mouth was dry. His voice was rusty. "The kids . . ." he croaked.

". . . are fine." Chad smiled. "The guards didn't even tell you that?"

"Nothing," Steve groaned, thinking of the last few days, when he had been so hungry for information.

"Thanks to you, the rescue was broadcast live," Chad said. He sounded pleased.

Steve had almost forgotten about pushing that green button. "But is Andrew okay?"

Chad grinned. "Yes."

Steve felt like crying, he was so relieved.

"After they took you here, to this prison"—Chad looked around with disgust at the cobwebbed room—"the kids managed to get Andrew inside the tent. He was dehydrated and weak, and his toes were badly frostbitten."

Steve had been afraid of that.

"Everyone in the whole country saw how brave and strong the kids were. The audience witnessed how close Andrew came to dying. They understood how risky *Historical Survivor* is." Chad lowered his voice. "So when the danger had passed, the viewers cut off their televisions!"

"You're kidding!" Steve said.

"During prime time, the ratings of all shows dropped to zero," Chad said.

Steve tried, but he couldn't imagine billions of silent televisions.

"Then the President intervened."

"What do you mean?"

"The President put the Secretary of Entertainment on mandatory leave and obtained a copy of the *Antarctic Historical Survivor* script. The script showed that the Secretary had set up a rival Amundsen expedition. The actor-Amundsen was waiting nearby. He was supposed to beat the kids to the Pole just as the real Amundsen had beaten Scott.

"The President declared the game over and sent the actor to Antarctica to rescue the kids. The kids' parents met them in Tierra del Fuego. Doctors there gave them a clean bill of health. Polly, Andrew, and Billy are on their way home as we speak." Chad beamed. "You stopped a *Historical Survivor* game."

Just as he had feared, Steve had to be in a lot of trouble.

"But Robert and Grace decided to stay," Chad added.

"What do you mean?"

"Robert wanted to be the first kid to reach the Pole, and Grace wants to stay just a little while longer. They're halfway to the Pole now and doing fine."

"And what's going to happen to me?" Steve said.

"We haven't been able to find you. We had no idea that you were locked up right here in the DOE. Jacob sent out an e-mail telling the public what you had done. When the Department took the MVP vote, the viewers wrote in your name." He paused. "Or Birdie Bowers's name. It's the same thing."

"What?" Steve said.

"You're MVP on *Historical Survivor*, entitled to the prize money." Chad's grin grew wider. "The President has almost started taking credit for your intervention. She'd like to talk to you. A little while ago one of the Secretary's guards cracked, and we learned that you were hidden in the building all along. Lots of reporters want to interview you, but I came alone to get you. You're a rich man."

No goons were going to beat him up. He wasn't going to be an old man at seventeen. No *Court TV*. He wasn't going to get a public whipping. Steve felt so overwhelmed with happiness that he was afraid he might faint.

"There's more, but I'll have to tell you later," Chad said. "Let's go. After you've had a chance to rest and eat, the President wants to talk to you."

Steve tried to walk, but his legs were too shaky. He stumbled.

"Come on," Chad said kindly. "I'll help you." He gripped Steve's arm.

Jacob and a policeman Steve didn't recognize were waiting for them outside the room.

"Hi, Steve," Jacob said.

Steve smiled weakly at Jacob.

The policeman nodded. "There's a crowd up there, sir."

Steve tensed. He wasn't ready to face a crowd.

"The sooner we go, the sooner you'll get home," Chad reminded him.

"I'll get his other arm," Jacob said, moving next to Steve.

Together with Chad and Jacob, Steve followed the policeman down the long, dank hall. As they walked up the stairway, he heard a jumble of loud voices.

Several police officers were blocking a group of cameramen and reporters. When the news reporters saw Steve, they began yelling at him from the top of the stairwell.

"Mr. Michael, what will you do with your prize money?"

"Why did you choose the alias Birdie Bowers?"

"Those kids could have made it!" a man wearing a cowboy hat shouted at him. "Why did you stop the *Survivor* show?" He stuck a mike in Steve's face.

Steve had been alone for so long that the stares of the journalists made him feel light-headed. How should he answer the last reporter? He had to defend himself. Oddly enough, a quote that he had heard in teleschool popped into his mind. He hoped Birdie Bowers had said it, but he couldn't remember for sure. He cleared his throat.

"Survival is no child's game," Steve said.

Before he had time to say more, lights flashed, and Chad pulled him through the crowd.

"Mr. Michael will hold a press conference later," Chad said over his shoulder. "But now he needs to get some food and rest."

37

The President sat behind her desk in the Oval Office. She wore a purple suit and purple lipstick. Steve knew that she was seventy years old, but her face looked younger. He had heard that she had paid outrageous fees to grow new skin.

Now that Steve had had a good night's rest and was cleaned up, he felt as if he had brand-new skin, too.

An aide stood with him in the doorway, waiting for the President to acknowledge them.

Steve had great respect for the President, but he also knew that running a government crippled by deficits was next to impossible. Neither her courage nor her worries showed in her face. She looked like an ordinary middle-aged woman.

The aide cleared his throat loudly.

"Ah, Mr. Michael," the President said when she looked up. "Come in."

The aide let go of his arm, and Steve walked into the room.

"I'm sorry that we didn't find you sooner, but I'm glad to have the chance for a chat," the President said.

Steve nodded. "Madame President."

"Please sit down."

Steve sat in one of the chairs in front of her desk.

The President stared into his eyes. "I'll come right to the point."

"Yes, ma'am." It seemed incredible to him that the President was giving him even five minutes of her time.

"To reduce the crime rate and to distract ourselves from the pain of our poverty, we have become a nation of viewers." She paused. "But not you. On behalf of all of America, I want to thank you for taking action."

Steve didn't know what to say. The President of the United States had just thanked him. He wished that his family were alive and could be with him now.

"Do you know how much the Secretary spent on *Antarctic Historical Survivor*?"

Steve shook his head.

"Over one hundred million dollars," the President said. "Outrageous! I'm going to make it my business to see that we never waste so much on so little again."

Steve's anger at the Secretary helped him to overcome his shyness. "What's going to happen to the Secretary?"

"I've disagreed with the Secretary on many issues for a long time. But you have to understand that there are limits even to a President's power." The President's solemn face broke into a broad grin. "I'm pleased to report, however, that Congress has started an investigation."

Steve had read about congressional investigations in the newspapers. Once, various members of Congress had asked a former CEO over 6,000,000 questions, and the same question 250,000 times. But in Steve's opinion, being bored by Congress was not enough punishment for the Secretary. "What about the corneal implants? The kids didn't know about those. Didn't she break the law?"

"When they applied to be on *Historical Survivor*, the kids and their parents signed a release."

"But how can that be fair?"

"The implants were legal," the President said simply.

Steve felt his face fall. He was happy that the Secretary had lost her job and was under congressional investigation. She was a bad person. But eventually congressional investigations ended, and Steve guessed that the Secretary would talk her way into another job.

"We are taking some action, however," the President said, as though she had sensed his disappointment. She paused. "I've asked your friend Chad to tell you about the Secretary's other troubles. While you've been unavailable, I've met with him."

Chad? What had Chad talked to the President about?

"We'll talk some more later, but I wanted to ask you if you'd help me greet the kids and their parents."

"Sure," Steve said.

"They're landing at the air force base this afternoon, at five o'clock. I'd like you to come with me."

So much was happening so fast. "That would be great."

"In that case"—the President signaled to one of her aides— "see that Steve gets a Presidential pass."

"Thank you," he said.

The President of the United States stood up and shook Steve's hand. "I'll see you in the helicopter."

As Steve was escorted out the front door of the White House, he carefully put his pass in his shirt pocket. He was more excited than he used to be on Christmas mornings. In a short while, he would meet three of the kids!

Outside the gate, he found Chad and Pearl waiting for him. Pearl didn't have her broom, and someone had styled her hair. As always, her eyes were downcast.

"The President mentioned—" Steve began.

"We have to talk," Chad interrupted. "I didn't have time to tell you everything yesterday."

"When?" Steve asked.

"How about right now?" Chad said.

Steve sat across from Chad and Pearl at a coffee shop around the corner from the White House. He sipped his coffee and waited.

"When you learned Pearl's story, you didn't ask a key question," Chad said.

What was Chad talking about?

"With all the blood and gore of *World War I Historical Survivor*, how did the Secretary ever witness Pearl's act of kindness?"

Chad was right. Steve hadn't thought about that.

"Well, it's simple, really." Chad stirred his coffee. "I was the head of the day shift then. Pearl was my assistant. The Secretary had these digicameras that she wanted to try out. Pearl was a guinea pig for one of the earliest models."

Steve looked at Pearl, stunned.

"The early models were crude. Incapable of picking up voices. The scenes they relayed were like silent movies."

Looking at Pearl across the table, Steve realized that he had never seen her eyes.

"When that soldier crawled to her, Pearl probably forgot

about the implant. All she saw was the suffering of another human being. But unwittingly she broadcast the entire scene to the editing room. The images weren't as clear as the ones today, but I stood next to the Secretary as she watched the intervention on a monitor: Pearl leaning down to give the soldier a cup of water. The blood on the man's forehead. His chapped lips moving to say 'Thank you.'"

Chad's voice rose. "And later I saw the Secretary shout at Pearl. Then two beefy goons appeared.

"I saw them pound Pearl." Chad's voice broke. "I waited as they held her in isolation and denied her food, day after day. I knew that I should try to help her. But I was a coward. I *am* a coward." He grimaced, and Steve remembered Chad's scared face in the editing room when he insisted that Steve go home and leave Andrew in the crevasse.

"I feared that they'd do the same thing to me—so I just waited." Chad looked over at Pearl, who was staring down at the table. "I know she's forgiven me for this, but that doesn't make it any easier for me to live with myself." He sighed.

"Of course, after it was too late, I rescued Pearl and took her to a hospital. Her appearance had changed so much that she didn't need a disguise when I brought her back to work. I just told her to keep her eyes on her broom. Shortly after that, I was transferred to the night shift. That's why the Secretary has left the night shift alone all these years. She knows that I have something on her, but because I've never spoken out, she's assumed that we had a deal. I guess we did, of sorts."

So that was why Chad had been able to get him transferred so easily, Steve thought.

"I never had the guts to stand up to the Secretary, but to try to make it up to Pearl, the night crew and I engaged in minor acts of sabotage. That is, until you joined us, Steve."

No one said anything for a minute, but Steve felt sure that Chad was trying to thank him.

"So what does this mean?" Steve said.

"I saved Pearl's tape," Chad said. "I have it all. I didn't think that the day would ever come when I could use it. If I had given it to the police earlier, the Secretary would have talked her way out of the crime. You were a little boy when the Urban Trash Wars were raging, so you may not remember. When the Secretary took over the DOE and started better programming, the wars virtually came to an end. She was a national hero.

"But now . . ." Chad smiled. "Thanks to you, we've got her. Taking you on was the best decision that I've made in twenty years."

Steve just nodded, but he felt proud. He had been scared, too, but he had acted anyway.

Chad patted Pearl's arm. "You've waited a long time, Pearl, but justice is yours." He faced Steve again. "I've discussed Pearl's case with the President. She gave the tape to the police. They're already prosecuting the Secretary for assault and battery. After all, the police have an open-and-shut case. It's all on the Secretary's own tape." He paused. "Show him your eye, Pearl."

Pearl looked up at Steve. Her gray hair framed a sad face, but her eyes were the clearest blue. It was unmistakable. Right in the middle of her left pupil, a clear glass lens shone.

Steve had to look away. "Why didn't you"—he searched for the right word—"remove that awful device?"

Chad shrugged. "The early models were tricky to implant and difficult to remove. Pearl had suffered so much . . ." He took a sip of coffee. "Are you going with the President to meet the kids' plane?"

Steve nodded.

"So in just a little while you'll get to see them?"

Steve nodded again. He couldn't wait.

They grinned at each other across the table.

"Well, you proved it," Chad said.

"Proved what?" Steve stirred his coffee.

Chad's face was solemn. "That the time hasn't passed."

Without asking, Steve understood what time Chad was talking about. Steve knew that he had made a difference, and it was the best feeling in the world.

38

The helicopter that was carrying Steve and the President was the length of five cars. It whizzed over the crowded city toward the air force base.

After greeting Steve, the President had begun talking on her cell phone. Steve caught an occasional phrase, such as "free trade" or "religious wars." Mostly his attention was fixed on the people sitting in traffic below while two Secret Service men, on either side of the President, glared at him.

Finally the helicopter passed over the barbed-wire fence of the base. The parking lot was packed. Thousands of people were waiting outside the fence to see the kids land.

The helicopter started its descent.

The President closed her cell phone and looked at Steve. "Grace and Robert have almost reached the Pole," she said.

"They'll be the first kids to make it to the Pole on their own, won't they?" Steve said.

"Yes," the President said with a heavy sigh. "The world needs brave deeds now more than ever."

Abruptly, the propellers stopped.

A Secret Service woman opened the door.

"We'll escort the President to the runway, and then you can follow," one of the Secret Service men inside the helicopter said to Steve.

Steve peered out the window at the crowd.

Security surrounded the President as she walked toward the runway.

Looking out the window, Steve saw a crowd of demonstrators outside the fenced runway. One little girl, her cheeks streaked with dust, hoisted a sign that said, ALL KIDS DESERVE AN EDUCATION.

A boy about Steve's age was carrying two oversized dice stuffed into a trash can. TRASH THE GREAT EDU-DICE TOSS was written in big letters on the side of the can.

A woman held up a sign with the words GIVE OUR KIDS A FUTURE superimposed over images of the faces of the *Antarctic Historical Survivor* kids.

The pilot called back to Steve: "They've given me the signal. You can get out now."

Steve walked down the stairs onto the tarmac.

Someone shouted, "That's Birdie Bowers!"

Steve heard the name Birdie Bowers called out again and again. It was fitting, almost two centuries after his death, that a brave man's name had become alive once more.

Steve passed a special area on the other side of the fence marked PRESS. The reporters seemed to lunge for him.

"Mr. Michael, can we talk to you?" a voice demanded.

"My newspaper will pay for an interview!"

Steve ignored the shouts and kept walking toward the President, who was surrounded by a group of aides. He walked up to her.

"I'll greet the kids," the President said. "Then you may."

"Now, if you'll excuse us," an aide said to Steve, "we'll take photos with the kids and the President first, then we'll get a photo of you together."

A different staffer took hold of Steve's elbow and directed him off to the side: "Stand here."

A big plane with the emblem of the U.S. government came into view.

From the loudspeakers came the strains of "God Bless America."

The plane descended and came to a stop twenty yards away. Steve stared at the plane windows, trying in vain to catch a glimpse of one of the contestants. He found it strange that he knew so much about the three of them, and they so little about him.

A group of men dressed in bright-orange suits rushed a set of stairs to the plane.

A long drumroll came from the loudspeakers.

A cleaned-up Billy walked down the steps first. His face looked tense, as though he expected to be booed. But when a kid in the crowd shouted "Hurrah!" he raised a bag of Chocobombs, and the crowd outside the fence roared.

Billy grinned and kept walking down the flight of stairs.

Polly wore a short black skirt. She had pulled her hair back in a ponytail. She was just visible at the top of the stairs when the crowd started cheering.

Polly burst into tears and hid her face with the book she was carrying.

Behind her, Andrew hobbled down. He had a crutch under one arm. Even at this distance his face looked drawn and white.

One foot was swathed in a bright-green bandage, and Steve wondered if the doctors had had to amputate his toes after all. It was only then that Steve realized how close Andrew had come to dying. He felt tears choke his throat.

Andrew smiled such a sweet smile that Steve wanted to hug him.

Then Andrew's dad started down the steps. The sight of the large crowd stopped him.

A few people booed. From the interviews of Mr. Morton that Steve had seen on EduTV, he hadn't liked the man either.

Two stewards carried Mrs. Pritchard down the stairs in a wheelchair.

Mr. and Mrs. Kanalski followed. Mr. Kanalski had a big grin on his face. Mrs. Kanalski was crying into her handkerchief.

Billy reached the bottom of the stairs. He walked over to the President as if he had known her all his life.

The President shook Billy's hand and congratulated him.

Lights flashed, and Billy grinned.

Steve guessed that Billy's dad would post the photo on Billy's website.

Polly approached the President. She walked hesitantly, as if she were afraid.

Billy stepped aside and looked around. He spotted Steve standing all alone a few paces away, and a puzzled look crossed his face.

The crowd, sensing the drama unfolding, began chanting Birdie Bowers's name.

Andrew, barely on the ground, stopped. He seemed to be listening to the crowd. He slowly turned and looked at Steve.

Polly squinted at Steve in the bright sun.

Andrew turned red, then white. He veered away from the President and started hobbling as fast as he could toward Steve.

Polly and Billy joined him.

Why am I standing here like a fool, watching? Steve rushed forward to welcome the kids home.

Acknowledgments

Carol Bennett, Dean Burkhardt, Franci Crane, Jill Jewett, Elena Marks, Gail Gross, Ellen Susman, and Michael Zilkha have read and helped me with countless drafts of many manuscripts, and I will always be grateful. My book group, composed of Sarah Cortez, Bettie Carrell, and Rachel Weissenstein, has been a constant source of encouragement and wisdom. I appreciate the friendship and professional editing of Amy Storrow, Emily Hanlon, Gail Storey, and Nora Shire. But for the patience of my husband, Bill White, I would not have stuck with writing. Thanks to my mother, Patsi Ferguson, for reading a yet unpublished novel. Thanks to Gar Bering for technical help.

Chas Jhin, Andy Marks, Craig Smyser, and Stephen, Elena, and Will White were my most faithful young readers. Thanks to Colton Bay, Winston Chang, Brent Doctor, Ashley Helm, Drew Jackson, Meghan Lewis, Salima and Shamsa Mangalji, John and Patrick Scully, Georgiana and Claire Smyser, Colleen Thurman, Sam Wilburn, and Daniel Zilkha, who also read my book and gave me valuable feedback. Finally—and most important—thanks to Marni Hettena and her fourth-grade class— Alex Bennett, Sam Bursten, Ryan Cooper, Dominique Dawley, Thomas Deskin, Julia Eads, Madison Feanny, Will Flanders, Graham Gaylor, Marion Hayes, Evan Henke, Michael Kumpas, Taylor Mattingly, Bruce Veyna, Stephen White, Elizabeth Wright, and Jeffrey Zuspan. You believed in me as a writer before I believed in myself.

After nine years of hard work, Ann Tobias, my agent, was an unexpected and wonderful gift to me. Sally Doherty, my editor, vastly improved the book with her many thoughtful comments. It takes a village to publish a first book, and I thank mine.

Endnotes

Abbreviations refer to the works cited in the Bibliography. Material cited here in *italics* is a direct quote; information based on works cited is roman.

vii	*"We are not going forward like a lot"*: HRB 1911; Coldest 290-292
37	"Scott's team had to hike seven hundred": Worst 327
59-60	*"In November 1910," "the vessel* Terra Nova," *"carried an international,"* and *"Scott kept a detailed"*: SLE back cover
65	"Scott's ponies had gotten": Worst 150
66	"Captain Scott used ponies": Worst 565; SLE 4-5, 395
73	"the Scott expedition boasted": SLE xx; Coldest ix, 54; Cherry 335
73	"the Ross Ice Shelf": Coldest map 2, 15; SLE 15
74	*"Scott began his ascent"*: Coldest 184
110	"Five men had continued": SLE Foreword xiii, xvii, 384, 430
111	"Captain Scott started writing": SLE 432
111	*"We had fuel to make"* and *"For God's sake look"*: SLE 432
114	*"But this I know"*: Worst 278
115	*"Amongst ourselves we are"*: SLE 424
115	*"We are in a very tight"*: SLE 425
115	*"Had we lived, I should"*: SLE 442
115	*"For God's sake look"*: SLE 432
144	*"As far as the eye"*: Worst 143-144
146	*"Killer whales ... were cruising"*: Coldest 98; Worst 158
160-61	"on the Scott expedition, Birdie Bowers": Coldest 56; SLE 265
162	*"He slept through the night"*: SLE 430
163	"Scott's men had described": Worst 247
173	"The plan was for them to man-haul": Coldest 128; Worst 367
174	*"... Proceeding Antarctic"*: Cherry 75
174	*"Great God! This is an awful"*: SLE 396; Coldest 217
174	*"Captain Scott ... has taken"*: HRB 1912; Coldest 219
175	*"We had four courses"* and the following five extracts: SLE 378-379

Bibliography

Cherry

Wheeler, Sara. *Cherry: A Life of Apsley Cherry-Garrard.* New York: Random House, 2002.

Coldest

Solomon, Susan. *The Coldest March: Scott's Fatal Antarctic Expedition.* New Haven: Yale University Press, 2001.

Debenham

Debenham, Frank. *In the Antarctic: Stories of Scott's Last Expedition.* Banham, U.K.: Erskine Press, Norfolk NR16 2HW and London: John Murray, 1952.

Evans

Evans, Edward R.G.R. "Rise and Shine in the Antarctic." Cambridge, U.K.: Scott Polar Research Institute, 1959.

GCS

Simpson, G. C. Text of a lecture given in Simla, India, in 1914. Collection of Simpson Letters and Papers, National Meteorological Library and Archives, National Meteorological Office, Exeter, U.K.

HRB 1911

H. R. Bowers. Letter to E. Bowers, October 27, 1911. Archives, Scott Polar Research Institute, University of Cambridge, U.K.

HRB 1912

———. Letter to May Bowers, January 18, 1912. Archives, Scott Polar Research Institute, University of Cambridge, U.K.

Lashly

Lashly, William. *The Diary of W. Lashly.* Reading, U.K.: Reading University Department of Fine Art, 1939.

SLE

Scott, Robert Falcon. *Scott's Last Expedition—The Journals.* New York: Carroll & Graf, 1996. First published as *Scott's Last Expedition: Being the Journals of Captain R. F. Scott, R.N., C.V.O.* 2 vols. London: Smith, Elder, 1914.

Wilson 1

Wilson, E. A. *Diary of the* Discovery *Expedition to the Antarctic Regions, 1901–1904.* London: Blandford, 1972. Orion Books, U.K.

Wilson 2

———. *Diary of the* Terra Nova *Expediton to the Antarctic, 1910–1912.* London: Blandford, 1972. Scott Polar Research Institute, University of Cambridge, U.K.

Worst

Cherry-Garrard, A. *The Worst Journey in the World.* London: Constable, 1922; New York: Carroll & Graf, 1997.

Permissions

The author and publisher gratefully acknowledge the following for permission to reprint pieces from the copyrighted material listed below.

Cherry: A Life of Apsley Cherry-Gerrard
By Sara Wheeler
Random House, New York, 2002

Letter to E. Bowers, October 27, 1911, and *Letter to May Bowers*, January 18, 1912
By H. R. Bowers
Archives
Copyright, Design and Patent Act (1988)
Permission granted by Scott Polar Research Institute, University of Cambridge, U.K.

The Coldest March: Scott's Fatal Antarctic Expedition
By Susan Solomon
Yale University Press, Copyright 2001

Diary of the Discovery *Expedition to the Antarctic Regions, 1901–1904*
By E. A. Wilson
Permission granted by OrionBooks

Diary of the Terra Nova *Expedition to the Antarctic, 1910–1912*
By E. A. Wilson
Permission granted by Scott Polar Research Institute, University of Cambridge, U.K.

The Diary of William Lashly (1939)
By Mr. W. Lashly
Department of Fine Art, University of Reading

In the Antarctic: Stories of Scott's Last Expedition
By Frank Debenham
Appears by permission of the publisher, Erskine Press